The Long Ears

The Harp of Elvyth

Dear Charlotte,
Welcome to Lizzie's worlds.
Enjoy the adventure!
love
Debbie x
Nov. 2013

Debbie Daley

Published in 2013 by FeedARead.com Publishing – Arts Council funded

A CIP catalogue record for this title is available from the British Library.

This book is dedicated to the memory of my beloved dad, Ernie, and my brother, Russell, who were taken from this world way too suddenly and much too soon, thereby inspiring me to follow my dream.

Acknowledgements

I'd like to extend my love and thanks to all those people who have believed in me and given me every encouragement to pursue my dream to see this work in print. There are too many of you to mention but special thanks must go to Richard Ommanney for persuading me to take my first leap of faith into the literary world via Kindle; Gina Carpenter who has proven to be my greatest advocate and supporter – my unrewarded publicist and friend; to the amazingly talented and far too modest Sarah Aumeer, whose cover illustration has brought Lizzie so stunningly to life; to Sheila Sykes and my beautiful daughter Elenya for their patience and eagle-eyes when proof reading, and their editorial suggestions, thereby making it a better read; and last, but far from least, to my wonderful family who have loved and supported me and been much of the inspiration for the characterisations within the story.

Chapter 1 – There it is again!

The pupils of 6F Chislewick Primary School were having a great afternoon doing pretty much as they pleased; laughing and messing around, singing songs, playing games and basically winding down on the last day of term before the Easter holidays. To one side of the classroom, taking no part in the frivolities, sat a young girl, staring out of the window and looking for all the world as though she would rather be anywhere else than where she actually was.

Lizzie Longton gazed glumly out of the classroom window at a grey and gloomy Friday afternoon. Heavily laden clouds overhead looked ominously like a storm was about to break, and Lizzie watched as the rain began lashing noisily against the glass; pinging off the pane like thousands of tiny glass beads. As a huge gust of wind whipped through the playground, the ancient oak tree at its far end waved its gnarled and knotted branches around as if angry at having to stand out in such dreadful weather. A blinding flash of lightening rent the sky and an almost instantaneous clap of thunder let all beneath it know that the storm had broken right above their heads.

The lights in the classroom flickered momentarily and, whilst some of the children let out screams of surprise and fright, others in acts of bravado whooped with feigned delight.

"Well that's just great! Go on," thought Lizzie, to some higher-being who was directing the drama unfolding outside, "make my birthday even more miserable than it already is."

Today was Lizzie Longton's eleventh birthday, and she could think of dozens of ways she would rather be spending it than being in school with a bunch of kids who couldn't care less if it was Lizzie's birthday or not. Suddenly…

There it was again!

Lizzie spotted a flash of green disappear behind the old oak at the far end of the playground. She craned her neck, trying to get a better look.

It wasn't the first time Lizzie had glimpsed something green flitting by, just at the edges of her line of vision. There had been lots of other occasions over the years, but whenever she had turned her head towards it, whatever it was had vanished. Just lately, though, the flashes of green had become more frequent. Coinciding with them, Lizzie had developed an acute sensation of being watched or followed every time she stepped out of her front door. She got that creepy, tingly feeling you get in the back of your head and neck (you know the one, when you just know someone's staring at you) but whenever she looked around, there was never anyone nor anything to be seen. She had begun to wonder if the green flashes and sensation of being stalked were connected, or whether she was becoming paranoid.

Now, peering through the pouring rain, still pelting against the window, she was once again unable to make out whatever it was that had just disappeared at the end of the playground. There was just no getting away from the fact that, whatever it was, it was bloomin' quick.

*

Out in the grounds, and leaning heavily against the old oak tree, a green clad creature bent over; its hands gripping its waist, as rain dripped from every available surface of its small lithe body.

"I'll be glad when this is all out in the open; I'm sick to death of all this cloak and dagger stuff," it grumbled to itself irritably. Just then, another blinding flash of lightening and a deafening clap of thunder split the air. The green clad creature looked up nervously through the oak's branches.

8

"Oh dear, this really is not the best place to shelter," it thought grimly; and, with that, made a bee-line for the bicycle sheds.

*

"Lizzie! Lizzie! Elizabeth Longton, are you still with us?" Lizzie was brought abruptly back to the present by the slightly impatient tone of her teacher, Miss Finley.

"Sorry, Miss," Lizzie apologised, shaking her head as if she'd just been woken from a dream. She looked down at her desk in embarrassment as she hated having attention drawn to her. The reason for that soon raised its ugly head...

There came a sound that always made Lizzie's heart beat just that little bit faster, her skin flush just that little bit hotter, and her blood run cold in dreaded anticipation.

"Oi! Oi, Long Ears. Away with the fairies again are yer?"

Accompanying the hateful sound of one of her dreaded enemies, was a sharp poke in her back. Lizzie glanced back quickly at Regina Bray; her podgy round face with its small piggy eyes that glinted cruelly under their folds of fat. Sitting smugly beside her was her non-identical twin sister, Veronica; tall and skinny with a hooked nose and hooded eyes, she couldn't have been more unlike her short fat twin than it was possible to be. Veronica was like a bird of prey; a vulture to be exact, always waiting to get her fair share of the pickings. Her sharp and vicious tongue ready to tear into its victim just like a vulture used it's talons to rip into some poor defenceless creature.

"Saddo!" Veronica spat, making sure she got her pennyworth in.

Lizzie swung back to face Miss Finley - her fingers automatically sliding up towards the tips of her ears as if to protect them from her horrid nickname.

9

The Bray twins made Lizzie's life a misery with their horrible name-calling and digs and jibes. It was because of the Bray's influence on the other kids in the village that most of them either ignored Lizzie or joined in with the taunts and insults. Lizzie's grandmother said that the Brays were mean because they were "just jealous" of how clever and pretty Lizzie was, but it didn't help Lizzie knowing that she had no friends because the Brays were "just jealous". Anyway, Lizzie knew that no-one in their right mind would consider her pretty. No, Lizzie knew that the Brays were mean because Lizzie was seen as being "different" to most people.

Lizzie had always been aware that she was kind of different to most of the other kids. For a start, she looked quite different with her straight, silvery blond hair and almost translucently pale complexion. Her large liquid blue eyes dominated her face with its slender nose, wide mouth and small pointed chin. But the one feature, which was undeniably her most noticeable, and she really wished they weren't, were her exceptionally long and pointed ears. Anyone seeing Lizzie for the first time couldn't help but stare at them in undisguised surprise.

Lizzie had tried keeping her ears under wraps from the first time she'd been made aware of how odd they appeared. She'd grown her hair long and combed it over them; she'd tried wearing a series of hats (which just resulted in more name calling and taunting); she'd worn wide hair-bands to cover them, but no matter what she did, they would defiantly wriggle their way out to be seen in all their pointed glory. Lizzie's ears were the bane of her life, as it was them that had earned her the hateful nickname - Lizzie Long Ears.

With the end of the school term finally upon them, Miss Finley wished the children a happy Easter holidays and warned them against indulging in too many chocolate eggs. She then watched sadly as little Lizzie Longton quickly grabbed her things and ran out to the cloakroom to put on her raincoat and wellington boots. It was like that every day

10

for poor Lizzie. No matter what Miss Finley had done to try to integrate Lizzie with the other children, nothing seemed to work. In Miss Finley's opinion, Lizzie was what people called a 'victim'.

Miss Finley liked Lizzie a lot because she was bright and polite, and always tried her hardest at everything she did. However, Miss Finley did her best not to show Lizzie any favouritism in case it resulted in Lizzie having an even harder time at school. It wasn't really surprising that Lizzie sometimes drifted off into her own little world, because that was where she spent a lot of her time – on her own in her own little world. Now the Bray twins were another matter all together. Miss Finley didn't like *them* at all.

Miss Finley eyed the Bray twins warily as she watched them sniggering together as they made their way out of the classroom. They were sneaky because they were careful not to take a step out of line in her presence. They brought her little gifts and were overly polite, trying to wheedle their way into her good books, but Miss Finley saw straight through them; she was under no illusions at just how devious they were. She knew that the twins would wait until either her back was turned or she was nowhere around before they'd start their nasty bullying of the younger or smaller pupils at the school. She'd lost count of the number of parents who'd been to into the school to complain about their children being bullied by the Brays. But the Brays were clever because they'd then befriend their victims so that their gang of followers became ever larger - giving the twins an increased sense of power.

Miss Finley had wanted to have them excluded, but the Headteacher refused because the twins father, Trevor Bray, was Chair of the Board of Governors and chief benefactor to the school. Trevor was pretty influential in the village, as he liked to think of himself as a gentleman farmer and landowner. Miss Finley knew that if she kept vigilant, she'd catch the twins red-handed one day - that was a promise, and then...

Out in the cloakroom, Lizzie had quickly put on her raincoat and was just struggling into her boots, when in trudged the Brays and their gang.

"Well, look who we have 'ere; if it isn't little Lizzie Long Ears," sneered Regina. Veronica and the rest of their gang sniggered and nudged each other in mirth. "Thought you'd get a quick getaway did yer?" Regina continued, nastily.

Lizzie looked up at her tormentor and tried to appear brave and unconcerned, but her stomach was doing a fine swan dive somewhere in the middle of her body, and her legs were trembling like a pair of jellies. She never quite knew what to expect when the twins got on a roll.

"So, why is it yer've got such weirdo ears, Long Ears?" piled in Veronica. "Oh, yeah, 'coz yer mum was from Greenland." The gang fell about in fits of laughter.

When Lizzie had first joined the village school, the other kids had shown great interest in her pointed ears and kept asking how come they were such a strange shape. Lizzie had no idea why her ears were that shape. She didn't have a mother and never saw her father, and so lived with her grandmother and her grandmother's ears were quite normal. However, she had often been told by her grandmother that she took after her mother for her looks, and so Lizzie said she had the same ears as her mum. As the kids got a little older and more inquisitive, they started asking where her mother had come from because they didn't know anyone with ears like Lizzie. Lizzie had asked her grandmother where her mother was from, but as Lizzie's mother had been an orphan, Mrs Longton said she didn't really know but that she'd had a strange accent, so maybe she'd come from abroad.

One day, having been bombarded at school with the same old question about her ears, Lizzie decided to invent a story to put an end to it. Lizzie's grandmother had an old globe at home and so Lizzie spun it and pointed her finger. It alighted on Greenland. Lizzie thought Greenland sounded nice and so had told the kids that her mum had come from there and that lots of Greenlanders had pointed ears like her. The story had lived to haunt her.

"Oh, yeah," laughed Regina. "That's right, ain't it Long Ears. Yer mum came from the Arctic circle - like Santa Claus and the elves." She collapsed in a fit of laughter, falling against her sister and almost knocking her over.

"Was yer mum a Christmas elf then, Long Ears?" Veronica smirked. "Suppose she couldn't stand living down 'ere 'coz of the heat. Yeah, she died 'coz she frazzled up like a bit of bacon."

There was a sharp intake of breath at this. The laughter on some of the gang's lips stopped, and there were some hesitant sniggers as if this remark had somehow overstepped some limit. The twins, however, thought they were hilarious and continued falling about in glee at what they perceived was their witty repartee.

Lizzie looked at them with eyes welling up with tears but was determined not to let them see her cry. Pulling the hood of her raincoat over her head, she ran out into the playground towards the gate that eventually led to the safety of home. The rain was still teeming down, and she bent her head against its onslaught and began running as the raindrops splashed against her face; mingling with the tears that were now flowing freely down her cheeks.

At the corner of the road, she turned quickly to check that the other kids weren't following her and was relieved to see that there was no sign of them yet. Rubbing her sleeve across her now runny nose, she suddenly spotted something green dart behind the hedge of one of the cottages on the other side of the road – Granny Fimble's cottage.

People gave Granny Fimble a wide birth, as the local gossip was that she was a witch. Lizzie's grandmother said that it was nonsense as there were no such things as witches, and that Ada Fimble was just an eccentric old lady that liked cats, of which she had several. Lizzie's grandmother's other name for Granny was "Daft Ada", because she had always been a bit odd. Lizzie wasn't so sure that there weren't such things as witches and so kept her distance from Granny Fimble's cottage just in case.

Part of Lizzie desperately wanted to run over and take a quick look over the hedge to see if she could see the mystery creature but, as well as not wanting to risk seeing Granny Fimble, the bigger part of her wanted to get home before the Bray twins and their nasty little gang caught up with her. Self preservation won out and Lizzie began running once again towards home.

Lizzie was an excellent runner. Her teacher often praised her by saying that she could run in the Olympics one day. Little did her teacher know that Lizzie was actually holding back, as she could run even faster when she wanted to. When she was on her own, Lizzie would sometimes push herself harder. The sensation of running fast was exhilarating as the world whizzed past in a blur. But if she'd done that at school then the kids would think she was even more peculiar than they already did.

At the end of the lane leading to Lizzie's home, sure that she'd put sufficient distance between herself and her tormentors, she slowed down and began to walk. Considering how fast and far she'd run, she was barely breathing hard at all. The rain had eased as she sloshed her way through the puddles in the lane, and she took some time to look out over the fields that surrounded the village.

Lizzie loved living in the countryside. Everywhere she looked, she saw brilliant shades of green with fresh buds and the early signs of crops beginning to sprout out everywhere. Daffodils and grape hyacinths poked their rain battered bedraggled heads from out of the long grass under the hedgerows at the side of the lane. Their bright yellow and purple colours cheered Lizzie and she started to hum to herself as she skipped along contentedly. School was over for a few weeks and it was her birthday, what could be better? Perhaps she and her grandmother could do something exciting this Easter holidays. At last Lizzie could see the gates of home looming ahead and she began running again. As she turned into the drive that led up to the welcoming embrace of her home Longton Hall, she gasped as a blur of green whizzed past her line of vision – there it was again!

Chapter 2 – Winning Ways!

Lizzie lived at Longton Hall with her grandmother, Amelia Longton. The Hall was a ramshackle old building, well past its best before date, with ancient glass in its windows and a pan-tiled roof. Inside the Hall, there was lots of oak panelling and wobbly wooden floors. Ivy and wisteria smothered its exterior walls and the whole place had a slightly spooky look. In the village, it was rumoured that the Hall was haunted. Lizzie has no problem with that at all as it kept the Bray twins at bay - like all bullies, they were cowards at heart. There were times when Lizzie herself had thought that maybe the rumours had some substance to them. On more than one occasion, late at night when she was tucked up in bed, she was sure that she'd heard footsteps creaking along the corridor outside her bedroom; long after her grandmother had gone to bed. She'd never felt threatened though; more the feeling that if there was any ghost creeping about, it was just looking out for her.

The Hall was Lizzie's refuge from the cruel world outside, and she loved the place like an old dear friend. The Longtons had lived at Longton Hall for several generations and, although Lizzie and her grandmother rattled around its many empty rooms (most of which were locked up because it saved having to keep dusting them – so her grandmother said), they wouldn't have considered leaving it for a moment. Evidence of the previous generations living at the Hall was shown in the numerous portraits that lined the panelled walls of the entrance hall and staircase. Lizzie had often stared up into the haughty faces of some of the portraits' occupants, just to check that none had the same ears as her, but none ever did. The fixed stares of her long dead ancestors in their grand poses just made her feel even more inadequate.

Lizzie and her grandmother lived very frugally at the Hall as money was tight for them. Much of the Longton's wealth had been diminished over the years in the way of inheritance and other taxes. Mrs Longton had made some money from the sale of land that had been in the family for hundreds of years and, although it made her sad to sell it, she knew that the money raised would be enough to see her and Lizzie through the years ahead. That and some stocks and shares she still had.

The Hall was set in large gardens, which again had clearly seen better days. As Lizzie made her way through them to the house, she could see old Bob Crowther from the village disappearing into one of the battered old greenhouses over by the old boundary wall. Bob spent lots of time at the Hall, looking after the gardens and doing odd jobs around the place. Although Lizzie's grandmother was unable to pay Bob much, he did well from the fruit and vegetables that he grew there and a generous supply of eggs that came from the few chickens they kept. Bob's wife, Mary, also helped out in the Hall with a bit of cooking and cleaning, and she and Bob were the only true friends that Lizzie had. In fact, Bob and Mary were more like family.

Lizzie loved playing in the gardens with her two main companions, Basil and Rathbone - her two very boisterous brown and white springer spaniels. Occasionally, there would be other small wild animals that visited, such as rabbits and hedgehogs. Foxes too would come brazenly close to the house, but would soon skedaddle with Basil and Rathbone in hot pursuit, barking crazily.

Lizzie also enjoyed watching the different types of birds that came into the garden. Bob had made her a bird table from bits of old wood that he'd found around the grounds, and she would make sure there was plenty of nuts, seeds and other hanging things for the birds on it. She would sit by the window in the living room, watching the birds flitting on and off the bird-table. Squirrels often came and pinched the bird food, performing acrobatics in their attempts to steal the nuts out of the feeders, but just recently a couple of magpies seemed to have taken up residency at the table. When the squirrels came near, the magpies would suddenly appear and chase them away. Bob said that it was because magpies were very territorial. Mary, his wife, said that at least there were two of them, which was a good omen. She said that there was an old saying that went, "One for sorrow, Two for joy," which meant that something good was going to happen for Lizzie. Mary was superstitious like that. Lizzie was just smiling at the thought, when...

There it was again; a green blur had just disappeared behind the old fir tree at the end of the terrace. Lizzie stopped in her tracks. Now was her chance. There was nowhere for the thing to escape to from there; unless it could jump the old boundary wall which was at least ten feet high.

"Should I run over there as quickly as I can, or should I try creeping up on it?" Lizzie thought to herself. She decided that creeping was the best option, as she could catch it unaware.

Lizzie crouched down behind the low terrace wall and made her way slowly along it, keeping her eyes peeled on her target. She jumped the final few feet and put her back against the tree's lower branches. With her arms outstretched, the tree's prickly pines tickled her palms as she inched her way around its perimeter. Lizzie's heart beat hard in her chest and she suddenly felt quite scared.

"What will I do if I catch it?" she thought. "What if it's dangerous?"

This suddenly didn't seem such a good idea after all. If the green thing wanted her to know what it was, it wouldn't be so elusive, she concluded, her bravery waning rapidly. And then she had the ideal get out clause as she heard her grandmother calling to her...

"Lizzie! Lizzie!"

Lizzie moved away from the tree and looked over at the front door to the Hall to see her grandmother standing in the doorway waving happily. Amelia Longton had once been a society beauty, and that beauty and elegance still shone through, even though she was now in her mid sixties. Admittedly she looked a bit frayed around the edges now; her once bright red hair was now almost completely white and a little wild and could have done with a trip to the hairdressers. Her well cut clothes were also well worn but, as she liked to remind herself and Lizzie, when she spruced herself up a bit, she could still turn a head or two.

"Hi, gran," Lizzie called back, and ran towards her grandmother. As she reached her grandmother, Lizzie flung her arms around her waist and, almost knocking her over, hugged her tight. Lizzie loved her grandmother with every fibre of her body.

"Oh, yuck, you're all wet," Mrs Longton laughed, kissing the top of her granddaughter's blond head and releasing her enough to help her take off her wet raincoat. "So, birthday girl, how was school?"

"It was okay." Lizzie shrugged her thin little shoulders, slipped out of her coat and passed her grandmother into the front hall. Even though she'd tried to disguise it, Lizzie's face had told Mrs Longton all she needed to know; that today had been just like any other, despite it being Lizzie's birthday.

Mrs Longton knew that Lizzie would have spent playtime avoiding the other children and, the rest of the time, just lost in her lessons or her own little world. Mrs Longton was well aware of the horrible things that were said to and about her granddaughter by the other children, as she'd wheedled it out of Lizzie on too many occasions. It broke her heart to think that her granddaughter led such a lonely existence. Although Lizzie always tried to hide her hurt from her grandmother, Mrs Longton knew; you didn't have a child with you every

19

day since it was born and not know these things. Her thoughts went back, as they so often did, to that fateful night when Lizzie was thrust so dramatically into her care:

* * *

Tom Longton fell to his knees, his hands covering his face as his body shook with the sobs that were wracking it to its very soul. Dropping his hands to his knees, he tried to gasp in deep breaths of air, but the vice-like pain in his chest made it almost impossible. He had always known that it might come to this, but he'd never imagined that it would cause him to feel this terrible physical pain as well as such an emotional one. So, this was what was meant by heart-break.

The young doctor standing in front of him looked on helplessly. She leant forward and gently placed a hand on his shoulder.

"I'm so sorry, Mr Longton. We did everything we could to try and save her."

Tom shook his head from side to side in grief, rocking back and forth on his heels. Slowly, he looked up at the doctor's face with dark rimmed, haunted eyes that seemed to have died along with the wife he had just lost giving birth to their first child.

The doctor dropped her hand back to her side. This was just so dreadful. This wasn't meant to happen; childbirth was supposed to be a time of great joy.

Standing nearby, rooted to the spot like a statue, watching this nightmare unfold, was a middle-aged woman. Her bright red hair, now liberally peppered with silver and white, bore a striking resemblance to the young man kneeling on the hospital corridor floor. It was obvious to anyone who met them that this was Tom Longton's mother. Staring wide-eyed in shock, her hands clasped to her mouth

20

as though trying to suppress the anguished scream that ached in her throat, Amelia Longton felt like she had fallen into some terrible nightmare. Surely there must be some mistake and she'd wake up any moment.

Ria Longton had shown no distress, no complications during what seemed to have been a straight forward child birth. Having delivered her baby daughter, what seemed like only moments before, she had taken the baby in her arms from the beaming midwife, smiled down into its tiny wrinkled face, gently stroked its funny shaped little ears, and kissed it's tiny forehead. Ria had then quietly laid her head back against her pillow, closed her eyes and died.

At first, the midwife and doctor had thought she was drifting into sleep through exhaustion. But then the realisation that she had stopped breathing had hit them like a thunder bolt. Organised pandemonium broke out in the delivery-room as the baby was quickly whisked away and every effort made to revive its mother, but it had all been in vain.

"I know you did everything you could, doctor, and for that I thank you," said Tom, his voice small and cracking with emotion. The doctor lowered her eyes; the pain in this poor man's face was too awful to witness. Tom then turned to his mother.

"I have to go now, mum," he said slowly, getting to his feet. Tom stared intently into his mother's eyes and she looked at him in confusion, slowly shaking her head; his words made no sense.

"I, I don't unders-," Mrs Longton began, beginning to tremble uncontrollably.

Tom took his mother's hands gently in his own and looked down at them. "I have to go," he said again, more earnestly this time. "You must take the baby. She's to be called Elizabeth." Then, looking back up into his mother's ashen face, he said, "Look after her and tell her I love her."

These last words seemed to trigger something in Mrs Longton's fuddled mind and she suddenly found her voice.

"What do you mean, you have to go? Go? Go where?" she snapped, squeezing Tom's hands and shaking them, her eyes were bright with unshed tears.

Tom drew his mother into his arms and hugged her tightly, as if he never wanted to let her go. His mother clung to him as if her own life depended upon it and she began to sob.

"You, you can't go Tom. I... I don't under.., understand. We need you here," she stammered, her head buried in his broad chest.

Pulling back, his hands now holding tightly to her shoulders for support, he looked down into his mother's tear-stained face. "I can't explain but I must leave. I can't look after the baby. You must do it. I'll be in touch soon." Tom's voice was close to breaking.

His mother looked at him in disbelief. He was walking away from his baby. This was crazy, he couldn't be serious. It was the shock of losing Ria, that's what it was. This was her little boy, her darling Tom, and he was hurting and she couldn't take away the hurt this time - the way she could when he was small and had fallen and scraped a knee. Amelia felt helpless. Tom probably just needed some air, some space to start dealing with what had just happened.

"Okay, my darling," she said sadly. "You just get home and try to rest. Mary will be there and she'll look after you until I get home."

Tom nodded at his mother mutely, then turned and, with shoulders hunched and head down, he walked slowly along the hollow corridor of the hospital's maternity wing; his footsteps echoing off the stark white painted walls as he went. His mother sadly watched his retreating back, wrapping her arms around herself as if they would hold her together when she felt she was falling apart. How was she to help him? She had to be strong for Tom and his baby's sake.

Further along the hospital corridor, hidden in the shadows of a recess, stood a small white haired man in a long green overcoat. The scene he'd just witnessed weighed heavily on him. He hung his head sadly as teardrops dripped from the end of his pointed nose and the white moustache that warmed his upper lip, which was trembling uncontrollably. Drawing himself up to his diminutive height, he pulled the collar of his coat up around his ears and, taking a deep breath, stepped out of the shadows.

Amelia Longton watched her son through a haze of tears and thought how kind it was that this small stranger had placed a comforting hand on Tom's back, and accompanied him out into the cold spring night and out of her and his baby's lives.

* * *

Mrs Longton followed Lizzie down to the kitchen and watched her as she hung up her raincoat. At that precise moment, Basil and Rathbone came bounding in, barking excitedly, almost knocking Lizzie over with their enthusiastically wagging brown and white bodies; it was as if just wagging their stumpy little tails wasn't demonstration enough of their pleasure at seeing their young mistress. Laughing, Lizzie bent down and ruffled their ears and stroked their bodies roughly, just the way her 'boys' liked it.

"Hi you two, did ya miss me?" she giggled, as the dogs tried to lick her face clean of every trace of skin. "Have you been chasing those magpies again?" she admonished them, as she took in their muddy feet and coats.

Smiling as she watched her granddaughter, Mrs Longton took an envelope out of her apron pocket and said brightly, "Oh, Lizzie, a letter's arrived for you."

"Do you think it's from daddy?" asked Lizzie excitedly, taking the envelope from her grandmother and scanning the writing on the front of it expectantly. Mrs Longton looked away quickly as a lump in her throat appeared and threatened to choke her.

"I'm afraid not, my darling, but it looks terribly important all the same," she said, with false cheeriness, swallowing the lump away.

Tom Longton didn't write home very often and, when he did, his letters were always addressed to Mrs Longton and never to Lizzie. They contained just enough information to let his mother know that he was still alive; only the stamps on the envelopes gave some clue of where in the world he was at any particular time. The letters rarely, if ever, mentioned Lizzie and, as he never gave a forwarding address or contact number, Mrs Longton was never able to let Tom know what was happening in Lizzie's life. Tom was sure to be so proud of her if he only took the time to see her.

When Lizzie was younger and unable to read, it had been easy for Mrs Longton to elaborate on the contents of Tom's letters by including a mention of Lizzie that wasn't there. As soon as Lizzie could read, however, it became difficult for Mrs Longton to explain Tom's lack of interest in her. Mrs Longton always made excuses for him, telling Lizzie that his work as an archaeologist kept him away and busy that his mind was always on other things. Lizzie always defended him by saying that he must be very busy with such an important job and she couldn't wait until she was old enough to go and help him. Mrs Longton would never get used to seeing the hurt and disappointment that showed in Lizzie's eyes, despite the forced smile on her lips. Oh, how she wanted to give that son of hers a good hard thwack!

Surely, after eleven years he should have come to terms with what had happened on the night Lizzie was born. Mrs Longton believed that one day Lizzie would give up on her father and it would be too late for him to make amends.

"Look gran, look at this beautiful writing. It looks really special," Lizzie said breathlessly, holding up the envelope and plonking herself down at the big old kitchen table. Mrs Longton watched as Lizzie turned the envelope over in her hands; she had done the same thing herself numerous times since its arrival on the doormat that morning. There was strange quality to it as the ink glistened, like a snail trail of shimmering, silvery green liquid crystal scrawling its way across the envelope's surface.

The address was written in a script that neither Lizzie nor her grandmother had ever seen before. There was no stamp on the envelope, but instead there was a crest in the corner that contained two creatures that looked like a Unicorn and a Griffin entwined in some kind of struggle. Lizzie wondered if perhaps it had come from abroad and that maybe it was from her father after all. As she turned the envelope over to open it, she saw that there was a green wax seal on the point of the flap. She was surprised as surely only very important documents warranted such special treatment. At that moment, Bob Crowther's wife, Mary, came into the kitchen.

Mary was like an old mother hen. Her large floral apron was, as usual, stretched tightly across her rather rotund body, clear evidence that she loved eating the wonderful cakes and pies she baked almost as much as she loved making them.

"Oh, 'ello there me ducks," she smiled. "And an 'appy birthday to you. Oh, what you got there then, another birthday card?"

"Thanks, Mary. I'm not sure yet, although it doesn't feel like a card," smiled Lizzie, squeezing the contents of the letter between her fingers.

"Shall I make a pot o' tea, Mrs Longton?" asked Mary. Mrs Longton said that would be lovely and they would all have a large slice of the scrumptious chocolate birthday cake that Mary had made for Lizzie to go with it.

"Will Bob come and join us?" asked Lizzie, keen that Bob didn't miss out. Mary said she'd give him a call, as Bob was rather partial to a slice of cake.

As Mary bustled about the kitchen, filling the kettle and setting it to boil, Lizzie turned her attention back to the envelope in her hand.

"Well, open it then," Mrs Longton urged Lizzie impatiently, and sat down next to her at the table. "Don't keep us in suspenders."

"Oh, gran," Lizzie giggled, as she began to open the envelope with great care; she didn't want to spoil it by opening it too quickly and ripping the delicate material. Lifting the flap, she took out a sheet of pale green tinted parchment, and saw that the writing was once again written in the same unusual green ink and strange script that had been used on the envelope. Lizzie carefully unfolded the parchment, as suddenly light from the sun that had finally come out from behind its blanket of cloud flooded through the kitchen window. Its bright rays caught the beautiful writing and the green ink glistened like liquid emeralds. Scanning the words closely, Lizzie read the letter aloud to her grandmother.

"Dear Miss Longton,

I would like to offer you my most sincere felicitations on the 11th anniversary of your birth."

Lizzie raised her eyebrow and she and her grandmother gave each other a quizzical grin.

"That's a very posh way of saying happy birthday, isn't it," grinned Mrs Longton.

Lizzie continued: *"In celebration of this auspicious occasion, it is with the greatest of pleasure that I write to inform you that you have won a holiday to stay at our exclusive establishment, Elvedom Castle Hotel."*

Lizzie's head snapped up in shock. She stared at her grandmother, whose mouth had dropped open in amazement. "What... How...?" she began, but her grandmother grabbed the letter from her hands, stunned by what she had just heard and read the remainder of the letter.

"You are, therefore, cordially invited, together with your grandmother, Mrs Amelia Longton, to come along to Elvedom Castle on Monday 17th April where our top class accommodation awaits you. We trust that you will make full use of our unique facilities.

Elvedom Castle is located in some of the most beautiful West Country countryside. We are sure that you will have a rewarding and unforgettable time during your stay at our exclusive and hallowed establishment.

Travel details and documents are enclosed.

Your servant,

Eldora Cherrytree

Head Housekeeper"

"Wow!" beamed Lizzie. "I've won a holiday. Yay!" She jumped up and hugged her grandmother's shoulders as Mrs Longton stared at the letter in her hands in confusion.

Running over to Mary, who was standing by the kitchen sink drying her hands on a tea towel, Lizzie grabbed her by

27

her still slightly damp hands and began dancing around with her. Mary laughed at Lizzie as she joined in the excitement.

"Whoa, whoa, whoa," Mrs Longton's abrupt tones brought Lizzie and Mary to a halt. "Now just a minute Lizzie, I wouldn't get too excited here. This could all be a hoax. I mean, neither you nor I have entered any competition to win a holiday as far as I'm aware."

A look of realisation hit Lizzie's face like a thunderbolt. It was quite true that they hadn't. So how could she have won a holiday? How would this Elvedom Castle Hotel have got her name and address and know that today was her birthday? She sat back down at the table next to her grandmother feeling deflated.

Mrs Longton asked Mary if she wouldn't mind finishing off making the tea while she and Lizzie tried to work out whether the letter was genuine or not.

"It's very odd that the Housekeeper's signed the letter; it sounds very formal signing it 'Your Servant'," Mrs Longton said, looking at the signature at the bottom of the parchment. "Most hotels would have their letters signed by the hotel manager. I suppose it's possible if it's a very old-fashioned sort of establishment. It's surprising that they haven't included a leaflet or brochure showing photos and giving details of their facilities."

"Maybe it's a scam!" chipped in Mary. "I've heard all about scams like this on the telly," she added, placing a steaming cup of tea in front of Mrs Longton and a large glass of cold milk by Lizzie. "They don't usually target kiddies though," she continued knowingly.

Mrs Longton thought it was particularly strange that there was no address, telephone number or any other contact details for the hotel contained anywhere in the letter or amongst the travel documents. The 17th was this coming Monday, only three days away. So how were they to

28

respond? How could they say that they were or weren't coming? Whoever this Eldora Cherrytree was, she was obviously confident that Lizzie and Mrs Longton would accept the offer and travel in exactly the way the documents instructed them and not by their own means.

"I think before we get too excited about this, we should try to investigate this hotel a bit further," suggested Mrs Longton. "It's Saturday tomorrow so we'll go to the village library and borrow their computer to check it out on the internet."

The Longtons didn't own a computer, even though Lizzie had tried on numerous occasions to persuade her grandmother to invest in one. Lizzie nodded in agreement, silently praying that the letter was genuine. It would be a brilliant birthday present if it were.

"This is strange; look at this Lizzie," Mrs Longton said, holding what looked like a glittering credit card between her finger and thumb and turning it so that the light bounced off its reflective surface. Lizzie took it hesitantly into her own hand and found it mesmerising.

Mrs Longton then took another identical card from the envelope, and the two of them held what were the most unusual looking train tickets that either of them had ever seen. Holding them up to the light, they shimmered and flashed with an almost diamond-like quality. As well as the two diamond-like tickets, there were two normal train tickets to travel from and back to their nearest railway station in Markham Town, and a further document giving full travel instructions for the day. It instructed them to go to Paddington Underground station in West London and take the escalator to the Diamond Line.

The document advised them that the train for Elvedom Castle Hotel would leave platform 11 at 11.00 hours and requested that they please ensure they arrive in good time, as the train taking them to Elvedom Castle was the only one travelling that day. There was a small map contained on the card, with a clear illustration of Paddington tube station ticket hall, and showed an escalator leading down to platform 11 and the Diamond Line. The Diamond Line train would then take them to Elvesham station where a car would be waiting to take them on the rest of their journey to Elvedom Castle.

"But gran," said Lizzie, looking up at Mrs Longton quizzically. "We've been to London loads of times and we've never seen a Diamond Line."

"That's because it doesn't exist, Lizzie. This letter has to be some kind of joke after all," she exclaimed.

"These tickets look real though," said Lizzie doubtfully, turning the one she was holding from side to side again as it glittered and gleamed brightly in her hand.

Mrs Longton looked at the glittering ticket in her own hand. It certainly appeared real enough.

"Well, as we don't have anything else planned for the Easter Holidays, we may as well go and see what this is all about," Mrs Longton decided.

"Absolutely," agreed Mary, enthusiastically. "Now, you two go off and sit yourselves down in the sittin' room and make your plans while I prepare somethin' nice for your supper," she said happily, and trundled off to the stove to do just that.

So, Lizzie and her grandmother took the letter, and its contents, at its word. They would get to the bottom of this mystery and discover why Lizzie's name had been put forward for some competition to win a holiday. Mrs Longton said that if they were going to play at being detectives then she was going to go up into the attic to retrieve her husband's old deerstalker hat. If she was going to act like

Sherlock Holmes then she might as well look like him. He was, after all, her favourite detective.

"We may as well have a bit of fun while we're about it," she grinned, as she tried on the battered old hat later that evening.

Chapter 3 – The Journey Begins

On Saturday morning, the day after receiving the letter about winning the holiday, Lizzie and her grandmother had gone into the little library in Chislewick Village and borrowed their computer to search the internet. Luckily, Lizzie had used computers at school and so knew just what to do but, as expected, they found nothing about either Elvedom Castle Hotel or the Diamond Line. Having drawn a blank, they had gone and had hot chocolate and cake at Mrs Crockford's tea shop, and discussed all the people they knew who could possibly have hatched such a hoax, should it turn out to be one.

Neither of them could believe that anyone would have taken the time and spent the money on producing such an elaborate joke. Even Regina and Veronica Bray, who had played some pretty cruel tricks on Lizzie over the years, weren't that imaginative. Having the amazingly beautiful tickets specially printed would have cost a small fortune and, although the twins were totally spoiled by their indulgent and adoring father, it was unlikely he would have wasted his precious fortune on something he would deem so trivial as tricking one of the inconsequential Longtons.

*

When the day of the journey arrived, the rain had finally stopped, but the gun metal grey skies overhead still threatened the earth below with a deluge before the day was out.

Lizzie and her grandmother had risen early and, having packed their suitcases the night before, had loaded them and themselves into Mrs Longton's faithful old Jaguar car. They then drove the ten miles into Markham Town to catch the 7:45 train into London's Victoria Station. Once in London, they would take the Underground to Paddington station in time to make their 11:00 connection.

Lizzie had had a restless night. As she and her grandmother boarded the London bound train, her emotions were all over the place. She was excited about the possibility of a free holiday (Lizzie had never really had a holiday before) but she was also feeling apprehensive in case the whole thing turned out to be a hoax. Her stomach was fluttering about all over the place and making her feel a bit queasy, which wasn't being helped by the motion of the train as it hurtled towards London. Lizzie could understand why people called the feeling butterflies as it was just like having a whole flock of them inside her stomach desperately trying to escape.

Sitting in the packed carriage, squashed up against the window, Lizzie watched as the Sussex countryside whizzed past in a blur. When she and her grandmother usually went to London, they would be looking forward to visiting museums or art galleries, going shopping or even just walking along the Thames – taking in the sights, smells and sounds of the city. Lizzie loved watching the street entertainers such as buskers and those performers who pretended to be statues; Lizzie knew she could never be one of those because she would never have been able to stay still long enough. On the few occasions, they had taken in a show at the theatre and it had been wonderful. This time, however, their journey to London was going to be different as she really didn't know how the day would turn out.

"What is it, Lizzie?" asked Mrs Longton, resplendent in her deerstalker hat and taking absolutely no notice of the amused glances she was attracting. "You aren't worried are you? I've told you that everything will be fine. If you've won a holiday then we'll have a lovely time, I'll make sure of that, and if it's just a prank that someone's played then we'll put our cases into storage at Paddington station and spend the day in London. Maybe we can get some cheap theatre tickets and go see a show; you'd like that, wouldn't you?"

Lizzie nodded at her grandmother and smiled. She loved her quirky grandma very much. Mrs Longton smiled back and leant across from her seat opposite, patting Lizzie's knee reassuringly.

"If it does turn out to be a joke, I shall track down whoever did it and they won't know what hit them," she growled, doing her best to look as scary as she could. Lizzie giggled at this because she had once seen her grandmother in full flight when she had been angry at Trevor Bray and it had been a pretty awesome sight.

As the train continued its clattering journey towards London, Lizzie decided to distract herself by burying her head in a book she'd borrowed from the library. It had been in a special section entitled – Holiday Reading. She was just getting to a good bit, when suddenly; she got the creepy, tingly feeling that she'd had so often lately – the sensation that she was being watched. Looking around the carriage, she noticed a small man in a very unusual bright green suit and similarly coloured knitted hat pulled down low over his ears. He was so unusual looking that she was surprised she hadn't noticed him before. He looked even odder than her grandmother in her deerstalker, but he didn't seem to be attracting anywhere near the same amount of amused glances from the other passengers. Although he was obviously trying to be discreet, Lizzie could see that he was peeking at her from over the top of his rather large newspaper.

Lizzie was used to people taking double glances at her because of her unusual ears, and she normally tried hard to ignore them, but she was so wound up with nerves that she decided to brazen it out and stared right back at him, hoping to embarrass him out of ogling, and gave him a huge cheesy grin. Surprisingly, he didn't seem at all embarrassed and instead smiled politely back, inclining his head at her in a slight bow, then returned to perusing his newspaper.

Lizzie was taken aback. "How odd," she thought, and, after another quick look at the man, who now appeared to be engrossed in his newspaper, turned her back to him slightly and returned her attention to her book.

In what seemed like no time at all, the train pulled into busy, bustling Victoria Station. Lizzie clung onto her grandmother's arm as they and their luggage were swept along with the tide of commuters onto the platform and away to the Underground station.

Whenever Lizzie and Mrs Longton had travelled to London in the past, they had avoided the rush-hour, when all the commuters usually travelled, but today they had no option but to go with the flow. Mrs Longton bemoaned the fact that these days, the rush-hour in London extended to about five hours in the morning and much the same in the evenings. Grumbling as she went, she said she couldn't understand how people did this journey day in and day out just to earn a living.

Before they knew it, they were deep beneath ground standing on the tube platform for the next leg of their journey towards the mystery Diamond Line.

"Well, I hope that if the Diamond Line exists, it isn't as hectic as this," Mrs Longton puffed down at Lizzie, her face red with the exertion and her deerstalker hat, which had been knocked slightly askew during their buffeted journey between train and tube. Lizzie couldn't help laughing when she noticed a man standing next to them, giving her grandmother a very strange look. Lizzie whispered up to her grandmother that she wasn't sure if he thought she was odd because of her hat, or the fact that she'd mentioned some unknown tube line. Mrs Longton chuckled and said it was most probably that he thought she was some barmy old bat in a hat.

They clung together, pressed in on all sides, desperately holding onto their luggage whilst the tube train rattled along its journey towards Oxford Circus where they were to take another tube to Paddington. At Oxford Circus, they were poured out of the tube's doors and swept across the platform with a swath of bodies intent on making their way to the shops and businesses situated along the famous shopping street. Struggling against the flow, Lizzie and Mrs Longton made it onto the next platform for the line taking them to Paddington station.

This tube train was less busy, as most people had left the Underground in central London to go to their jobs in the offices and shops in the city, rather than heading north out of London towards the suburbs and commuter-land. Mrs Longton managed to grab a seat for the few short stops to Paddington, and Lizzie perched herself on her grandmother's knee.

"Will you be disappointed if this all turns out to be a joke?" Lizzie asked her grandmother.

Mrs Longton thought for a moment and then said, "I will, Lizzie. I'd be disappointed for you mainly and I shall be very cross if it is, as I am actually quite looking forward to a nice break. It's been a long time since I've stayed in a hotel."

Lizzie held on to her grandmother's arm tighter than ever as they got off the tube train at Paddington station. Her heart was beating so hard that she could hear the blood pounding in her ears, and her brain and nerve ends seemed to be buzzing.

Mrs Longton reached into her handbag and took out the travel instructions they'd received and looked at the little map showing them the way to platform 11. As they made their way up the escalators to the main ticket hall, Mrs Longton told Lizzie to look out for signs pointing them to the Diamond Line. They found none.

"Can you see any mention of the Diamond Line anywhere, darling?" Mrs Longton asked Lizzie, having scoured every sign herself. Lizzie stood in the centre of the concourse, her sharp eyes scanning each station sign again, just in case she'd missed something. Mrs Longton looked at the map again, turning it upside down and sideways on, just to make sure that she was viewing it from the correct angle; maps had never been her strong point.

"Well, judging from the map's layout, the escalator to platform 11 should be over there in that corner," she said, holding up the map and pointing to a dark recess to her right. They peered gloomily over at the corner concerned.

"It's just a battered old door, gran," groaned Lizzie, tears of disappointment pricking at her eyes. "It's all just a joke after all," she muttered.

"I'm going to go and ask someone in the ticket office; just to make sure," Mrs Longton announced, and was just about to march in that direction when she was brought abruptly to a halt.

"Excuse me," said a small, high-pitched voice from just behind them. Mrs Longton and Lizzie swung around, and there stood a young man. He was of diminutive height, slightly built and dressed completely in green. He wore an emerald green velvet suit with a paler green roll-necked sweater beneath the jacket, and he held a green woollen hat nervously in his hand; a newspaper was rolled up and tucked under his arm. Lizzie recognised him immediately as the man who had been staring at her on the train that morning. Was he following them, she thought suddenly. Then, she almost gasped with surprise as she noticed something else very odd about him, as well as his strange attire; he had very long, pointed ears that were remarkably similar to her own.

"I couldn't help overhearing that you're looking for the Diamond Line?" the man continued, politely.

As Lizzie gaped at the little man, Mrs Longton, although equally astonished at the man's appearance, asked, "Are you a member of staff? It's just that I thought the Underground's uniform was blue."

The man shook his head vigorously. "Oh, no, no! I'm not a member of London Underground's staff but I can show you the way to the Diamond Line if it would help. Please follow me." He beckoned them, and began walking towards the corner that Lizzie and Mrs Longton had been peering over at just moments earlier.

Lizzie and her grandmother looked at each other in bemusement, shrugged, and, with arms linked, proceeded to follow him. As they approached what appeared to be a battered old door from a distance, it seemed to change shape and appear vague and fuzzy around the edges until it no longer seemed to be a door, but the mouth of a tunnel. Lizzie and Mrs Longton hesitated and looked at each other uncertainly.

"Do you think it's safe to go in there, gran?" asked Lizzie hesitantly, pulling back slightly on her grandmother's arm.

As the little man stood smiling at the mouth of the tunnel, like some airline crew waiting to welcome passengers aboard some flight to exotic lands, Mrs Longton turned to Lizzie.

"Well, my love, there's only one way to find out. In for a penny, in for a pound, as they say," she said, patting Lizzie's hand reassuringly. So, with arms hooked together tightly, and dragging their suitcases behind them, they stepped into the tunnel.

Chapter 4 – The Diamond Line

A blinding white light suddenly hit the back of Lizzie and her grandmother's eyes like an electric shock, and they staggered back in surprise. As their eyes adjusted to the sudden change in light levels, they could see that the tunnel they were standing in appeared to be made of sheet ice or glass or some other transparent material, which glistened like cut glass or diamonds. Cascades of water, or some other clear liquid, ran like rivulets behind the surface of the walls, giving the impression that they were walking through a waterfall. It reminded Lizzie of pictures she'd seen of those large aquariums where people walked through a tunnel with sharks and other marine creatures swimming about over their heads. Lizzie gazed around her in stunned silence.

"Wow," she gasped, when she finally found her voice. "It looks like the walls are melting," Lizzie said.

"Wow indeed, darling," her grandmother agreed, squinting at her surroundings. "I certainly hope they aren't melting otherwise we'll get very wet," she added, as she looked up at the ceiling above them.

"Excuse me, ma'am, but do you have your ticket ready?" The little man had turned to Lizzie; in his hand he held an identical ticket to those that Lizzie and her grandmother had received days earlier. It was then they realised that they had come upon some extraordinary looking ticket barriers. They were, in essence, very like the normal Underground barriers that you see every day when travelling the Tube, only these ones weren't made of grey metal, but shone like burnished gold. Mrs Longton fished out the Diamond Line tickets from the recesses of her handbag, where she'd put them for safe keeping. Following the little man's example, they inserted their tickets in the appropriate slot and walked through the gates as they slid silently aside for them. Lizzie looked at her grandmother as they watched their companion walk on ahead of them.

"I've never been called ma'am before. Isn't that what you call the Queen?" Lizzie whispered to her grandmother. Mrs Longton eyed the strange little man keenly; he certainly was an odd character, and she hoped that they were doing the right thing in following him so trustingly.

"It's very fortunate that you overheard us looking for this tube line, Mr ...?" Mrs Longton called to the little man who was marching on ahead. He stopped in his tracks and turned to face them.

"Doogoody," he announced, bowing so low that his nose almost touched the pristine floor beneath them. "Elwood Doogoody, at your service."

"Doogoody by name, do goody by nature," quipped Lizzie, then squeezed her lips tightly together in an effort to stop the giggles that were bubbling up in her throat from bursting out. Mr Doogoody bowed his head once more.

"That is my motto, ma'am," he beamed happily, the colour rising in his pale face.

"Well, as I said, it's very fortunate that you were nearby when we were looking for this tube line," continued Mrs Longton, still eyeing him suspiciously; his behaviour and choice of words were most peculiar. "I was most disappointed to find that Paddington station was not more clearly signposted. There seems to be an awful lot of secrecy surrounding this particular Underground line. My granddaughter and I have spent the last couple of days searching for information about it and could find nothing."

"Indeed," was all Mr Doogoody said in reply, and he turned once more to continue on his way. Ahead of them, they could see an escalator stretching away into the depths of the underground for what appeared to be hundreds of feet. The escalator treads gleamed silver and it appeared that it was either very well maintained or hardly ever used.

"Please mind the step," announced Mr Doogoody, as he stood aside to allow Lizzie and her grandmother to step onto the escalator. The escalator surprisingly made no noise at all as it glided on its journey into the depths. There were no other people around and the eerie silence and solitude of their surroundings was quite unsettling for Mrs Longton. She turned to Mr Doogoody.

"Excuse me, Mr Doogoody," Mrs Longton said. "I'm interested to know how you knew where the entrance to the Diamond Line was, when there were no signs to be seen anywhere. It doesn't seem to be particularly well used."

"Oh, that's because this line isn't available for the general public's use. It is for use by special invitation only," replied Mr Doogoody, grandly.

"Oh, I see," she replied, not really seeing anything at all. She continued, "My granddaughter here appears to have won a holiday and, when we received the letter informing her of this, well, that was the first time we'd ever heard of the Diamond Line."

"The Diamond Line has a very exceptional heritage and is certainly not your common or garden tube line. Indeed not. Because of that, its existence is kept quite secret. We don't want any undesirables trying to use it now, do we?" said Mr Doogoody, conspiratorially.

"Special invitation? A secret line?" thought Mrs Longton. She was desperately trying to sort out the bizarre snippets of information she was gathering. Why were she and Lizzie the only 'specially invited' people to use it today? It must be a grand sort of hotel that used such an exclusive railway line as this. Of course, Mrs Longton knew that Lizzie was, in her opinion anyway, a special girl in lots of ways, but how on earth had she come to win such an amazing prize? She'd never even entered a competition. How and why had she

41

been singled out in this way? Maybe it had been some kind of lottery draw. Mrs Longton turned again to Mr Doogoody.

"From the little you've already told us, you seem to know quite a lot more about this particular tube line," Mrs Longton said, smiling encouragingly. Mr Doogoody puffed out his chest proudly and eagerly announced that, as a matter of fact, he did indeed happen to know quite a bit about the history of the line.

"Oh, please tell us?" said Lizzie excitedly; she found the strange little man in his bright green outfit quite fascinating, and was especially intrigued by his extraordinary ears, to which her eyes were constantly drawn. Mr Doogoody launched into what appeared to be a well-rehearsed lecture:

"The Diamond Line is *the* premier underground line in the Country, if not the world. It was completed in 1897 in recognition of Her Majesty Queen Victoria's Diamond Jubilee. It was built for her and her family's use and that of her most important staff and personnel. The line runs between London's Paddington station and what was her favourite home, Osborne House on the Isle of Wight. However, the Queen used it infrequently, as she was uncomfortable with the thought of being so far underground for any length of time. She also liked to be able to view her country and its people from above ground whilst she was en route to her various residences and so, therefore, preferred more conventional modes of transport. The Diamond Line reverted to the control of those who had built it upon her death and so it has remained," Mr Doogoody concluded, grandly.

Mrs Longton stared at Mr Doogoody in stunned silence. Finally finding her voice, she asked incredulously, "Are you saying that this line goes underground all the way to the Isle of Wight?"

"Yes, madam, but the final section of the route hasn't been used for many years. Not since Osborne House stopped being used as a royal residence in fact," Mr Doogoody said, nodding vigorously and smiling widely, showing pearly white teeth that shone almost as brightly as the lights of the tunnel. Mrs Longton suddenly collapsed into spasms of laughter. Lizzie and Mr Doogoody stared at her.

"But that's impossible!" she gasped, trying to regain her composure. "I'm sorry, but I've never heard anything so ludicrous in my life. There is absolutely no way that, in the 1800s, they would have had the engineering expertise to have built an underground railway line under hundreds of miles of the English countryside. I mean, I know the Victorians had some great engineers, Isambard Kingdom Brunel for one, but even he couldn't have managed that," she said haughtily. "Not only that," she continued, vehemently, "You're also asking me to believe that they tunnelled under the Solent and a chunk of the Isle of Wight, all the way to Osborne House. I'm sorry but that's absolute poppy-cock."

"I beg your pardon, madam," said Mr Doogoody raising himself up to his full height, which wasn't much, and barely concealing his indignation. He looked most affronted, his face had turned a very lurid shade of red, which clashed terribly with his green hat. "The engineers who built this railway are the most brilliant engineers on this planet," he announced proudly, and, turning his flushed face towards the bottom of the escalator, which was rapidly approaching, he marched down its remaining treads.

As they followed behind his retreating back, they found themselves on the platform of the station. The walls seemed to be covered in white mosaic tiles, and there were arched recesses along the platform's walls which contained mosaics of animals and birds, and what looked like mythological creatures. It then occurred to Mrs Longton that there was something distinctly missing from the walls of the place;

there were no advertisements. In fact, there hadn't been any adverts on any of the walls since they'd gone through the entrance to the Diamond Line. The sense of foreboding grew in Mrs Longton's head. She wasn't sure she liked the way this "adventure" was panning out. There was something decidedly weird going on.

Lizzie sensed that the atmosphere developing between her grandmother and their new acquaintance was turning noticeably frosty. In an attempt to pour some soothing oils onto what was beginning to look like some fairly turbulent waters sloshing around between them, she said, "Excuse me, Mr Doogoody, Sir?"

He turned to face her, once again inclining his head. "Oh please, ma'am, I am not a Sir. I should prefer it if you call me Elwood."

"Elwood," she smiled. "Thank you. I'm sure my grandmother didn't mean to offend you (*she glanced meaningfully at her grandmother whose face was fixed with a firm frown*); it's just that all this information about the Diamond Line has come as bit of a surprise to us." Lizzie looked hard at her grandmother for support but she was still staring at Elwood suspiciously, and so Lizzie continued.

"You see, we've often been to London, and we have lots of books at home about the history of London, but we've never heard of the Diamond Line. You also said that the engineers of this line *are* the best on the planet but surely you mean they *were* the best because they'd all be dead by now. I mean, you did say it was built over a hundred years ago."

Elwood suddenly looked flustered, as though he had said something he shouldn't have. "Yes, of course, were the best. Of course," he blustered. "I think you should be assured that all will become clear as the day progresses. So, if you'd be so kind, I shall refrain from saying anything further on the subject. Ah, here we are," he waved his arm in the direction of a tunnel at the end of the platform.

At that precise moment, from the gaping mouth of tunnel came the most amazing vision. Gliding swiftly and silently towards them was the most startlingly beautiful tube train that Lizzie could ever have imagined. The front of it looked as if it were gilded in gold leaf filigree that shone and sparkled as the lights of the platform struck it from all angles. The train's headlamps shone out like beacons, almost dazzling them in the process. As the driver's cab approached, Lizzie tried to look through the windscreen to catch the driver's eye as he pulled into the station, but the cab was encased in mirrored glass and so all she could see was her wide-eyed expression staring back at her.

The carriages of the train gleamed with equal brilliance. They seemed to be burnished silver and were covered with swirling, intricately entwined patterns along their panelled sides. When Lizzie tried to peer through the windows to see inside each carriage, once again she could only see her reflection gazing back at her. Lizzie and her grandmother became acutely aware of their drab, and somewhat dishevelled, appearances from their mirror images and Mrs Longton quickly whipped off the deerstalker hat she'd been wearing all morning. It now seemed totally out of keeping with the immaculate and stately surroundings they now found themselves in. She stuffed the hat unceremoniously into her handbag and quickly smoothed down her rumpled hair.

As the train finally came to a halt, its doors slid open with a barely audible hiss. Lizzie, Mrs Longton and Elwood stepped into the carriage nearest to them, and Lizzie had the sudden impression that she had travelled a couple of hundred years into the future. The interior of the carriage looked more like the inside of a private jet belonging to some multi-millionaire rather than that of a tube train. Each seat was a sumptuous grey leather armchair. Piped music was playing throughout the carriage; beautiful, relaxing music that seemed to seep into their brains, and they began to feel the tensions of the morning loosen in their bodies. Lizzie was so pre-occupied by examining her surroundings, and the relaxing music flowing through her brain, that she almost jumped out of her skin when a voice said, "Welcome to the Diamond Line, ma'am. May I show you to your seat?"

Swinging round, Lizzie saw a young woman standing to the left of the door that she had just walked through. She was dressed in a shiny silver coloured uniform, similar to that of an airline stewardess. The girl's clear blue eyes smiled down at Lizzie and then up at Mrs Longton.

"Follow me, please," she said, in a gentle sing-song voice as she walked over to two of the armchairs, about midway down the carriage, and indicated that they should sit down. Lizzie and Mrs Longton did as they were asked and lowered themselves into the two plush chairs.

"My name is Elvine and it is my pleasure to be your servant today," said the stewardess pleasantly, dipping her knee in a slight curtsey. "Should you require anything at all during your journey, you need only ask," she continued, bowing her head.

Lizzie looked up to thank Elvine, but was struck dumb as she looked at the girl more closely. Her mouth gaped open as she stared at the girl's ears. They were exactly like those of Elwood; in fact, they were exactly like those of her own. Lizzie suddenly realised that she was staring and quickly looked over at Elwood, who was taking a seat just across the aisle to where Lizzie and Mrs Longton were sitting. Looking at Elwood and Elvine, Lizzie thought how alike they both were. They had the same colouring and build, but most intriguingly - the same pointed ears. Lizzie wondered if perhaps they were related. The whole day was beginning to feel like a dream, so surreal that she started to wonder if perhaps she hadn't woken up yet and that she was in some prolonged dream.

"Gran," Lizzie whispered, leaning forwards so that only her grandmother could hear her. "Would you pinch me, please?"

"I know what you mean, darling," Mrs Longton said anxiously; the initial calming effects of the music were wearing off, as her nerves took over. "None of this seems quite real, does it? As lovely as this all seems, I just hope we're doing the right thing here. I feel decidedly uneasy."

Elwood looked across at them and smiled reassuringly. "Are you all settled in?" he beamed happily and, as Lizzie and Mrs Longton nodded mutely, said "Then the journey can begin." He then nodded at Elvine who, in turn, walked over to a small speaker set into the wall of the carriage and spoke into it briefly.

The doors of the train slid closed, with just a hint of a hydraulic hiss, and Lizzie and her grandmother felt the slight sensation of being pushed back into their seats as the train pulled away from the station. The train seemed to make no noise at all and Lizzie wasn't sure if that was because the sound of the music, which seemed to permeate everywhere, had drowned it out, or that the train actually didn't make any noise. As the lights of the platform suddenly disappeared, the view from the windows became momentarily black before suddenly springing into life.

In one window, she could see green fields and rolling hills zipping past. Another showed a mountain range, and in another there was a sandy cove and a rocky coastline stretching away to the distance, the sea pounding off the cliffs. Lizzie was mesmerised. She looked out of the window next to her to see a beautiful forest, where shafts of sparkling sunlight filtered through the leaves on the branches, lighting up the shrubs and plants below. A huge stag stepped out from behind a tree, his massive antlers blending in with the flora and fauna surrounding him in perfect camouflage. Lizzie knew that the train couldn't possibly be traveling through all these types of terrains at the same time, plus there was the irrefutable fact that they were traveling deep underground.

"This is amazing," she said wistfully as she gazed out at the scene from her window, her elbows leaning on the little table in front of her and her chin cupped in her hand. Elwood smiled brightly at her, his eyes twinkling in amusement.

"They are special images projected onto the glass to make your journey more pleasant, ma'am," he said. "It's a little boring just gazing out into blackness, don't you think?" Lizzie nodded in agreement.

Mrs Longton sat quietly in her seat, her eyes flitting from one window to another, as if lost for words. Her mind was working overtime trying to work out what was really happening. She was edgy and was feeling increasingly nervous about where they were going. Something was afoot; she didn't know what yet,, but she could feel it in her bones and she wasn't sure she liked it. She didn't feel that she and Lizzie were in danger, but there was definitely something bigger behind all of this; of that she was convinced. Elwood looked at her wearily. He could feel her disquiet and wanted to help her relax but was unsure of what to say or do. He decided to try and answer some of the questions that she was no doubt chewing over in her mind. Afterwards, he wished he hadn't.

"Mrs Longton," he began again. "Perhaps it would help if I explained briefly that I was sent to meet you at Paddington station and guide you to Elvedom Castle in case you should get lost on the way. Other than that, I'm afraid that I'm not at liberty to say too much at this time as I have been instructed to leave explanations to others. I am purely here to ensure that you reach your destination safely," he concluded.

Mrs Longton glared at him. "So you knew that we are on our way to Elvedom Castle Hotel? What else are you hiding from us, Mr Doogoody?"

"Elwood," it was Lizzie's turn now to have her say. Staring Elwood in the eyes, she said, "You weren't only sent to meet us at Paddington Station, were you?" Elwood's face reddened once again to the bright shade of crimson that was so unbecoming to him.

"Er, umm..." he spluttered.

Mrs Longton turned quizzically towards Lizzie. "What are you saying, Lizzie?"

"You were also on our train from Markham Town, weren't you? I saw you staring at me from across the carriage," Lizzie continued. Elwood seemed to crumple under the even fiercer glare now emanating from Mrs Longton; he looked like he'd been caught stealing from the cookie jar. His face fell and he hung his head; his crimson coloured face had spread through to the tips of his ears which seemed to wriggle in embarrassment.

"So, you've been following us?" fumed Mrs Longton, her colouring was rapidly starting to match that of Elwood's but for a whole different reason.

"I must own that you are right, but I must beg that you please do not ask me anything further," he pleaded. "I am just a messenger and I must allow others to answer any further questions you may have. I promise that all will become clear when we reach our destination," he said humbly, averting his eyes as if he would give in to Lizzie's demands if she stared hard enough.

"Humph," grunted Mrs Longton in frustration and flopped back into her seat, now turning her glare to the woodland scene outside her window.

In an effort to try and soothe her grandmother, Lizzie reached over and took her hand. "Come on, gran. We might as well enjoy the ride," she said, as she snuggled down further into the soft leather. "Remember what you said, it'll be an adventure. Well, you must admit it's all pretty exciting." Mrs Longton gave Lizzie a wan smile.

"I suppose you're right," she admitted grudgingly. "I did say that, so I suppose I ought to just go with the flow." She sighed deeply, leant back in her chair and closed her eyes. "And these chairs are very comfortable," she grinned, opening one eye and peering a Lizzie.

"That's the spirit," chirped Elwood, smiling brightly from across the aisle; he felt as if a great weight had been lifted off his shoulders. Then, noticing Mrs Longton's one eye swivel in his direction, he quickly gazed out of the window next to him.

As the train sped on its journey into the depths of the English underground world, Lizzie let herself relax, settled back into her luxurious seat and listened to the beautiful soothing music still filling the carriage. During the trip, Elvine, the stewardess, would appear silently from time to time, offering them refreshments; placing small silver trays in front of them with selections of lovely creamy, sugary cakes and small delicate sandwiches, beautifully presented on fine china. Lizzie and Mrs Longton chose from selections of teas or cordials – flavours so intense that they seemed to explode in their mouths. The whole experience of the ride and the food and the drink was almost magical.

"This is fantastic," Lizzie garbled through a mouthful of creamy chocolate cake. Her gran could only send a big creamy grin back at her as her mouth was full of strawberry shortcake. After wiping the crumbs and cream from their lips and fingers with small, hot floral scented towels, they sat back in their seats and relaxed. Mrs Longton's eyelids drooped and she snoozed whilst Lizzie gazed at the windows and thought about the day's events so far.

A short time later, Lizzie felt the sensation that the train was slowing down. As it came to a stop, Elvine appeared and announced that they had now reached their destination and should prepare to disembark.

"Thank you for travelling on the Diamond Line," she announced in her lovely tinkly voice. As the passengers rose to their feet, the doors of the train slid open with a gentle hiss and they could see the platform of a station through its gap.

As Lizzie and Mrs Longton stepped off the train and onto the platform, they could see that it could not have been more different from the one they had left behind at Paddington. There were no glistening white walls and floors here, but was more like having arrived in the middle of a forest. The walls, ceiling and floor were of every shade of green and brown you could possibly imagine. Dappled light shone from illuminations discreetly hidden up in the eaves of the roof of the platform, and it seemed to follow them as they walked towards a flight of steps that looked as though they were hewn from the huge trunks of trees. Lizzie felt that the whole experience was like being in some kind of fantasy film and she could almost imagine that pixies and fairies would suddenly flit out in front of them at any moment.

"This is getting more surreal as the day goes on," Mrs Longton whispered to Lizzie, out of the corner of her mouth, as she peered around at her surroundings.

Elwood strode on ahead. At the top of the steps, he called down to Lizzie and Mrs Longton, "This way please."

As Lizzie and Mrs Longton reached the top of the steps, they could see daylight flooding in through a large pointed archway that led out of the station. Elwood stood to one side and, with a grand sweep of his arm, announced, "The car awaits you, ma'am."

Lizzie and her grandmother stopped, looked at each other and then, linking arms and lugging their suitcases behind them, they strode out into the daylight.

Chapter 5 – Surprises in Store

"Oh my goodness! A Silver Ghost! Surely we can't be travelling to the hotel in this?" exclaimed Mrs Longton, stopping in her tracks, her eyes widening in awe. There, parked in front of the station, was the most beautiful car that Lizzie had ever seen. Its high classic lines were a lustrous shade of green that seemed to shimmer in the sunlight, bouncing off its reflective surface. The leather button-cushioned seats were a deeper shade of green and shone like they had been buffed to an inch of their lives. The chrome head-lamps, grill and footplates sparkled like mirrors. The car was a true credit to its creators, Messrs Rolls and Royce.

"But I haven't seen one of these for years. There can't be many left in the world; it must be worth a fortune. Elvedom Castle Hotel must be very exclusive if it can afford to send one of these to collect us," Mrs Longton said incredulously, as she caressed one of the car's curved mudguards.

Elwood beamed. "It's one of the earliest models too; having been built in 1908. I believe that it is considered priceless," he announced, proudly. Mrs Longton shook her head in disbelief. What kind of hotel was this Elvedom Castle to send a priceless motor vehicle to collect two ordinary guests?

A tall and very blond young man, wearing a smart, dark green velvet uniform, topped by a flat chauffeur's cap of the same colour, was standing towards the rear of the car. As Mrs Longton walked towards him, he opened the car's rear passenger door and Lizzie and her grandmother clambered up onto the running board and into the car's soft leather seats. As Elwood took the seat up front next to the driver, the car's engine purred into life and pulled smoothly away.

"Oh, this takes me back," Mrs Longton sighed, as she leant back into the comfort of the leather seat and looked around her at the stunning features of the open backed car.

"My grandfather used to have an old Rolls Royce Phantom when I was a little girl," she told Lizzie. "It had been in the family since before the Great War. I can remember my mother, grandmother and I piling into it and stuffing a picnic basket in the boot and off we'd fly – well it felt like flying – along the country lanes. My grandfather said he'd always wanted a Silver Ghost as it was the best car in the world," she reminisced.

"And quite right too, madam," agreed Elwood, turning to face Lizzie and Mrs Longton from his seat in the front. "Mr Royce himself said it was the best car he ever produced when he personally delivered this specimen. He said that he and his people had excelled themselves. I remember it like it was yesterday," he added wistfully. Lizzie noticed the chauffer shoot Elwood a glance as she and her gran stared at the back of Elwood's head. What was he talking about?

"How can you possibly remember that? Henry Royce died in the early 1930s," asked Mrs Longton.

"1933 actually," piped up Elwood, who obviously couldn't help himself when it came to showing off how knowledgeable he was. He suddenly hung his head and lowered his eyes sheepishly, realising that once again he'd said too much. Lizzie could see his ears turning a bright shade of pink in embarrassment.

"There; precisely!" exclaimed Mrs Longton, surprised not only by what he said but also by the fact that he'd heard what *she'd* said. "That's over 80 years ago and you can't be any more than what, twenty five or so? You couldn't possibly have met him, you're far too young," she said.

"Oh, it's very kind of you to say so," Elwood blushed and grinned broadly. "I do try to look after myself and keep my skin looking good." Mrs Longton and Lizzie gaped at each other in surprise; shaking their heads and shrugging their shoulders in disbelief. Mrs Longton was rapidly coming to the conclusion that the poor little man was slightly deranged.

Settling back into her seat, Mrs Longton was becoming increasingly uneasy about what they were letting themselves in for. There were some very odd things going on. She looked across at her granddaughter and saw her bright eager face watching the undulating countryside as they whizzed past. The weather in the West Country couldn't have been more different than the dreary day they'd left behind at the beginning of their journey. The sun beat down onto Lizzie's upturned face as she soaked in the view of black and white cows chewing on lush green grass, and white fleeced sheep grazing on the hillsides. It was the perfect picture of a typical English vista and Mrs Longton couldn't help but smile as her heart swelled with love for the little girl sitting beside her.

"Well, here we are," called Elwood over his shoulder, as the car began to slow. They had been travelling along an avenue of tall trees that lined the sides of the road, and in their midst appeared a huge pair of intricately woven wrought iron gates, supported by two large columns of grey granite. Lizzie held her breath as it suddenly hit her that their mystery destination would soon be revealed.

As the car approached the gates, they slowly drew apart and allowed them to enter the grounds of Elvedom Castle Hotel. The driveway to the hotel seemed to go on forever, but it gave them time to enjoy the view of the grounds of the castle, which were beautiful. There were an abundance of exotic looking trees and shrubs, many of them in full bloom; fruit trees with blossoms of the palest pinks, yellows, whites, lilacs and even pale blues could be seen dotted in amongst every shade of green. Carpets of daffodils and bluebells covered the ground beneath the trees.

As the car drew to a halt and its passengers stepped out of its comfort, Mrs Longton gasped. "Oh my; what a beautiful building!"

Lizzie found herself looking at the most amazing structure she'd ever seen. Elvedom Castle seemed to have been hewn out of the very ground it rose up out of. It was as if it was totally at one with its surroundings. The castle had turrets at each corner, which looked like giant ancient trees with gnarled trunks. Twisting vines and trailing plants wound their way up its enormous sides. The main body of the building was covered with more climbing and trailing vegetation; ivy and purple wisteria, together with some plant with huge white waxy flowers blooming in amongst the leaves, almost covered the walls. The scant bits of exposed masonry was seen to be ornately carved. Lizzie could just make out an occasional gargoyle or two. The Diamond Line and the car had impressed Lizzie and her grandmother, but this? This was truly spectacular. Lizzie felt something stir in her stomach that she couldn't describe. There was something about the castle that felt so familiar, an intense feeling that she had always known it, almost as if she had seen it before; like in a dream.

A small, polite, "Ahem" drew their attention away from admiring the castle to a small, elderly, grey haired man standing nearby. He looked to be either a doorman or butler as he was wearing a dark green uniform and a bright grin on his friendly, open face.

"Mrs Longton, Miss Longton, welcome, welcome. My name is Elbert and I am butler here," he squeaked, bowing low to Lizzie and Mrs Longton.

"Thank you Elfer, that will be all," he said to the chauffeur, who also bowed before turning and driving away. Elbert then spoke to Elwood, who was standing beside Lizzie and Mrs Longton's suitcases. "Elwood, could you please advise his Ma..., ahem, the Master, that our guests have arrived safely."

"Of course," said Elwood, giving Elbert a stern look as if the elderly man could have been about to say something he shouldn't. Elbert nodded briskly, and threw Elwood a knowing look. Lizzie watched the encounter between them with interest and was sure she'd spotted Elbert wink at their travelling companion as Elwood passed by. Lizzie looked at her grandmother to see if she had observed anything untoward but Mrs Longton was still staring in rapt admiration at her beautiful surroundings.

"Now, let's get your luggage organised and arrange a nice spot of tea for you. I trust you had a pleasant journey?" Elbert said, as he beckoned two young girls in smart green maid's outfits who had just come out of the castle. He instructed them to take Lizzie and her grandmother's cases to their rooms. Elbert's sprightly manner belied the looks of his obviously advanced years. "Please follow me," he chirped brightly, as he headed towards the doors of the castle.

As they passed through two of the biggest and most elaborately carved oak doors, they seemed to have been plunged into a dark cavern. Having left the bright sunny day outside, it took a few moments for Lizzie and Mrs Longton's eyes to adjust to the cool darkness of the entrance hall. Lizzie felt almost blinded by the difference at first but, as her eyes grew accustomed to what appeared to be a gloomy interior, she could begin to see that the hall was actually a vast vestibule, with doors leading off in all directions, and a huge sweeping staircase ahead of them, which appeared to go up into the castle's depths. The walls of the entrance hall weren't flat and even, but gave the impression of having been carved out of rock, a bit like the inside of a cave, and in the subdued light they seemed to glisten, as if they contained tiny flecks of metal or chipped glass. The reason it was so dark inside, though, was because the only natural light coming in was from the two huge front doors. Peculiarly, there were no windows.

In between each of the numerous doors leading from the hall were pedestals, each containing a statue of what appeared to be men and women dressed in medieval clothes. The men dressed in doublets and hose held swords or bows and quivers full of arrows, or other ancient types of weapons, such as axes or spears. The women wore long flowing gowns and carried posies of flowers or musical instruments, such as lyres or harps.

Lizzie sniffed the air, expecting it to smell damp and musty but it didn't in the slightest. It smelt clean and fragrant as if the flowers from outside had lent their fragrance to the castle inside.

The light in the hall gradually began to lift, as torches in sconces on the walls began to burn. Lizzie felt as though she had somehow travelled back in time by several hundred years as she looked at her surroundings. They had travelled on a futuristic train to this almost medieval castle. Mrs Longton looked around. Apart from there being no windows, there was something else missing. Mrs Longton addressed Elbert.

"Excuse me, but we appear to be the only people here today. I've been looking out at the grounds and haven't seen another soul about. Do you have many guests staying?"

"Ah, um, well, no, no, not many. No," mumbled Elbert, vaguely. Then, more clearly, asked them to follow him. As they followed Elbert across the vast floor space, Mrs Longton's feelings of unease returned in spade loads. "Where do we register then?" she asked, scanning the hall for a reception desk.

Elbert stopped and looked at her. "Register?" he quizzed, as if wondering what a register actually was. Then, as if suddenly remembering, he said, "No, no. That won't be necessary, thank you." And set off across the hall once again.

Trundling along behind him, Mrs Longton looked around her, "Well, where *are* the others guests?" Elbert did not reply, but walked on determinedly towards his destination.

"Are you expecting many more visitors, then?" continued Mrs Longton; like a dog with a bone, she didn't like to let go until she was satisfied.

Elbert was beginning to look increasingly uncomfortable under Mrs Longton's continued questions, and he ran a finger around the inside of his crisp white collar as if it was suddenly getting a little tight. Lizzie was astute enough to realise that her grandmother's questions were beginning to unsettle the little man. He was showing a distinct similarity to Elwood when he was under the pressure of Mrs Longton's questioning.

"Have any of the other visitors also won holidays here?" fired Mrs Longton at Elbert's back, as he walked ever more briskly ahead of them.

"Umm, err, I..., I'm afraid I don't have that information. Now, if you'd be so kind, all will be made clear shortly," Elbert replied, bouncing up and down on the balls of his feet as he rushed ahead. Lizzie and Mrs Longton hurried along behind him, looking at each other uncertainly. Lizzie was completely baffled now as to what on earth was going on.

"Curiouser and curiouser," Mrs Longton hissed into Lizzie's ear, as if reading Lizzie's thoughts. Finally, Elbert reached a large wooden door to a room to their right, opened it slowly, and invited them to enter.

Lizzie's stomach gave a lurch as, for some unexplainable reason, she suddenly felt an impending sense of destiny settle on her. She followed closely behind her grandmother as they went through the door.

The room they entered was as unlike the large medieval cavern they had just left behind as it was possible to be.

59

They had walked into what appeared to be a gentleman's study. A large, highly polished wooden desk, behind which was a deeply padded green leather swivel chair, dominated the room. The walls were covered in books, most of which appeared, from the look of their well-worn leather spines, to be very old. A large window, framed by deep green velvet drapes that fell in luxurious folds, filled the wall opposite the door. Through its panes, a stunning view of the spectacular gardens greeted the viewer's eyes.

On their left was an enormous stone fireplace, with logs burning in the grate that made the room feel warm and welcoming, even though the warm sun outside should have meant there was little need of a fire. Above the mantle of the fireplace hung a huge portrait of a small, silver haired man with the brightest, greenest eyes that seemed to follow the room's occupants no matter where they stood. The man was wearing a golden crown, studded with large green gems that sat low on his head and covered the tops of his ears. He was resting his hand on the hilt of a long, silver, jewel-encrusted sword. He wore the robes of a King or Lord of the realm; Lizzie had seen people from the House of Lords wearing similar robes on TV at the opening of Parliament, the only difference being that the man in the portrait wore green rather than the usual red. The proud tilt of his head showed him to be a man of some significance. It was the only picture in the room as there were no other portraits or photos to be seen. It was very much a man's room rather than a woman's room, which rather surprised Mrs Longton as she had assumed that they would be entering the office of the Elvedom Castle's head house-keeper, Eldora Cherrytree.

"Please take a seat and make yourselves comfortable; the Master will be along presently," Elbert said, indicating a large leather sofa to one side of the fireplace. Opposite it was a large wing-backed easy chair. Before Mrs Longton had the chance to ask who "the Master" was, and why they had been taken to his office, Elbert had backed quickly out of the room, bowing as he went.

It was the first time that Lizzie and Mrs Longton had been left alone since arriving at Paddington station and meeting Elwood. They looked at each other with similar expressions of wide-eyed bafflement. Mrs Longton flopped down on the sofa and let out a long sigh.

"Well, gran, this sure is turning into a grand adventure," grinned Lizzie, as she sat down next to her grandmother. "I don't know what you think, but this isn't what I expected of a hotel. There's not many people about, are there?"

Mrs Longton took Lizzie's hand in her own. "No, there aren't, and I have to say that I'm very suspicious about this hotel. It's certainly living up to its claim of exclusivity; I haven't seen any evidence of there being any other guests at all. Also, I haven't seen any sign of the usual facilities that you'd expect in a high class hotel."

"What do you mean?" asked Lizzie.

"Well, when I used to frequent the best hotels in my dim and distant past," smiled Mrs Longton, "There were things like tennis courts, swimming pools and recreational areas. I expected to see at least a car park. I suppose it's possible that they're all hidden out the back of the castle somewhere. The reception hall also doesn't have a check-in desk. It's all most peculiar."

"Actually, gran, now you mention the car parking, I've just realised that apart from the car that brought us, I don't remember seeing any others on our drive here from the station. Did you?" Lizzie asked. After a brief think about it, Mrs Longton acknowledged that she didn't recall seeing any either.

Lizzie got up to check that the door to the room was fully closed and then walked over to a large bookcase lining one of the walls. She took one of the books from a shelf and tried reading the title on the spine.

61

"Look at this, gran. Can you understand this writing?" she asked, as she tried to read some unintelligible script on the binding. Her grandmother walked over to join her and, taking her half-moon reading glasses from out of her jacket pocket, she placed them on her nose and peered closely at the writing on the book.

"Well, it looks a bit like ancient Egyptian, but actually I think it may be some form of runic writing," she said, peering closely at the lettering.

"What's runic writing?" asked Lizzie.

"Well, runes are a very old type of script that you usually associate with pagan religions dating back before Christianity. These days, people tend to associate them with witchcraft or magic of some sort. Actually, they're more symbols than writing. I believe that they were sometimes used for things like foreseeing the future and stuff like that," Mrs Longton explained, opening the book and flicking through some of the pages.

"Quite right, Mrs Longton," said a man's voice from just behind them. Lizzie and Mrs Longton jumped so violently that they nearly left their skins behind them, and they swung round to face the direction of the voice.

Standing in the doorway, with his hand still on the handle of the door, was the man who had looked down at them from the portrait above the fire-place. As he walked towards them, he held his hand outstretched in welcome. "Thank you so much for coming. Welcome to Elvedom Castle," he smiled warmly.

Lizzie's eyes sprung wide with surprise at seeing their host for the first time. Then, before Mrs Longton could take the man's hand in greeting, Lizzie suddenly blurted out, "You've got pointy ears like mine too!"

Chapter 6 – The Mystery Unravels

The stranger began to laugh. A deep, gurgling laugh that seemed to bubble up from his toes until it burst out of his mouth; infecting those standing closest to him, so that Lizzie found herself laughing too. Giggling at first, and then almost doubling over in fits of laughter as the nervousness she'd been feeling drained away. Mrs Longton looked at the two of them in amazement.

"I am so sorry Mrs Longton, this is very rude of me," the stranger gasped, taking a deep breath. "It's probably the release of all the built up tension of the day. My household and I have been feeling it for days whilst we waited for your impending arrival, and they do say laughter is the best medicine," he said, regaining his composure. He took a deep breath and offered his hand to Mrs Longton in welcome. As she shook it politely, she stared at the face of the man. He had a pleasant, open face, framed by a neat white beard and moustache. His bright green eyes sparkled as if he was storing a secret joke behind them. The white hair on his head was swept back from his high forehead and tucked neatly behind his (as Lizzie had so loudly observed) large pointed ears.

"I really must apologise for my granddaughter's impolite outburst," Mrs Longton said, casting a disapproving look at Lizzie.

"Not at all, not at all," the man exclaimed. "She was only being honest. There is no fault in honesty, as long as it is not used to wound. Don't you think?" he continued.

"Yes, of course," Mrs Longton agreed. She then asked if he would be so kind as to explain what was going on. "We are very baffled as to how Lizzie here came to win a holiday to your most unique hotel."

"Please, please, do sit down, there are indeed explanations owed," the man said, indicating that they sit once again on the sofa by the fireside. He was a very dapper little man. He was dressed in a high collared green velvet jacket, with gold brocade edging that complimented his green trousers; from which he took a crisp, white linen handkerchief. He wiped his face to remove the tears that had moistened his cheeks, and went to stand next to the fireplace. His portrait above him looked down upon the proceedings.

"Firstly," he said, sounding more formal. "I feel I should introduce myself. My name is Elfred, King Elfred," he swept a low bow to them both. Lizzie, who was still struggling to control her fit of giggles, stopped instantly and stared at the man.

Although he certainly appeared regal enough, every sense in Mrs Longton's body cried out fraud. She had an avid interest in world history, with current affairs with European royalty being one of her particular interests. She knew that there were numerous exiled royals from around the globe residing in England, but she had never heard of a King Elfred. He must really have come down in the world to be managing a hotel, even one as exclusive as this. All these thoughts tumbled through Mrs Longton's mind in an instant.

The man, claiming to be King Elfred, sat down in the large wing chair opposite them and stared intently across at Lizzie. His face suddenly showed traces of sadness that surprised his guests. Then, as if shaking himself out of some deep reverie, he smiled at them once again.

"My dear Mrs Longton, and Miss Elizabeth, I owe you an explanation about why you have been invited here today." Looking at Lizzie, he took a deep breath as if preparing to share some deep dark secret. "I'm afraid that you did not win a holiday."

Mrs Longton jumped out of her seat. "I knew it..." She began, but the little man quieted her by waving his hands in downwards motion, as if flagging down traffic. Mrs Longton dropped back to her seat.

He began again, "What I'm about to tell you will be difficult to believe, but believe it you must. Firstly, I must admit that the letter about the holiday was a ploy to get you both to come here. In hindsight, it was probably unfair, but I had to get you both here somehow and my advisors felt that telling you that Elizabeth had won a holiday would sufficiently arouse your curiosity without frightening you. At first, I was going to travel to your home to introduce myself and explain my story, but I was advised that you would probably throw me out as some kind of lunatic. Whereas, if you were persuaded to come here, I would be able to prove to you that what I am about to tell you is the truth." His eyes seemed to sparkle brightly, as though about to shed tears as he looked at Mrs Longton, and she suddenly felt a wave of sympathy for him. She sensed that there was a great sadness in him, despite his smiling expression.

The door opened and Elbert, the butler, came in carrying a silver tray containing a delicate white bone china tea set with an ivy leaf pattern. The distraction eased a little of the very palpable air of tension in the room. He set the tray down on a small side table and proceeded to serve the tea. The group sat silently until Elbert had completed the process and had backed out of the room.

The King lowered his eyes and stared into the cup of tea in his hand, swirling its contents like some gypsy fortune teller about to impart some tall story to a gullible client. He drained the cup and set it aside.

"So many times I have imagined this moment and now it's finally here, it is difficult to know where to begin," he started, leaning back and placing his elbows on the arms of the chair, his fingertips touching as if in prayer and resting gently against his lips. He closed his eyes as if deep in thought. Lizzie watched him keenly; there was something very familiar about him that she couldn't quite put her finger on. Finally, the King opened his eyes and the corners of his mouth curled upwards into a faint smile.

"I have deliberated for a very long time as to how I can ever begin explaining things to you, Elizabeth, but from what I know of you through my sources, I feel that you are intelligent enough, and have the right amount of intuition, to accept the total truth. So, that's what I am about to tell you both," he said, looking from Lizzie to Mrs Longton and then back to Lizzie again.

"As I said, you are going to find it beyond your belief, but I swear that everything I'm about to tell you is the absolute truth. I think that perhaps it is best relayed in the form of a story."

Mrs Longton sighed in exasperation, and squirmed in her seat impatiently, "I did not come half way across England to hear fairy tales!"

"Ahh," smiled the King. "You may change your mind about that when you've heard what I am about to tell you."

Lizzie turned to her grandmother. "Please, gran," she pleaded. "I'd like to hear the story. We've come all this way; we might as well listen. I know it's been a really weird day, so what if it does get even weirder?" Her eyes looked imploringly into her grandmother's.

Mrs Longton was beginning to get a sense of foreboding about how the day was panning out. She felt she was on the precipice of a whole new beginning of something she could not control, and she was uncomfortable with that. But her curiosity was getting the better of her, so she agreed that they may as well hear what King Elfred had to say for himself. As she and Lizzie settled back into their chairs, the King leant forward in his chair and began:

66

***

Many years ago, a King had two daughters. The King loved the two princesses more than life itself and indulged them totally. Anything they wanted, he did his best to provide, but they were not spoiled as they loved the King greatly, and so asked for very little. Everyone in the Kingdom adored the princesses, for they were not only beautiful, but kind and generous.

The older of the two girls, Princess Elethria, was an intelligent girl and would spend hours reading and learning from her father's many books and advisors. She was deeply inquisitive. She would wander the fields and forests spending time with the animals, creatures and people of her world. She collected various plants and flowers, which she would draw and paint or press and keep in volumes in her rooms.

The King's younger daughter, Princess Elenya, was also intelligent but she was more athletic and enjoyed running and hunting with her friends and courtiers from the King's household. She learnt to use the sword and could shoot an arrow from the bow more accurately and further than any of the King's other subjects.

When the King's eldest daughter was born, she had been betrothed to the son of one of the King's oldest friends and allies who lived in a county at the edge of the King's realm. The King and his friend hoped that the joining in marriage of their two children, Elethria and Eldorth, would cement their friendship and bring new life to the bloodline of the royal family.

As Eldorth grew, he became more and more unruly, and when Eldorth's father tried to discipline him the boy became sly and devious. Eventually, the King's friend became frustrated and disappointed in his son and so he told the King that he would understand if he wanted to break the contract of engagement between the two children. But the

King hoped that the goodness and loyalty of the father would in time manifest itself in the son; and so he would not end the betrothal.

Then, one day, the King's friend died suddenly. It was a shock to all who knew him, as he had been in robust good health. The circumstances surrounding his death were suspicious, and so the King sent some of his closest liegemen to investigate his friend's death and report back to him. But when they arrived at his friend's manor, they found that the body had been cremated in a ceremony totally lacking the pomp and recognition that such a highly born ally of the King deserved. The King was furious and demanded to know who had made such a decision without his consultation, and was told that the decision had been that of his friend's son and heir.

The King immediately commanded that Eldorth come to court where the King and his most senior advisors questioned him. The boy insisted that his father had just become sick and died. When questioned about the haste of the funeral, the boy claimed it had been because there was fear that whatever had killed his father could have been contagious and spread to others around him.

The King then had the members of his old friend's household questioned, but they told the King very little. The King and his advisors had the strong belief that his friend's staff were under threat of some terrible retribution should they say anything about what had truly happened to their old master. And so, with no real evidence of foul play, the King decided that he would have to accept the boy's story that his father had died of natural causes.

The King decreed that Eldorth, who was then 15 years of age, should therefore come to live at his court where the King would supervise his upbringing until he was of an age to take full control of his father's lands. At first the boy rebelled, saying that he was already capable of managing *his lands, but he could not openly disobey the King's direct order and so reluctantly agreed to live within the King's household.*

The King placed him under the tutelage of one of his most old and trusted advisors and, at first, Eldorth's behaviour seemed to improve. But as time went by, and the boy grew towards maturity, his deviousness and malevolence began to raise its ugly head once more.

One day, Eldorth's tutor sought an audience with the King and expressed his grave concerns with regards to keeping the boy within such close proximity to the King and his family. The King asked his advisor what was meant by such a statement and was told that, although the tutor had worked with Eldorth for a number of years, and had endeavoured to improve his naturally malicious tendencies, he had to admit defeat. The advisor said that he was sad to have to acknowledge this failure, but he felt that the King should accept that Eldorth was no good and was never likely to be. The King's advisor then told the King that he had made a terrible discovery about him – he had been meddling with dark magic. The advisor said that he couldn't stress strongly enough that the King should send Eldorth far away from court.

The King told his advisor that he should in no way blame himself for how the boy had turned out. He said that his old dead friend had told him many years before of his disappointment in the boy, and that he was no good and could not be trusted. The King said that, in honour of his friend, he had always lived in the hope that, with a firm hand and the right guidance, the boy would one day be redeemed.

The King said that nothing would have made him happier than to have joined the royal house to that of his late friend and ally, but he would not risk marrying his beloved daughter to someone of such a wicked and untrustworthy disposition. The King said that, now with knowledge of

Eldorth's dabbling in the dark arts, he had no choice but to end the boy's engagement to his daughter. The King thanked his advisor and told him that he would henceforth deal with the matter. The King then called for his eldest daughter to be brought to him.

The King spoke with his daughter and explained everything that his advisor had told him. Elethria breathed a huge sigh of relief and threw her arms around her father. She tearfully explained that she was relieved by his decision. She said that she had always found his friend's son cold and aloof, and that she had never been able to come to terms with his spitefulness and cruelty to the people and creatures around him. Elethria said that she had tried to talk to the boy about it but he had laughed at her and told her that when they were married, and he was King, she would do as she was told and he would do as he wished.

The King was angered by this latest information and asked his daughter why she had never told him of this before. She said that she had wanted to make her father happy by fulfilling his wish for her to marry the son of his oldest friend, and had hoped that as the boy matured, he would grow out of his wicked tendencies and see the error of his ways. She had never given up hope that he would change for the better.

The King's mind was now made up. He knew that he could no longer keep Eldorth in his household, but must banish the boy from the court and back to his dead father's lands. There, the King would set guards to ensure that he stayed within his own lands and that, by containing him there, the boy would be unable to cause any future damage. The King then sent for Eldorth.

The youth entered the King's chamber and stood before him; his contempt for the King was barely disguised beneath his scornful countenance.

"You requested my attendance, Your Majesty," he sneered. The King said that he did indeed have something of grave importance to discuss with the boy. The King told Eldorth of his decision that the betrothal between himself and Elethria was to be ended with immediate effect.

Eldorth's face coloured with rage and, in a voice quivering with barely suppressed anger, he demanded to know why. The King said that information had been brought to his attention that had made him conclude that the union between them was unsuitable. The King told the boy that he was aware of his misdemeanours and cruel tendencies and had, therefore, decided that he could not accept him as a son-in-law and that he was no longer welcome in his household. The King told Eldorth that he would return to his father's manor where he would reside under the King's custody, and that he should cause no further trouble.

Eldorth flew into a rage. He ranted at the King and flung himself at him, threatening him with violence. The King's guards intervened and restrained the boy. As he tried to wrench himself free from their grasp, he told the King in a frighteningly calm, cold voice that the King would live to regret his decision. He said that if he was not to marry the King's daughter, then she would be cursed. He said that if she ever married, then the union would bring nothing but pain and heartbreak to the King and his heirs; they would never find happiness and the house of Elderen would fall. He said that if the princess ever had a child, then she and the child would die in childbirth. As the guards dragged the youth from the King's presence, he screamed that he promised that the King's powers would be diminished and that he would never find happiness again.

Shaken by the vehemence of the confrontation, the King instructed the Captain of the Guard to escort the boy to his father's house under strict armed guard, and to keep a vigilant watch on all his activities. He told the captain to establish a company of soldiers to maintain order on the borders of the youth's lands and report regularly on any unusual activities. The King informed his courtiers that he never wanted to see the boy's face again.

Years passed and, as the young man grew into adulthood, he bided his time, causing no trouble to the King and his people. The King hoped that the episode was over and that the threats made to him and his loved ones were idle ones. But then it came to the King's attention that minor skirmishes were breaking out on and around the borders of Eldorth's lands. Although the King's watch tried to contain the troubles, reports were coming in from their outpost that the young man's lands were becoming a haven for some of the more undesirable elements of society. Eldorth had become the King's most dreaded enemy.

In the meantime, Princess Elethria grew into a lovely young woman. The King had regularly sent his ambassadors to different parts of the realm to seek out a suitable husband for her but, unbeknown to the King; his daughter had found a suitor of her own.

Elethria had fallen in love with a man from a different race to her own and from a different social sphere, and had for some time been meeting him in secret. The princess knew that her father would never refuse her anything, but she also knew that it would break his heart if she followed her own. But love is a wonderful, and sometimes terrible, thing and the princess loved the man so deeply that she was prepared to give up everything to be with him.

One day, she went to her father and sadly told him that she must leave his Kingdom in order to pursue a new life with her soul mate. She told the King all about the man, how good and kind he was, and how she wanted to spend the rest of her life with him. The King was distraught and tried to dissuade his daughter, insisting that marrying someone not of their own race was impossible. There would be terrible consequences and it could not end happily, but the princess said that she would marry the man and she would do so with or without her father's consent, although it would break her heart if he refused her. The King reluctantly agreed, and preparations were made for the princess to leave her home to be with the man she loved. The King knew that once the princess left his realm, he would never see her again. But he put in place protection for her, whereby, one of his most trusted servants would watch over her and regularly report back to him. The day that the princess left her father's household was one of the saddest of the King's life, but worse was still to come.

Some years after the princess's marriage, she fell pregnant and the old curse placed upon her by the King's enemy came back to haunt the King. With all the powers at his disposal, he did his best to counteract the curse, but as his enemy had said, events had since occurred that had diminished some of the King's power.

Against the advice of his people, the King went to be near the princess on the night of the birth of her child and endeavoured to protect the daughter he loved so much, but it was to no avail. When the princess gave birth to her child, the King was unable save his daughter. As his daughter slipped away, the King's power did one good thing; it saved the life of his grandchild.

Overcome by grief, the princess's husband placed his daughter into the care of his own mother. And there the child remained; loved and cared for by her grandmother, for the past 11 years – until today.

***

The King stopped and looked at Lizzie with such deep intensity, tears glistening in his bright green eyes, that she could almost feel his pain physically reach out across the room and touch her. She was stunned.

73

Mrs Longton had sat in silence, enthralled by the story until its end. Rooted to her seat, she was unable to believe the implications of the story that she and Lizzie had just been told. She tried to absorb the enormity of what the King had said. The whole story sounded like a fairy tale, it only needed a few fairies and dragons and she would have said the Brothers Grimm had written it. She eased herself to her feet and began slowly pacing around the room. It was something she tended to do that when she needed to think clearly. If she understood the King correctly, he was implying that Lizzie was his grandchild. If that were true, and she couldn't believe that it was, this would have an enormous impact on Lizzie's life and, of course, upon her own too.

She quickly came to the conclusion that this man must be some kind of lunatic, and possibly a dangerous one. This must be some kind of mad, cruel prank and she would make him pay. She stood and faced the King and stared him straight in the eye. Raising herself to her full height, and with all the strength and control she could muster, she said, "Let me get this clear; am I to take it that you are telling us, through this story of yours, that my granddaughter, Elizabeth, is also your granddaughter?"

Lizzie stared at her grandmother and then across at the King. This wasn't possible; she couldn't be this man's granddaughter. She just couldn't. It was crazy, but the King nodded his head sagely.

"Yes, that is correct," he confirmed, his voice gentle and full of emotion.

Mrs Longton suddenly felt angrier than she had ever felt in her life. What was this man doing, telling such terrible lies to a small and vulnerable child? She exploded with disbelief.

"That's impossible. Lizzie's mother's name was Ria. Not Elethria, or whatever you called her; and anyway, Ria always told us she had no family. Why would she say that if it were untrue? And, if you loved her, as you claim you did, how is it that you were never there for her whilst I knew her? And, where have you been during Lizzie's young life? And, all this nonsense about curses and such like..." Mrs Longton looked at the man in front of her, not disguising her contempt for him. "You sit there telling us that you're some kind of King, that Lizzie's mother was a princess. You expect us to believe all this baloney about malevolent forces and dark magic and such nonsense? What is this place?" she added, looking about her as if seeking answers. "Some kind of asylum for lunatics?"

Trying to regain her composure, she turned on him once again. "Sir, what you have done today is cruel and totally unacceptable. Why are you doing this? Who's put you up to it? And how did you found out about Lizzie's birth and what she has been doing until now? If I find out who put you up to this, I shall sue both of you." Then, grabbing her bag and bending to take Lizzie's arm, she stormed, "Come on, Lizzie, we're going home. We will not stay here a moment longer and have our intelligence insulted and abused in this way."

A small voice from the child sitting on the sofa said, almost to itself, "Daddy didn't want me?" The words brought Mrs Longton down to earth with a shattering bump. She sat down quickly beside Lizzie and threw her arms around her.

"Of course he wants you. It's just his work that keeps him away," she gabbled, trying to cover over what she had being trying to hide from Lizzie her entire life. Then, turning on the King with venom spitting from her eyes, she hissed through gritted teeth, "Are you satisfied now?!"

The King stood and put out his hands, trying to soothe the woman in front of him. His face looked sad and weary.

"Mrs Longton, I wouldn't hurt Elizabeth for the entire world; she is my only grandchild." Then, turning to Lizzie, he said, "Of course your father wants you, but there are things preventing him from being with you which will be explained to you at some other time." Turning once more to Mrs Longton, he said, "I know that what I've just told you sounds completely implausible to you, but I assure you that it is the truth. If I could have done things differently I would have, please believe me. I've done my utmost to protect Elizabeth, but it's most important that she now knows and understands the roots of her mother's family and, consequently, her own heritage. There was no easy way to break this to you both and I'm sorry that you have reacted this way," said the King, trying to pacify them. He then turned to Lizzie and looked at her with such love that there could be no doubt of his honesty, and Mrs Longton was rocked to her soul by the power of it.

The King squatted down in front of Lizzie and took her small hands into his own. "Elizabeth, of course your father loves and wants you. Your grandmother is quite right, his work is one of the things that has kept him from you, but it's also true that Elethria was indeed my daughter's, your mother's, name. Ria was the nickname given to her by her beloved mother. When Ria came to me and told me that she had fallen in love with your father, she told me that he knew her only as Ria. She said that the name Elethria would sound strange in your world and she knew that people would ask its origins and this, in turn, would raise questions about her past. She said that the name Ria was one that people would be more likely to accept. There is also something else that I must tell you, something that I have so far omitted. If you are finding what I have already said hard to believe, then I'm afraid that this next piece of information will probably seem even more unbelievable to you."

"I think that's highly unlikely," scoffed Mrs Longton, holding tightly to Lizzie shoulders, as much for her own reassurance as for Lizzie's.

The King looked at both Lizzie and her grandmother, his face showing the uncertainty he was feeling about divulging this next piece of the puzzle. He looked as if he were trying to find the right words. Then, taking a deep breath, he said clearly and precisely, "There is no easy way to say this, so I shall say it straight; the realm of which I am King is called Elvedom."

Lizzie's eyes flew wide with surprise; she'd already guessed what was coming next. The King nodded, "That's right Elizabeth, I am an elf."

Chapter 7 – Early Lessons for Lizzie

It was now Mrs Longton's turn to collapse onto the sofa in convulsions of laughter.

"Oh, pur-leeze," she wheezed as she tried to pull herself together; she was beginning to feel that she was on the verge of hysteria. Lizzie reached over and took her grandmother's hand.

"I believe him, gran," she said with conviction. She felt that she'd never been surer about anything in her life. "It all makes sense. Well, perhaps not all of it, but there have been so many things that have happened over the years that haven't made sense. Hearing and seeing things that other people can't. Being able to run much faster and jump much higher than the other kids at school. I've always been different to the other kids; you know I have, that's why I've never fitted in properly. Now after what we've heard today, I just know King Elfred's telling us the truth. I really do. You must admit that it's been kind of magical. I mean, look at the Diamond Line, that car and well, Elwood." She looked at her grandmother pleadingly. "Please let the King go on. I really need to know."

Mrs Longton's amusement was turning more to anger with each passing moment. This man, claiming to be not only a King, but an elf, had somehow fooled Lizzie, she thought, and she was going to get very hurt if Mrs Longton didn't put a stop to his antics there and then.

"Lizzie, darling, it's all lies; it's just stories. There are no such things as elves and magic. You are just cleverer and more athletic than the other children and they're jealous of you. I don't know what your game is," she said, turning on the man sitting opposite them and glaring at him accusingly, her face puce with anger, "but whatever it is you're up to, you need to be putting away. I've a good mind to report you to the police. Look at that poor child; look what you've done to her, making her believe your lies."

The King and Lizzie watched her sadly and silently, and something suddenly hit Mrs Longton like a slap in the face. The two pairs of eyes watching her were the same iridescent blue; the same eyes that had once belonged to Ria. It took the wind right out of Mrs Longton's sails and she said, "All right then; you claim to have lured us here to prove that what you've just told us is true, so go ahead, prove it."

The King stood and walked over to a table, on which stood a small box with a hand-piece on top, something akin to a small telephone-like apparatus. With his back to them, he lifted the hand-piece and spoke into it quietly and then turned back to Lizzie and Mrs Longton.

"I know you have both had a long journey here and I would ordinarily suggest that you relax for the remainder of the day and I show you around tomorrow. However, given your reaction to events so far, Mrs Longton, I feel that delay would not be the right option. So I have organised for you both to accompany me on a brief tour. Though there is something that I want you to understand from the outset, as there has been much talk of magic. We elves do not perform magic, well not in the sense that we cast spells or enchantments; we leave that to witches or wizards," he said, with almost a dismissive wave of his hand. "Our 'magic' is in our physical and mental powers. We tend and care for things, grow and nurture them. We can also communicate with other creatures. Our bodies can function at a higher level than humans, in that we can see and hear things better. We can, as you said, run faster, jump higher and are stronger than humans of similar size. As today goes on, I am sure these things will become clearer to you."

At that moment, Elbert walked into the room.

"Sire, I have asked Elwood to arrange for the transport to be made ready, as you requested. Shall I make the necessary arrangements for the ladies to stay the night?" he asked.

Mrs Longton swung her head in his direction and glared at Elbert, as though staying the night would be the last thing in the world she'd ever do.

"I think I shall reserve judgement on that decision until we have seen this so called proof of who you are and where we are," Mrs Longton said loftily. Elbert looked startled that anyone should speak to or of the King in such a way.

The King turned and smiled at the elderly elf. "I think it's a little too early to say just at the moment," he said gently. "But please ask Eldora to prepare the accommodation, just in case."

Elbert nodded and backed quickly out of the room, the look of shock still etched on his lined face.

Lizzie, still sitting rooted to the sofa, was in turmoil. Her emotions were all over the place. She looked at the man claiming to be her grandfather standing there in front of her. With her head leaning a little to one side, she asked in a small voice, "Why have you waited until now to contact me?"

King Elfred looked at her, with his sad smile once more playing on his lips. "I wanted to take you away with me the night you were born, Elizabeth, but I could not have done that because it would not have been safe to do so. I could also never have done that to your grandmother. She had lost too much already," he said, looking at Mrs Longton understandingly. Mrs Longton looked surprised at this demonstration of kindness, considering how hostile she had been to him. She opened her mouth to ask what he meant by that, but before she could, the King said, "Yes, Mrs Longton, I was there the night Elizabeth was born. I was there to be close to my daughter and to try and provide her with the

80

strength to survive Elizabeth's birth. Sadly, as you know only too well, I did not succeed."

The King sat down heavily in his chair and bent his face into his hands. Lizzie watched him with a heavy heart. The King looked up at them both; the pain of the memory seemed engraved on his face.

"As I said, I couldn't take you with me because I knew that you would have been in grave danger from Duke Eldorth. Eldorth is the boy from the story that I have just told you and he has grown into my worst enemy," the King explained. "I am sure that if he knew you had survived, and were here in Elvedom, he would have done everything in his power to have you harmed, possibly even murdered. Being so young, you'd have had no powers of your own to protect yourself. Even though my people and I would have done our utmost to protect you from harm, I couldn't take that risk. That is why I had to wait until you reached the age of eleven to bring you back into my world."

"Why eleven?" Lizzie quizzed.

"Eleven is the age when an elven child begins to develop their own special powers and discover their strengths. The word eleven is an old elvish word for pre-coming of age. Coming of age in our world is not the same as in yours where it means becoming an adult. An elven child still takes years to mature, but at eleven they will discover that they have other attributes and abilities they've never felt or experienced before. I had to contact you when you reached this age so that I, and my people, can help you control and enhance your own special qualities. You will truly come into your powers at the age of seventeen, but each year until then, you will gain more and more skills and abilities. My people and I need to do everything in the coming years to help you identify and develop these special skills and powers before you reach that age.

"You have said that you don't fit in with the other children in your world because you can run and jump faster and higher. You may also have found that you are able to absorb knowledge quicker too and maybe could do certain other things better than they can. You have probably experienced difficulty relating to other children because of this?" Lizzie nodded in agreement. He was right; it was all these things that made the other kids bully her.

"Well," the King continued, "from now on, you will probably find that you will fit in with them even less. That will be very hard for you, and possibly for them, if you were left to your own devices and didn't understand what was happening to you. You may find yourself in some difficulties, but more than that; extremely lonely. People who are different find it hard to make friends. Without our guidance, who knows what might happen?" He smiled at her knowingly.

"I don't really have any friends now anyway," said Lizzie, sadly.

"I'm sure that we can change that," smiled the King. "We are not sure what powers you will eventually possess, what with your being Half-Human, or a Half-Elf as we say for ease of reference. We couldn't take the chance that the powers within you would begin to manifest themselves before you understood what was happening. These powers uncontrolled would cause you, and those around you, shall we say, problems. In the time you have been in the human world, I have had you watched. I placed a guardian to oversee you until the time was right to bring you here. He has watched over you, as he did your mother before you. As well as ensuring your safe keeping, he has kept me informed of how you have grown and of the things you have been doing. He has seen some of the special qualities you have begun to demonstrate, and as time goes on these need to be examined properly and, eventually, to be developed and enhanced."

"Elwood!" said Lizzie assuredly, and a look of realisation lit up her face. She suddenly remembered the green flitting figure that she had seen on countless occasions in and around Longton Hall, and at last she knew what, or rather who, it was that she had glimpsed all those times. And his turning up on the train and at Paddington Station that morning had been no coincidence either.

"It's Elwood that's been watching me, isn't it? I've seen him lots of times out the corner of my eye. I told you that I wasn't imagining seeing fairies in the garden, gran" she grinned over at her grandmother. Mrs Long smiled at her sceptically, and sank down onto the seat next to Lizzie, her mind was reeling with all the information it was trying to absorb; she was still reserving judgement on whether or not she should believe any of it.

"Yes, it was Elwood, although I'll have to have a few words with him. It would seem that he must be losing his touch if you've been able to see him. Still, maybe I'm doing him a disservice. It may just be that your eyes, like an elf's, are quick at seeing things," smiled the King. "Elwood has observed your upbringing and reported back to me. He was under strict instructions that if there was ever any hint of danger to you, he must get you to me as quickly as possible. It was safer, however, to keep you in the human world for as long as we could."

Mrs Longton had been watching this exchange with mounting disbelief. "Do you mean to say that we've been spied on for years?" she asked indignantly. "What a cheek. In our world it'd be seen as an infringement of our privacy. Don't you have privacy laws in Elvedom?"

"I'm sorry for any offence you may feel about this, but as you learn more about Elizabeth's heritage I think you will understand why I had to have Elizabeth watched over. Think upon it as a security service; I don't believe those are against the law. We are fortunate that Eldorth does not yet appear to

83

know of your existence," he said, turning back to Lizzie, "but my sources say that his suspicion has been aroused. As far as we know, he was given to understand that Elethria's child had not survived the birth. You see, Elizabeth, you are very special in our world as the only child of my first-born. You are, my dear, my direct heir."

Lizzie's mouth dropped open and a shock, like that from electricity, stung her body. This wasn't possible. She was just beginning to believe that her mother was an elven princess, but it hadn't occurred to her that it would also make her one. Heir to the elven throne: no, this wasn't possible! This was all too much to take in. Mrs Longton was gaping stupidly at the King; she felt emotionally and physically drained. She couldn't even summon up another objection to what had become such an extreme situation; it defied everything she believed in. She tried to find the words she sought, but her mouth just opened and closed like a goldfish gasping for air.

Lizzie was the first to find her voice, "B.. b.. but, that's impossible; I can't be. I thought you said you had another daughter? In your story you mentioned you had two daughters. Where's she? Why isn't she here with you? Surely she's your heir; not me," she blustered.

"My other, younger, daughter is not here at present. I thought it would be best to meet you alone in the first instance, as she can be very excitable. She wants to meet you very much, though. My daughter, Elenya, is currently staying with some of my people in the North. She frequently travels around the realm, partly to ensure that she is never anywhere for too long. This is because she must also be protected from Eldorth, as he currently believes her to be my heir. We do not want to allow him the opportunity to infiltrate our defences, thereby reaching her and harming her. It is also a good education for her, as she's able to learn much about the work of our people, and it gives her the opportunity to help them in some way. I am sure that in time you will become good friends, Elizabeth.

But returning to your question about who is my heir, it is as in your world, Elizabeth. The line of succession falls to the eldest child of the eldest child, and so forth. As your grandmother will know, if anything should happen to your queen, and her eldest son is no longer there to succeed her, then the crown will go to his eldest son; not to one of the queen's other three children," said King Elfred. He smiled reassuringly at Lizzie and her grandmother.

Lizzie's grandmother clapped her hand to her forehead. "I must be going mad," she exclaimed, shaking her head. "I'm actually starting to believe all this nonsense. What you are saying all sounds incredibly plausible, but it goes against everything that my rational and logical mind believes and knows to be true. There are no such things as elves and magic. They are figments of the imagination that have been passed on through myths and legends."

"That is what most humans have been led to believe," nodded the King. "It suits my own and other magical folk for humans to believe it so. Children believe because they are born with the instinct that magic exists. It is as they grow that that instinct is destroyed by adults who have learnt otherwise. Many hundreds of years ago, there was a much closer relationship between our people and yours. But then humans became greedy and brutal and were only interested in what they could get out of what you call "mythical" people. Humans began exploiting elves and the other magical folk, such as fairies, goblins and sprites, to achieve their own ends. They began to turn on them and abuse them. Eventually, our two worlds grew further apart.

You may have learnt in your history lessons, Elizabeth, how cruel humans were to witches and warlocks during your medieval times. Then, over recent centuries, humans exploited the very thing that gives them life; the Earth itself.

You can see the damage and destruction that they've wrought on this planet. Elves were appointed the guardians of Mother Earth, and it is taking the combined efforts of most of the magical communities around the globe to keep her functioning, as she should. But we can only do so much. Humans have to begin to learn that they cannot continue this abuse and destruction, or else Mother Nature will, in turn, destroy them.

In the hope that we may teach humans how they can assist us in protecting the Earth, we have allowed, over many centuries, certain members of your race to be aware of our existence. The people we have contact with are those who have most influence over their fellow humans. There are also some tribes and clans of people who live in remote areas of the Earth who know and communicate with us, but the rest of the human race have been taught to believe that we are imaginary figures, created by storytellers from a dim and distant past." Mrs Longton just sat and stared at the King during this long speech, her eyes agog. Just then, there was a knock at the door and in walked Elwood.

"The transport is now ready as you requested, Sire," he said grandly, bowing very low. The King thanked Elwood and stood, holding out his hand to Lizzie.

"Come, my dear, allow me to show you around my world, soon to be your world," and looking at Mrs Longton, he said with a smile, "And let's hope that I can prove to you, once and for all, that what I have been telling you is true."

Chapter 8 – Into Another Realm

As Lizzie followed the King from the room and walked out into the entrance hall to Elvedom Castle, she now saw it in all its glory. The torches in the wall sconces had been lit whilst she and her grandmother were meeting the King, and the grandness of the hall was now very evident.

Lizzie's first impression, when they had arrived, was that the hall was like a large, gloomy cave, but she couldn't have been more mistaken. It was large, cavernous even, but not gloomy. The walls glistened as if peppered with gold and silver chippings that reflected the light from the torches. To her left, she could see that the enormous oak front doors to the building were now closed and that they were ornately carved. They were attached to their frame by massive, elaborately engraved brass hinges.

Directly parallel to the front doors, to her right, was the largest and grandest staircase that Lizzie had ever seen. It was made of white and grey veined marble, with vast pillars to either side of it that stretched up to the ceiling high above. The ceiling itself was difficult to see clearly due to its height, and the fact that it was also shrouded in the flickering shadows caused by the flames of the torches. She could, however, vaguely make out that there were paintings of what looked like Greek gods and other mythical creatures; in a style similar to the paintings of the great artists that used to adorn the ceiling of the great stately homes of Britain. Between each of the smaller wooden doors, that led off at intervals along each side of the huge space, were magnificent statues. In the improved light she could see that they were figures of elves. It was the ears that gave them away; pointed ones just like Lizzie's own. The statues were beautifully sculpted, almost lifelike, and Lizzie could imagine one of them suddenly stepping down from its base and walking over to greet her. It was disconcerting how the eyes of each one seemed to follow her every move.

Lizzie followed behind the King and Elwood, holding onto her grandmother's arm. She glanced up at Mrs Longton to look at her expression and could see that her grandmother was just as impressed as she was. Their footsteps echoed around the entrance hall as they walked across its shiny granite floor. She turned and looked up into the faces of each of the statues as she passed. Suddenly she became rooted to the spot. As she looked up into the face of yet another beautiful woman, she found herself staring into the face of her own mother. Lizzie knew the face immediately; she'd seen it hundreds of times gazing out at her from photos in the albums her grandmother kept in the study at Longton Hall.

Lizzie suddenly had a terrible sharp pain in her chest as if her heart was about to explode, and she felt as though she couldn't breathe. Her arms felt weak and her legs like lead weights. The statue was so life-like, she felt that her mother, Elethria, would reach down and touch her at any moment. Lizzie felt a sudden urge to run to the statue and hug it tight, but her legs just wouldn't move.

"What is it, Lizzie?" her grandmother asked. She had been yanked to a halt when Lizzie had stopped so suddenly. "What is it, darling?" she asked again, this time with concern when she saw the look on Lizzie's face. Then, following the direction of Lizzie's eyes, she too looked into the face of the statue and gasped, "Oh my; Ria!" The King and Elwood stopped and turned to look at what had brought Lizzie and Mrs Longton to such sudden standstill.

"Ah," said the King softly, when he realised what was causing the disturbance. He walked back and stood beside Lizzie and placed a hand on her shoulder.

"It's my mother," whispered Lizzie, her voice was barely audible. Mrs Longton took Lizzie's hand and gripped it tightly. What could she say to her granddaughter? This statue alone seemed to be evidence enough that the King had been telling the truth. Why else would he have such an accurate replica of Ria here in his home if he weren't in some way related to her?

The King smiled up into the face of the statue. "Actually, Elizabeth, this isn't your mother," the King said gently. "This is my wife, Eldorene, your maternal grandmother." Lizzie whipped her head around and looked up at the King's face as he stared at the woman's image.

"But she looks just like my mother; I've seen photos of her," she said with certainty.

"Yes; Elethria was very like her mother but I assure you, my dear, this is my wife Eldorene," the King said softly. "You are very like them both. I was struck by the likeness when I entered my study and saw you standing there. As the light caught your hair and it glistened like spun silver, it was exactly the same shade as your mother's and grandmother's. You're bigger in stature than they were, but that is not surprising given your human blood, but your features are the same; beautiful, gentle, intelligent." He smiled at Lizzie and reached out a hand towards her face, but he pulled back at the last minute as if the gesture was inappropriate. Lizzie could sense the love the King had for her and it felt odd to feel the strength of emotion coming from this man who, what was after all, a stranger. She put a hand on the King's arm and squeezed it gently.

"Where's my grandmother now?" she asked.

"Sadly, she is no longer with us; she has passed over," he said and he looked unhappily into Lizzie's eyes.

"I'm sorry. How did it happen?" Lizzie probed.

"That," he said, "is a story is for another time, Elizabeth. Come, let's continue with our tour." He smiled gently, placed a hand on her shoulder, and began to lead her away from the statue.

Mrs Longton had been watching the exchange between Lizzie and the man claiming to be her grandfather and felt her resolve beginning to crumble. It was pretty clear to her now that, whoever this man was, he had suffered terrible losses and sadness in his life. If he was who he said he was, she didn't really understand why he had waited until now to make contact with Lizzie, despite his earlier explanation, but she could sense that he now needed this contact with her very much. Against every rational bone in her body, she had begun to realise that the impossible may actually be possible.

"King Elfred," Mrs Longton began, tentatively, her voice was gentle for the first time since she'd met him. "Please forgive me for having been so hostile since my arrival. I hope you understand that I have only had Lizzie's best interests at heart. Lizzie has been my whole life for the past eleven years and I'd protect her to my death," she explained. "She sometimes has a very hard time where we live. Children can be very cruel if they feel that someone's a little different from themselves. I couldn't bear it if someone set out to deliberately hurt her or play cruel jokes on her." She looked back up at the statue and said thoughtfully, "But this …"

Mrs Longton turned to the King again. "This couldn't be a hoax. It would be just one thing too far. I am still struggling to get my head around everything you've told us because so much of it goes against everything I have grown up to be certain of, but I have to admit I'm beginning to actually believe that you've been telling us the truth."

The King smiled. "Thank you, Mrs Longton," he said. "I do understand why you have been so suspicious. Perhaps I should have approached things differently and I fully appreciate that you were only trying to protect Elizabeth. I have no doubt that I would have reacted in much the same way had I been in your position. However, please allow me to continue showing you around. I have some very special places that I would like you both to see."

Mrs Longton felt as though a huge weight was suddenly lifted from her. She had been so agitated and angry about everything that had happened since they had met Elwood at Paddington station. She decided that for the moment, maybe it was best to just relax a little and let events take their course. Que sera, sera, she told herself - What will be, will be.

The King took Lizzie's hand in his own and then, linking her arm over his, he led her and Mrs Longton to a door that Elwood had just opened, who was quietly standing by to let them pass. As Lizzie stepped through it, she expected to find herself in similar room to the one in which she had met her grandfather. Instead, she found herself in a cobbled courtyard surrounded by what appeared to be the cloisters of an old monastery, but it wasn't her surroundings that Lizzie found most amazing, it was what was standing in the middle of the courtyard that caused her to take a sharp intake of breath.

There, in front of her, was a carriage painted a deep shade of red, beautifully decorated with golden gilt, and an elf in ornate green livery sat on the seat holding the reins loosely in his hands. But what Lizzie found most incredible was what was harnessed to the carriage. The King of Elvedom didn't have some ordinary old nag pulling the carriage; that wouldn't have done at all. Harnessed to the carriage was a creature that Lizzie believed only existed in mythology. There in front of them, in all its dazzlingly beautiful whiteness, was a splendid winged horse. The creature tossed its magnificent head and snorted impatiently. It looked like illustrations of the Greek mythological Pegasus that Lizzie had seen in books and on the internet. The creature rustled its great folded wings and then stretched and flapped them, as if impatient to be soaring its way across the sky.

Mrs Longton appeared to be getting into the swing of things, for she suddenly clapped her hands together and let out a squeal of delight.

"Oh, how wonderful!" she exclaimed. "Is it real?"

"Indeed *she* is," smiled King Elfred, as the huge animal flexed her wings and peered around at Mrs Longton, her soft brown eyes seeming to narrow at her as though insulted that she should not believe in her. The creature snorted loudly once more.

"Please allow me to introduce Pegasa," announced the King. The great creature stretched her front right leg and bent her left knee in a graceful bow, and Lizzie and her grandmother dipped their heads respectfully. The winged horse stood up and stretched proudly. "Pegasa is a direct descendant of the legendary horse of the gods, the great Pegasus," explained Elwood, sharing a bit more of his boundless knowledge.

Lizzie and her grandmother smiled ecstatically at the beautiful creature before them. Lizzie looked up at the delighted expression on her grandmother's face and it made her happy to see that she was finally beginning to relax a little and enjoy the experience. The King led Lizzie around the carriage and assisted her into one of its sumptuous seats. Mrs Longton, almost childlike, clambered up and sat opposite Lizzie, clasping her handbag to her waist with the Sherlock Holmes hat protruding from its front pocket. She leant across and took one of Lizzie's hands into her own. She looked into Lizzie's face and smiled brightly.

"Lizzie, my love," Mrs Longton said, her eyes sparkling. "It really is all too much to take in. I mean, it's like some amazing dream and my arm is going to be black and blue in the morning with the bruises I've made each time I pinch myself. To save any more harm to my arm, I've decided to allow myself to just believe what's happening and go with the flow. Bless you, darling; it must all be terribly confusing for you."

Lizzie squeezed her grandmother's hand and nodded mutely. She didn't know how to put into words how she was feeling, as she was experiencing a whole multitude of emotions; shock, amazement, confusion and happiness were just a few. Part of her felt as though she'd fallen into some mad dream, but she agreed with her grandmother and decided that, for the moment, she too would just sit back and go with the flow. When the time was right and she'd sorted out the myriad of thoughts racing around her brain, she would be asking a whole heap of questions.

The King and Elwood climbed into the carriage beside Lizzie and Mrs Longton and, without further ado, Pegasa flapped her wings and began to take a short run – her hooves clattering across the cobbles of the courtyard. The carriage lifted smoothly off the ground and rose into the air above the castle.

Everything below them shrank rapidly, as the great winged horse flew high into the atmosphere. They travelled at such speed that nothing could be seen below but a blur of colours. Lizzie tried to see Elvedom Castle and its grounds, but it was gone. Mrs Longton turned and asked the King about where it was they were going.

"I should like to show you both some of my Kingdom and for you to meet some of my people. It is important that Elizabeth begins as soon as possible to learn about our world, and most significantly about her mother's kin," he announced, smiling fondly at Lizzie.

As they flew towards their mystery destination, Mrs Longton asked questions about the beautiful animal pulling the carriage. Elwood took up the role of lecturer as he explained that Pegasa was indeed descended from the great winged horse of the gods Pegasus, famed for carrying the God Zeus' lightening bolts. Although Pegasa was not as famous as her ancestor, she too had a long and proud history; it was just much less chronicled which was why Lizzie and her grandmother had probably never heard of her. Pegasa's main role in life had been to convey various dignitaries, to and from the home of the gods on Mount Olympus. Elwood told them that the Kings of Elvedom had been great allies of Zeus through the ages and so, after assisting Zeus in battle many years previously, Zeus had made a gift of Pegasa to the King.

"How old is Pegasa?" asked Lizzie.

"That I do not know," said Elwood.

"That makes a change," mumbled Mrs Longton, continuing to gaze out of the carriage at the earth far below.

"I do not know because, like the gods she serves, Pegasa is immortal. She was created many millennia ago." He continued that Pegasa only carried out very important duties, and so it was deemed that His Majesty's first meeting with his granddaughter and her grandmother was one such occasion when Pegasa's services were required. Elwood informed them that when the journey was over it would be, as was customary, proper to thank Pegasa in the manner that was appropriate to her eminent status.

In what seemed like the twinkling of an eye, the great horse began to slow her wings, so that they were scarcely flapping, and they began a gliding descent slowly back down to earth. They touched down with barely a bump, and Elwood quickly jumped out of the carriage and went and stood directly in front of the winged horse. He bowed low and thanked the creature for honouring them with her kindness and prowess. Pegasa bowed in return and dipped her great head. As Lizzie, Mrs Longton and the King departed from the carriage, they also thanked Pegasa and then left the great animal resting; her beautiful white coat glistening in the sunlight.

Lizzie followed behind Mrs Longton and the King and listened to them as they discussed the journey they had just taken. Ahead of them she could see that they had landed close to the outskirts of a small village. The fields around the village were a mixture of different coloured crops; bright yellows, greens, purples and russets that appeared to have been splashed across the landscape by some giant artist's paintbrush. The King beckoned Lizzie to him.

"This, Elizabeth, is the village of Elvenholme. It is a typical elven village in one of our farming communities. I should like to show you around so that you may see how most of my people live. Working the land is of vital importance to both this and the human world."

As they walked towards the village, which was made up of small thatched cottages and huts of varying sizes, Lizzie could see a man, or rather a male elf, walking towards them. He was smiling broadly as he approached and, as he reached them, he stopped and bowed low.

"Welcome Sire, welcome," he said.

"Good day Elmer. How are things in Elvenholme?" asked King Elfred, smiling at the proud elf standing before them, offering his hand which was shaken warmly and firmly by his subject.

"Excellent Sire, excellent," enthused the elf. He was of a similar height to the King, but more slender in stature. He had a high, proud forehead, surrounded by silky white hair that fell to his shoulders. His demeanour was grand and commanding and it was obvious that he was an elf of some elevated position within his community. The King turned towards Lizzie and introduced her to the man.

"Elmer, please let me introduce you to Elizabeth, my granddaughter," said the King proudly. With a sweeping motion, the elf bowed low to Lizzie.

The King then turned to Lizzie and introduced Elmer. "Elmer is the chieftain of the village of Elvenholme, Lizzie.

He, together with the leaders from all the villages and settlements in this realm, report to me and my council regularly on what is happening in their particular part of the realm; whether it be good or bad." Elmer extended his hand to Lizzie and, taking hers in his own, bowed low over it and kissed it. Lizzie blushed shyly.

"It is a pleasure to meet you at last, ma'am," said Elmer with great reverence. The King then introduced Mrs Longton, explaining briefly her relationship to Lizzie. Elmer bowed to her in turn. "I am honoured to welcome you both to my home and to show you around our village," he said, turning slightly and sweeping his arm towards the settlement behind him.

As the small party walked towards the village, the King turned to Lizzie and her grandmother and explained that there were villages and settlements all over Elvedom that specialised in skills. This enabled each and every one of his subjects to care for the environment around them. Some, like the villagers of Elvenholme, lived in rural communities that tended the land; growing crops, rotovating and fertilising the soil, enriching it to ensure its future health and prosperity. Other settlements specialised in tending the woodland and forest areas, and others specialised in coastlines or rivers.

As they approached the first of the cottages on the outskirts of the village, some children ran out and stood staring at the strangers in their midst. Suddenly, one of the older children recognised the King and fell to his knees. Elmer cuffed a couple of the younger children gently around the ears and they all, like their older companion, dropped to their knees in reverence.

"Hail, King Elfred, our Lord and Liege," they cried in practiced unison. King Elfred smiled and extended his upturned hands towards the prone children.

"Arise my children," he said, smiling down at them. "Come, join us. This is my granddaughter, Princess Elizabeth." As he swept his arm towards Lizzie in introduction, the children knelt and looked up at Lizzie, wide-eyed with wonder.

"Hail, Princess Elizabeth, our sovereign maid," they chanted in unison. Lizzie smiled down at them in embarrassment. Normally she did her best not to draw attention to herself, but that was going to be difficult here.

"Please, please do get up," she grinned, as a bubble of nervous giggles desperately tried to escape her; she often giggled at the most inappropriate times when she was nervous, and her nerves were definitely rampaging through her right now. She held out a hand to the nearest and smallest child and, taking the tiny hand in her own, helped the little girl to her feet, as the child gazed up at her in awe.

By now, their arrival was attracting the attention of other villagers, and a small crowd was forming as people came out of their huts and cottages. Lizzie could hear the general burble of excited murmurs at what seemed to be their unexpected appearance. As Lizzie, still holding the small child's hand, and her party approached the centre of the village, the crowd began crying out.

"Hail, King Elfred, our Lord and Liege." They bowed their heads in reverence.

"Good morning, good citizens of Elvenholme," said the King formally, smiling around at the crowd. "Thank you, for your warm welcome on this fine day."

The villagers stood watching the party as they passed through their throng. Once the royal party had passed them, people began dispersing and there began a general buzz of activity as people started organising what looked like an impromptu fete or feast in the middle of the village square.

Lizzie watched the proceedings with interest. She was finding the whole experience extremely strange and a little amusing, as everything was so formal here. The words of greeting between people were so old-fashioned. Was she supposed to speak in the same way? She didn't think she'd ever be able to because the idea of doing so was so foreign to her. Lizzie looked over at her grandmother to see how she was coping and saw that she actually looked to be in her element. Lizzie knew that her grandmother had had quite a formal upbringing herself, as her parents had been wealthy aristocrats. Nannies had been employed to look after her when she small before she was sent away to boarding school. Lizzie supposed that because of these early experiences, her grandmother was better prepared for these sorts of behaviours and manners. Lizzie thought her own background was much more normal. But, what then was normal? Lizzie wasn't sure anymore.

As Lizzie gazed shyly around the crowd in front of her, the King went through the formalities of greeting the villagers. It made her uneasy to see dozens of pairs of eyes looking at her furtively, as the people of the village were obviously too polite to stare openly. Lizzie didn't like being the centre of attention in this way, as at school it would usually lead to her being teased and taunted mercilessly afterwards by the Bray twins and their cronies. When she was being stared at in school, it was usually with malicious glares, not looks of interest and awe that she could see and sense here. Although she felt awkward and self-conscious, Lizzie took a deep breath and tried to relax a little.

Out of the corner of her eye, Lizzie noticed a young boy elf. He looked much the same age and height as her and a cheeky smile played on his lips, causing a small dimple to crinkle in his cheek. His bright carrot-coloured hair glowed like a beacon and he had warm brown eyes; having seen that Lizzie had spotted him, he winked one of them at her mischievously. Lizzie grinned and looked down at the ground quickly, trying not to giggle. She glanced over at him again and she could see that this time he was grinning broadly and he winked again in a much more obvious way. Lizzie had strong urge to poke her tongue out at him but wasn't sure how it might be interpreted in Elvedom and so, as she didn't really want to offend him, she winked back at him instead. She could see him laugh quietly to himself and Lizzie warmed to him immediately.

"My good people, I should like to introduce to you my granddaughter, Princess Elizabeth." Lizzie was brought back to the proceedings with a jolt as the King swung his arm around to her by means of introduction. Lizzie was unsure of what she should do next. Should she curtsey or bow or, heaven forbid – make a speech, so she decided smiling politely and waving was the safest option. The crowd cheered and applauded and the King smiled down at her encouragingly. Lizzie looked over at her grandmother for reassurance and she too smiled at Lizzie, her hands clasped together against her chest in pride; unshed tears glistening on her eyelashes. Wow, thought Lizzie; this is something else!

Elmer had begun speaking and was inviting the whole village to prepare a feast to welcome the royal party. He told the villagers that whilst the preparations were in hand, he and his son, Elrus, would take the King and his party on a tour of the village and surrounding lands to show them the work that was being undertaken and the progress that was being made.

The King took Lizzie's arm gently and, with Mrs Longton and Elwood behind them, followed Elmer towards a large cottage at the top of the village square. As the royal party departed, the villagers began to disperse, chatting noisily amongst themselves as they disappeared into their homes to prepare for the feast. As Lizzie looked back towards her grandmother and grinned, she saw to her surprise that the winking boy was also following them.

Chapter 9 – Country Cousins

As Lizzie entered the building, she was surprised at how large it was inside, as it had appeared quite small from the outside. Looking around her, Lizzie could see that they were in a large hall, at the end of which was a grand wooden chair sitting on a raised platform. The hall was simply but tastefully furnished. Lizzie looked at the boy, who was still staring at her, and wondered who he could be, just as Elmer placed a hand on the boy's shoulder and introduced him as his son, Elrus.

"Hello, Princess," said the boy, the cheeky grin still fixed on his face. As Lizzie tried to return the greeting, she suddenly burst out laughing and everyone looked at her in surprise.

"What's so funny, Elizabeth?" asked the King.

"I'm sorry, grandfather," she blurted, and then turned to the boy and apologised to him too. "I'm sorry, I didn't mean to be rude, but it just sounds so weird being called Princess. Everything today has been weird. So much has happened that I can't really take it all in. I'm so used to being a nobody, that it's difficult to think that I'm actually a somebody."

The King smiled reassuringly and told her that it was all right. "Of course, it will be strange for a while, but in time you'll get used to your status here and will learn the correct way to behave in certain situations. Learning this, together with all the other skills you will be trained in, will help you prepare for being a great royal princess."

A woman appeared from one of the doorways leading from the hall. She was carrying a tray containing a number of glasses and a jug of liquid. Elmer went to her and took the tray from her hands and placed it on a table at the side of the room. He then introduced the woman to Lizzie and Mrs

Longton as his wife, Elmara. The woman extended her hand to Lizzie and shook it gently while curtseying low, her head bowed.

"An honour, Princess," Elmara said, smiling politely.

The woman was very beautiful, with sharp chiselled cheekbones and a delicate straight nose. She was very elegant in a flowing dress of simple sky blue cotton and with long red hair which shone and fell like silken threads as she moved, pinned back from her face with what looked like carved ivory or bone combs. Elmara then turned and curtseyed low to the King, who reached down and took her hand in his own as she straightened up. He thanked her for her hospitality at such short notice.

Elmara then turned to Mrs Longton and, politely shaking her hand, offered her some refreshments. Mrs Longton thanked Elmara and said that a cool drink would be most welcome, to which Elmara then went over to the tray and prepared the drinks.

As Elmer talked to the King and Mrs Longton about the activities of the village and the achievements of the villagers, Lizzie looked at her surroundings. It was like being in a history book, as it looked as if it had come out of the Middle Ages. The walls of the building appeared to be made of whitewashed wattle and daub, supported by heavy oak timbers. There were tapestries hanging on the walls and the wooden floors were polished to a high shine. The furniture was heavy and, again, looked to be made of oak; some pieces with intricately carved adornment. Lizzie found it all fascinating and, as she looked at her surroundings, she suddenly noticed Elrus out of the corner of her eye. He was still staring at her. She glanced at him shyly and he grinned, walking over to her.

"Well, I suppose this must all be a bit strange to you, Princess," he said. "I've heard that you're not from around these parts."

"Please call me Lizzie," she replied, in a half whisper. "Princess doesn't really suit me yet."

"Okay then… Lizzie," answered Elrus, slightly hesitantly, as if he was unsure whether it was really appropriate to be that informal. Then he said in hushed tones, "But I'd better not let my father hear me calling you that or my ears will be ringing for a week from the clip he'll give them. So it's Princess when he's listening, okay?"

They laughed together and Lizzie nodded. "Okay, it's a deal," she smiled. "You're right; this is all very different from where I'm from. It's all been a bit of a shock. Up until today, I was just Lizzie Longton from Longton Hall, but now I've discovered a whole side of me that I didn't know existed."

As the adults talked, Lizzie briefly told Elrus about how she'd received the letter and ticket to get to Elvedom Castle, and how she'd met her grandfather for the first time that day. She said that finding out that she was a Half-Elf had been surreal enough, but then discovering she was royalty to boot, well, that was just the stuff of fairy tales.

Elrus told Lizzie that all elven children were taught from an early age about the story of Princess Elethria and Duke Eldorth and the curse he'd placed upon her. He said that up until recently, it had been believed that Princess Elethria had perished during childbirth having left Elvedom to marry a prince from a foreign land. He said that although Lizzie had never been specifically included in the story, there had always been rumours that one day the true heir to the throne would return to Elvedom and take their rightful place beside King Elfred. Elrus said that it had only been a few days before that his father had been sent a message saying that the

King was preparing to bring forth this 'rightful heir', and that he would be introducing the child to his people. Elrus said that his father had told them that Lizzie's arrival had to be kept secret until then for the security of the heir. It was then that all hell had broken loose with elves from all over the Kingdom, frantically preparing for the great day.

"I have to say," said Elrus with a grin, "You're not quite what we were expecting."

"Wow," exclaimed Lizzie. "I feel more special than ever," she said sarcastically, pretending to look hurt. "So what were you expecting, then?" she smiled.

"I'm not quite sure," Elrus said, grimacing slightly and placing a finger on his chin. "Perhaps I was expecting someone with more regal bearing and not someone so funny-looking" he said, cheekily. "Is it true you're a Half-Elf?" he asked, his eyes twinkling mischievously.

Lizzie punched him playfully on the arm and he feigned great pain. They laughed together and the adults looked over and smiled at them.

"Yes, it's true," she said, still not believing it herself.

"You should have seen my mother flapping around the place, trying to make sure that everywhere was clean and tidy and that the larder was full. She might look cool, calm and collected now," Elrus said, glancing over at his mother standing serenely next to Mrs Longton, "but you should have seen her this morning; her face was as red as her hair!" Lizzie looked at the beautiful, composed Elmara and couldn't imagine her flapping in a million years. She thought that perhaps Elrus was prone to exaggeration.

The King's voice caught their attention. "Well, Elmer. Shall we go and see what the good people of Elvenholme have been doing on the land before we have the pleasure of spending some time feasting with them? I'm getting hungry and can't wait to sample their food. Are you hungry yet, Lizzie?" He asked, turning towards her.

"Oh, yes – starving," Lizzie nodded enthusiastically.

As the little party left the home of Elmer, Elmara, as wife to the Chieftain, went to join the other villagers to supervise the preparations for the feast. Lizzie and Mrs Longton looked at their surroundings with interest. The village was much larger than they had first thought, with roads spreading out from the central square; along which were cottages and other dwellings, as well as a variety of small shops. Elmer pointed out a bakery to their left from where a wonderful smell of baking bread and cakes emanated. Lizzie's stomach grumbled loudly in protest at having to pass by the shop without being fed. Embarrassed, she pressed her hand to her stomach and hoped no-one had heard it, but judging from the smirk on Elrus's face, his sharp ears most certainly had.

They also passed a butcher's, where cuts of meat were displayed on trays and hung on hooks, just as they would be in the world that Lizzie and Mrs Longton had left that morning. A shop that particularly caught Lizzie's eye was displaying a fantastic selection of confectionery; sweets of every colour and description filled the jars and bowls in the shop window, and her mouth watered with the imagined taste of them. As though the shopkeeper had read her mind, she came running out with some bags of multi-coloured fruit sweets, bowing low as she gave them to Lizzie and Elrus. Lizzie thanked her warmly and the woman beamed happily, her round rosy face lighting up in pleasure as she watched Lizzie popped a purple pastille into her mouth.

"Mmm, lovely," mumbled Lizzie, dribbling a little as she tried to get the words out of her sweet-filled mouth. The sweet was certainly the most delicious blackcurrant pastille she'd ever eaten; the flavour exploding in her mouth.

Mrs Longton asked what the local currency was in Elvedom, and the King explained that trade was mostly through bartering and sharing produce. However, there was a coinage for some items. The smallest coins were coppers, and there were eleven coppers to a silver, and then eleven silvers to a gold.

"Bartering?" Lizzie asked, peering into her bag of sweets to make her next choice.

"Yes, bartering," piped up Elrus. "It means that someone can exchange something they have for something they might need from another person; if, of course, the other person wants to swap."

As they continued through the village, they passed a green-grocer's, a blacksmith's, a small tea shop with little tables outside, and an inn which smelt as though they brewed their own beer, as a strong smell of malt and hops hung in the air.

Once they'd passed the last of the village dwellings, they could see that the countryside around the village was lush and productive. Elves working in the fields appeared to really be enjoying their work, even though it looked like extremely hard labour. There were no great tractors or combine harvesters here, but large oxen-pulled ploughs and horse-drawn carts carried barrels of seed. Elves walked along behind the ploughs and threw grain from large wicker baskets hanging on their hips. In orchards, other elves could be seen pruning back trees and others were planting vines in the vineyards that were dug into the slopes behind the village.

Mrs Longton turned to Elmer and asked why they used such old-fashioned methods of farming when the elves obviously had the technology to use engines and other more updated methods; she mentioned the fantastic Diamond Line and its train.

"We are very conscious of the effects of machines and the pollution that they emit into the atmosphere," Elmer said. "The effect of pollution on our planet is devastating. It is the elves' lot in life to protect our Mother Earth and repair some of the harm that humankind has so thoughtlessly wrought upon her. We do not have the desires of power and control that your kind does, if you don't mind me saying so." He looked a little embarrassed at having spoken so bluntly.

"You are quite right, Elmer," said Mrs Longton, looking apologetic. "I often feel ashamed to belong to a race that thinks so little of the planet they live on. I feel privileged to have this opportunity of seeing what's being done to salvage some of what my race has inflicted. I only wish others could see this."

"To finish answering your question," Elmer continued, "we use the 'old' methods of farming because they cause the least damage to the environment. From what I've learnt, I understand that in your world you would call it being *eco-friendly*?"

"Ah, yes indeed," smiled Mrs Longton, and looked at a group of young elves in the field close by throwing corn seeds into the furrowed field, singing happily as they went. It was like travelling back in time by several hundred years.

In another field, they could see an elf herding some cattle towards a barn in the distance. And away on the hills beyond, a flock of sheep grazed; the white of their fleeces dazzled in the spring sunlight. Lizzie found the whole scene captivating. Like her first impressions when she'd arrived that morning at Elvedom Castle, everything here seemed so much more vibrant and alive than they were where she came from.

"Well, I wonder if that feast's ready yet, Elmer," said the King rubbing his hands together vigorously. "I'm famished."

"Oh, yes. I could eat a horse!" exclaimed Lizzie in agreement. There was general assent within the little group and so they began heading back towards the village, Elrus running ahead to let Elmara know that they were on their way.

Chapter 10 – Feting, Frivolities and Fear

As they approached the village, they could hear music and laughter. The sight that greeted them was almost overwhelming. When they had left, there were only a few trestle tables being set up, but now! There now seemed to be dozens of tables and each one had a crisp white cloth over it which was covered with plates, cutlery, goblets and posies of pretty spring flowers.

In the small trees that surrounded the village square were bowers and garlands of more spring flowers linking each one. The trees shaded the tables from the unseasonably warm sun that was beating down from the clear blue sky above. The whole scene reminded Lizzie of one of those elaborate American celebrity weddings that she'd seen photos of in the gossip magazines that Mary, back at the Hall, loved to read.

The King and his party seated themselves at a long trestle table sited on a platform at one end of the square. From there, Lizzie could look out over the rest of the tables lining the square, as well as see a long table that contained the feast's food. There were large platters of cooked chickens and hams. Wonderful freshly baked loaves of varying shapes and sizes sent their mouth-watering aromas drifting across to where Lizzie sat. Golden-crusted pies and flans glistened in the sunlight. Terrines of fresh vegetables, including round, fat potatoes dripping in rich creamy butter, sat steaming in their bowls; cheese boards containing cheeses of all colours and shapes; huge bowls of fruits and berries, with jugs of fresh cream sitting close by ready to compliment them. There were pitchers of fruit juices, wine, cider and beers. Each and every piece of the feast had been produced by the elves for their own use and enjoyment. Lizzie was amazed at how quickly they had put the feast together and she couldn't wait to tuck in to the wonderful food.

Once the villagers had sat down, and the general hubbub of chatter and clatter of people settling down to eat had quietened, the King stood and addressed the crowd.

"Good people of Elvenholme, I should like to thank you on behalf of myself, my granddaughter, Elizabeth, and others of my party for your kind hospitality today. The feast we see before us," he said, swooping his hand towards the food laden tables, "is a tribute to your hard work and dedication to the lands in which we are privileged to live. I have been much impressed by the work you have done here and the rewards it reaps. The fields and orchards abound with plentiful crops and fruits. The livestock are healthy and happy. All this contributes to the well-being of our great Mother Earth and we are all the better for it. So without further ado, let us enjoy this magnificent feast."

Representatives from each of the tables began serving food and pouring drinks. Lizzie tucked into warm hunks of bread, with spit-roasted chicken and steaming buttered potatoes, accompanied by fresh spring vegetables. She took a sip from a goblet of freshly pressed apple juice. It took her by surprise that the juice was ice cold. How could it be so cold on such a warm day? In fact, now she'd come to think of it, how were they keeping the meats and vegetables hot and the drinks cold out here in the spring sunshine? She caught her grandfather looking at her in amusement.

"Cold, Elizabeth?" he asked. The cold had caught Lizzie's breath and she nodded. "How …?" she began.

"Let's just say a little magic's involved," he whispered, cupping his hand to the side of his mouth in conspiracy. Lizzie's eyes widened; she had a lot to learn.

The feast continued in earnest and the burble of conversation, singing and background music made for an enjoyable time for all. Elrus was seated a few of chairs away from where Lizzie was sitting, at the middle of the table

109

between her grandparents, and Lizzie could feel him watching her before she actually spotted him doing so. He smiled, his cheeks bulging with food, and he waved merrily at her. She waved back. Perhaps she'd actually made a friend at last, she thought.

As the plates emptied and began to be cleared away, Elmer stood up and addressed the revellers. "On such an auspicious occasion as this, we should have music and dancing," he announced grandly; and, clapping his hands together, said, "Bring on the music."

Elves from each table around the square scurried off into various cottages and homes and reappeared with numerous musical instruments; fiddles, lutes, small harps, flutes, drums, and a variety of other rustic instruments carved out of wood that Lizzie hadn't seen before. Meanwhile, villagers had moved the tables to the sides of the square, creating enough space for performing and dancing. The air was buzzing with the excitement and enthusiasm being generated by the villagers, and Lizzie felt herself caught up with it. Some of the musicians formed into a small group in the corners of the square and struck up with an energetic tune, something akin to an Irish jig. People rushed onto the dance-floor and began swirling and flinging themselves around the dance area, laughing and singing along to the music. Lizzie found herself laughing along with them. She was so pre-occupied with the scene in front of her that she almost jumped out of her skin as someone touched her on the shoulder. Looking up, she saw that it was Elrus.

"Come on," he said, jerking his head towards the dancers. "Let's dance."

Lizzie blushed brightly; she didn't dance – well, maybe when she was on her own in her bedroom listening to her CDs, or around the kitchen with Mary or her grandmother, but never with a boy.

"No thank you. I think I'll just watch if you don't mind," she said, shyly.

"Oh come on, don't be such a spoil-sport," he urged, throwing back his head and laughing. Before she knew what had happened, he had grabbed her hand and dragged her onto the dance-floor.

"But I don't know how to dance to this," Lizzie said in panic as she looked around at the elves twirling and spinning past her in a blur.

"Just do whatever you want. Nobody cares. It's just about having fun and letting go of your inhibitions," he said, throwing his arms and legs around in abandon. This was going to be so embarrassing, Lizzie thought to herself. She'd never let go of her inhibitions before; she'd always been pretty self-conscious. She began gently swaying slowly, looking around to make sure nobody was looking at her.

Elrus stopped leaping and writhing around and watched her with a surprised look on his face.

"What on Earth are you doing?" he asked her incredulously. Lizzie's bright red face stared back at him in discomfort. "I'm dancing," she said bashfully, stopping suddenly.

"That's not dancing. You look like you've got a broomstick stuck up your back, you're so stiff," he declared in mock horror. Then, grasping her hands in his and whirling her around, he announced eagerly, "This is dancing!"

Lizzie found herself being spun and whizzed around the dance-floor by Elrus, holding her by her hands or by her waist. It was dizzying, exciting, exhilarating even, but it was also pretty exhausting. As the music suddenly stopped, Lizzie was sent spinning to a halt.

"Whoa, that was actually fun," she said breathlessly, holding her hands to her waist and bending over as she gasped air back into her heaving lungs.

The musicians struck up another song, but this one was a little slower than the last and some of the villagers formed a ring and began to dance a sort of folk dance. Not knowing the steps, Lizzie walked back to the high table to sit it out and watch with interest as the dance continued. Mrs Longton smiled at her as she approached.

"Well, that looked like fun," she grinned; taking in Lizzie's glowing face and glittering eyes. Lizzie smiled back at her and said that it certainly was once she'd got over her fears of making a fool of herself.

"I think that's the whole point," interjected the King who had been talking with Elmer, but had stopped as Lizzie sat down next to him. "Humans take themselves far too seriously. Life is for living and enjoying. Never waste a moment of it," he said and turned once more to watch the dancing while clapping along with the tune.

Lizzie and Mrs Longton had a wonderful time dancing and humming along to the wonderful music. Eventually, it was just the youngest and fittest left dancing on the dance-floor when the music finally finished and the King stood to speak.

"Well, my good people of Elvenholme, thank you again for your wonderful hospitality. You have made us most welcome and we've had a thoroughly enjoyable afternoon. However, before we take our leave of you, I would make one request and that is to Elmara." Elmara stood up and faced the King. "I would be glad if you would perform Elvyth's Ode for us?" Elmara curtseyed and said that she would be honoured to do so and, with that, two elven men went to her cottage and returned with a beautifully carved wooden harp.

Elmara sat on a stool at the harp and began to pluck the strings. The most beautiful, haunting music emanated from the instrument and when Elmara began to sing, Lizzie felt that she had never heard anything more enchanting. The words of the song echoed around the square as everyone sat in rapt silence.

"In days of old,
So we are told,
There lived a great musician.
He plied his art,
Songs he'd impart,
By ways of good tuition.

His tool of trade
Was specially made
By otherworldly creatures.
Hewn from a tree
For all to see,
A Harp with magic features.

And so it came
That his name
Was known from near and far.
And folks would cheer,
As he came near,
"Our Hero, Elvyth, hurrah."

Some called him "King"
As his songs seeped in
To each and every mind.
He took control,
Of every soul,
Of all of elven kind.

An elven King,
Named Elderin,

Heard of Elvyth's renown.
Unconcerned,
He then soon learned
Elvyth planned to take his crown.

The King declared,
Elvyth would not be spared,
He must remove his power.
So Elvyth was took,
And his life forsook
His harp locked in a tower.

And so it came
That this same
Harp was hidden safe away.
And there it stayed
Not to be played
Until a fateful day…

When Elvyth's Harp was stolen clean away."

As the haunting notes from the harp drifted away, Lizzie joined the rest of the villagers in applauding and cheering the performance. Elmara stood and curtseyed once again to the King before turning and doing the same to the rest of the crowd.

Suddenly there was a cry from a small child. "Look mummy, what's that?" it yelled, pointing up into the sky.

"What on earth is it?" gasped Mrs Longton.

Lizzie turned to look in the same direction as every other pair of eyes in the company around her. A huge shadow passed across the lowering sun and Lizzie saw, to her horror, a creature that she could never have imagined. It looked for all the world like a pterodactyl; a large flying dinosaur with huge leathery wings and a long pointed head and face. It let out a spine-chilling screech, and people clasped their hands over their ears and began running into buildings for cover, carrying babies and dragging small children with them.

"Quickly, inside," the King shouted urgently, and, taking both Lizzie and her grandmother by their elbows, almost pushed them into Elmer's house. Through the window of the house, he stared up angrily at the creature as it wheeled around once more overhead, then flew off into the distance.

Lizzie was badly shaken by what had just happened and began trembling uncontrollably as Elmara put a comforting arm around her shoulders. Looking shocked and dishevelled, Mrs Longton sat down heavily on the chair offered to her by Elmer. The elf turned to the King.

"Do you think it saw her, Sire?" he said anxiously.

"I don't know and, even if it did, I'm not sure it would know who she is," the King said; his face strained and pale. He looked extremely angry.

"I didn't know he still had those creatures at his disposal," Elmer said, shaking his head in disbelief.

Lizzie looked up at the King as he turned towards her and he could see the terror in her eyes.

"What was that thing? Why was it here?" she asked.

The King took Lizzie's hands in his own and looked earnestly into her eyes. He told her that the creature was an ancient beast called a pterotorial and that for many years it was believed that the creatures were extinct, just like their close cousins - the pterodactyls which had inhabited her world millions of years ago. However, some many years previously, a small colony of the creatures had been discovered living and breeding on a remote island off the far northern coast. The King explained that the creatures were highly intelligent and for many years were allies of the elves,

115

sometimes carrying out surveillance for them in troubled times. Their huge wingspan and highly developed eyesight meant that they could cover large distances in a short amount of time and were able to fly high enough to keep out of view. For many years, the creatures lived peacefully and undisturbed in their isolated home.

"Some time ago, we discovered that Eldorth had captured some of the pterotorials and had begun breeding them, using them for his own evil purposes. Some pterotorials have been known to attack remote elvish settlements, something never before heard of. I think it's safe to assume that the one we've just seen was scanning the lands for any signs of unusual activity. Today's celebration is one such occasion," the King said uneasily.

"We don't have such large acts of spontaneity very often. Usually we are too busy working the land but today, it couldn't be helped – my people are very excited about you, Elizabeth, and it was worth the risk just to see everyone so happy. Now, we'll have to wait to see what Eldorth does next," he said anxiously.

The King then turned to Mrs Longton and saw that shock and fear at what had just happened had turned her face a grizzly shade of grey. He asked her if she was all right.

"I… I'm not really sure," she stammered. "I've never seen anything like that before."

The King then called Elwood to him and told him to go and arrange for Pegasa to prepare to return to Elvedom Castle.

"I think we've had quite enough excitement for one day," the King announced.

"Will it be safe to fly back with that *thing* up there somewhere?" asked Mrs Longton, nervously. The King smiled reassuringly and said that the pterotorial was probably half way back to its master by now. He then turned and thanked Elmara and Elmer once more for their hospitality and, ruffling Elrus's hair as he passed, walked outside, closely followed by Lizzie and Mrs Longton who scanned the skies nervously as they went.

Pegasa was now re-harnessed to the carriage; her brilliant white coat gleaming with a golden sheen as it reflected the late afternoon sun and her wings quivering in anticipation to be off.

As handshakes were exchanged between the departing guests and their hosts, Lizzie turned to Elrus.

"Thanks so much for making today such fun. It's just a shame that thing went and spoiled it," she said, looking nervously up at the skies again. Then, turning back to him, she said, "I hope we see each other again sometime."

"Oh I'm sure we will," grinned Elrus, with an exaggerated wink, giving Lizzie the distinct impression that he knew something she didn't.

Elwood opened the carriage door as the King took Mrs Longton's hand and helped her climb in. He then turned and assisted Lizzie to do the same, said a final goodbye to Elmer and, with a nimble leap up the carriage steps, sat down next to Lizzie for their journey back to Elvedom Castle. Elwood, sitting next to Mrs Longton, scanned the skies once more before asking Pegasa to make haste for home.

As Pegasa soared off into the sky, Mrs Longton kept her eyes peeled for any sign of the pterotorial returning and Lizzie took the opportunity of pumping her grandfather for answers to some of the many questions buzzing through her brain.

Why was Eldorth so interested in finding her?

How did he communicate with the pterotorial creature?

117

Why were the people of Elvenholme so happy that she was there?

What was the song that Elmara had sung all about; and why did it end so abruptly?

What on earth was going on here?

The questions came tumbling out of her in a torrent and the King held up his hand in an attempt to stem the flow. The events of the day seemed to have tired him and Lizzie thought his eyes gave away the fears he was feeling, even though his lips smiled at her reassuringly.

"I will answer each of your questions in good time, Elizabeth," he assured her. "But I know that the answers are likely to give rise to even more questions, so for now let us leave them and rest for a while. I'm sure that all that vigorous dancing must have tired you. " He looked out of the carriage window and gazed down at the ground rushing past them far below.

Lizzie lay back against the soft leather seat of the carriage and thought about all that had happened to her in such a short space of time.

Only yesterday, she was odd little Lizzie Longton of Longton Hall with decidedly dodgy ears. An outcast and loner with no real friends for company and only her grandmother for family; her father hardly counted as she never saw nor heard from him. Now look at her; she was a somebody. She was an elf princess no less, with a whole new family and a whole new race of people to come to terms with and get to know. At last she was beginning to feel that she fitted in somewhere. She wasn't made to feel the odd-bod in this new world she belonged to. Okay, so she wasn't a full elf, but at least people seemed to accept her here and not be prejudiced against her because she wasn't exactly the same as them. In this world it was her grandmother who was different with odd ears because everyone here had just the

118

same sort of ears as Lizzie. It still felt as though she would wake up at any moment and discover it had all been a dream after all. In her heart she knew this was real and that she had found a home and place in her late mother's world. She felt that there were big things in store for her; she just wasn't sure what they were yet.

Lizzie felt the carriage starting to descend as Pegasa flew in to land close to Elvedom Castle. Elbert, the King's butler, was standing close to the doors of the building. He was standing with a number of other elves, wearing similar green livery, that ran forward to assist the King and his small entourage to disembark from the carriage. The King thanked Pegasa, who bowed her head respectfully, and Lizzie and Mrs Longton also thanked the beautiful creature who bowed her head to them in return. Lizzie wanted to reach out and stroke Pegasa's beautiful, brilliant white mane but then decided that if she did so, she may break some rule of etiquette or other. So instead, she too just bowed her head in thanks.

They entered the huge oak doors of the castle and walked through the fantastic entrance hall towards her grandfather's sitting room. Lizzie looked at her grandmother and realised for the first time how exhausted she appeared. She had to admit that she was pretty tired herself after everything that had happened, and yet they still had the long journey home to undertake before the day was out, if her grandmother didn't agree to stay. As if reading her mind, the King turned to Mrs Longton and invited them to stay for at least the night.

"This day must have been very tiring for you both," he said. "Events took something of a dramatic turn with the arrival of the pterotorial, and I feel sure that you could both do with relaxing and gathering your thoughts before your journey back to Longton Hall. I took the liberty to instruct my servants to prepare rooms for you in the eventuality that you agreed to stay. There are fresh clothes and anything else you may need laid out for you in your rooms. I would be most honoured if you would accept my hospitality." He looked hopefully at Mrs Longton.

Mrs Longton smiled and thanked King Elfred, and said that she and Lizzie would be most glad to spend the night. The King clapped his hands together and beamed happily at Lizzie. He then went over to a small side table and spoke into a telephone-like contraption, and advised whoever answered that Princess Elizabeth and her grandmother would be staying in the guest suite. In the twinkling of an eye, there was a knock at the door and a woman elf entered. She was thin faced; her bright blue eyes piercingly sharp and her grey hair pulled back into a tight bun at the back of her head. She looked somewhat stern, but when she spoke her voice was warm and friendly.

"Your Majesty; the guest suite is ready. Would you like me to show Her Highness and Mrs Longton to their rooms?" she asked.

"Thank you, Eldora," the King replied. Then, turning to Lizzie and her grandmother, he introduced the elf as his housekeeper, Eldora Cherrytree.

"Eldora will ensure that you have everything you need to make your stay as comfortable as possible. However, if you need anything further, please do not hesitate to call for Eldora. You will find communicators in your rooms," he indicated the telephone-like contraption that he'd used to summon Eldora. "Now I must ask you to excuse me. Following today's events, I must meet with some of my advisors. I wish you a pleasant evening and I will see you tomorrow." With that, he bowed to them both, smiled brightly at Lizzie, and turned to walk towards his large desk.

"Thank you, Your Majesty, for a lovely and most interesting day, except for that horrid creature of course," Mrs Longton said politely, with a wry smile. She felt somewhat taken aback at the abruptness of their dismissal, but then she looked at her watch and expressed surprise that the hour was so late. "Oh my goodness, where has the time gone? It's 8.30 already Lizzie. No wonder I'm exhausted, we don't seem to have stopped since we got up this morning."

Lizzie went over to her grandfather and placed her hands on the desk between them. The King looked up into her face.

"Thank you for today," she said. "I'm so glad you decided to finally ask me to come here. I'm sure everything's going to be okay."

The King smiled tenderly. "I'm sure you are right, Elizabeth. Now, don't worry, just go and get a good night's sleep. Arrangements have been made for Elwood to give you a tour of the castle and grounds in the morning before you leave for home," he said, reaching across and patting her hand gently. "Unless, of course, we can persuade your grandmother to stay a while longer," he whispered.

As Lizzie reached the door of his study, she turned to give her grandfather a final look and saw that his shoulders appeared to sag as though they were carrying the weight of his world upon them. Getting a good night's sleep didn't look like they were on the cards for him.

Chapter 11 – A Sorceress Scorned

A shadow passed over the handsome features of the man sitting, staring through narrowed dark eyes at the woman standing before him. He was sitting in a huge, almost throne-like, chair on a dais at the end of a large hall. Tapestries and drapes hung around the walls and rugs were strewn about the stone flagged floor. Mullioned windows let in a little light, but the braziers burning in the corners of the large space were the only things sending any warmth across the Duke's cold countenance.

"So the child survives?" he said, his voice deep and silky smooth.

"So it would seem, me Lawd," replied the woman, her eyes cast down. She was short and squat with straggly, mousey brown hair and she spoke with a rough common accent. Her brown robes were dusty and unkempt and her whole appearance was that of someone who wasn't particularly bothered by the niceties of personal hygiene.

There were several guards standing at strategic places around the room and their eyes furtively moved in her direction; each taking a secret pleasure in the woman's discomfort.

"But I seem to recall you assuring me that the curse would destroy the mother and any child that she carried," the voice was still calm and silky, but it had an edge to it that sent a shiver down the spines of those present. Duke Eldorth's elaborately ringed fingers gripped the arm of his chair so that his knucklebones shone white through his tanned skin. His displeasure was clearly evident.

Melificent raised her pale, watery eyes to face him. "And so it should 'ave. I can only fink that that pain in the rear end, Marvin, had summink to do wiv it," she said through gritted teeth. She rubbed her hands agitatedly and pursed her slippery lips in annoyance. Her fat, slobbery tongue flicked over them, licking away the beads of sweat that had formed on the upper one. She was not a pretty sight.

"That curse I gave ya was strong enough to kill an ox - a whole bloody herd of 'em. Marvin must 'ave eiver countered it or else..." she hesitated, her brow furrowed in thought. "It could be that the King's powers weren't weakened enuf. There were still four relics we needed to get our 'ands on at the time," she concluded, clenching her hands as if imagining them doing just that.

Duke Eldorth leaned forward in his chair, his arm resting across his thigh. "So what do you propose to do about the situation?" he said, his voice almost a whisper.

Melificent began rubbing her hands together nervously. Her face worked as her brain considered her options. Eldorth drummed his fingers on his knee as he waited impatiently for her reply. Realising that she had to give some kind of response, before Eldorth really lost his temper, she simpered, "Well, me Lawd. I need to 'ave a bit of a fink about this one. I'll go and 'ave a look at me bits and bobs to come up wiv a few ideas, shall I?"

Eldorth narrowed his eyes further, his glare almost burning holes through Melificent's blotchy face. "I suggest you do that," he hissed, the colour rising in his face as he tried to control his temper. Melificent dipped in a quick curtsey and turned to leave the room. As she did so, Eldorth stopped her in her tracks.

"Oh, and Melificent," he called. She turned sharply to face him. "Don't mess up again." Melificent bowed her head briefly in compliance and scurried from the room.

Eldorth watched her rapidly departing and then slumped back in his chair. He was angry. He hadn't been this angry for many years; not since the day that he had been dragged from King Elfred's court screaming the curses that he had gone away to fulfil; with the help of the woman who had just left his presence. He had learnt to control his anger over the following years and channel the energy of it in a more positive and destructive way. He could now coldly and calculatingly work some of the dark magic that would eventually bring down the royal household of Elfred. He still had a lot to learn, but when he was ready he would take over, just as he'd always planned. He took a deep breath and relaxed a little. He beckoned to a young elven girl that was standing in the shadows to one side of the room holding a tray.

"Wine," he called, and she stepped forward, bowed and offered him a goblet of wine. He glanced up at her and saw the look of adoration in the girl's face as he took the goblet from the tray. He smiled at her, put out a hand and ran his finger down the girl's cheek. She looked down shyly, her long white hair falling in a curtain across her face and hiding it, and she seemed to shiver with pleasure at his touch.

"Thank you, Ella," he purred softly. This is what he sought, the power to draw people to him and be adored, worshipped. When the time was right, he would use Elvyth's harp and then thousands of faces would look at him in the same way. The Harp was protected by some old magic that was still preventing him from using it to its full effect, but once that magic was broken, then… That's if the old crone, Melificent, pulled her finger out, he thought, and the anger suddenly flared in him again. He took a large gulp of the wine and, as its warmth seeped through him, he relaxed a little again. For now, though, they had to concentrate on doing something about Elethria's child.

"But it's just a child," he thought to himself, "and a girl at that. Why, she's not even a full elf. She's just a Half-Elf." He allowed himself a smug smile and an icy laugh. Then, with a snap of his fingers, he said in his cold, calm voice, "I could snuff her out like that!"

Chapter 12 – A Good Night's Sleep?!

Lizzie and her grandmother followed Eldora up the large marble staircase of the entrance hall; the stairway seemed to illuminate at every step they took. As they reached the first landing, a long corridor stretched away to both their left and right and further staircases branched off the corridors behind them, curving up and around from either side to more levels above them. The whole appearance of the building was of some kind of warren or labyrinth. The corridors appeared like tunnels as they disappeared off into the distance. Due to their subdued lighting, Lizzie couldn't see their ends.

"This way, please," Eldora invited and walked off towards her right.

As they followed along behind Eldora, Lizzie looked at the paintings and portraits that adorned the walls of the corridors. Elves and other magical creatures filled the frames, as well as landscapes and seascapes. Lizzie would have loved to ask Eldora who they were, but she found her a little intimidating and so decided to wait for another time. At least she hoped there would be another time.

Eventually they stopped outside a large oak door. Like all the others they'd seen in the castle, it was beautifully carved – not as elaborate and imposing as the front entrance doors, but obviously crafted by an equally trained master woodcarver. Eldora opened the door and stood aside to let them enter. The room was beautiful. It was a bright and airy sitting room and it contained a number of soft, squashy sofas and a small dining table, laid with what looked like a light supper of drinks and sandwiches. Elves obviously liked regular intakes of food because Lizzie didn't think she'd ever eaten so much in one day.

Two doors led off to either side of the room and the windows looked out over the grounds of the castle. But as Lizzie approached them to see the view, the darkening sky prevented her taking in its full glory. There was a fire burning in the grate and the room, although light and airy, felt warm.

"I hope you'll be comfortable, ma-am. If you need anything further, please let me know. Someone will be along in a while to remove your supper things. There are books and articles over in the bookcase there for your entertainment," said Eldora, pointing to a large bookcase in the corner of the room. "There are also towels and bedclothes in your rooms," she indicated the doors to either side of the room. "I'll take your leave now, unless there is anything you'd like to ask me."

"Oh, there is just one thing. Will we receive a wake up call in the morning?" asked Mrs Longton.

"Indeed, madam. Myself, or one of the other staff, will bring breakfast here at about 8 am. I'm sure you'll need a good long rest after today," Eldora smiled at them. Then, curtseying low, she backed out of the room.

"Well, Lizzie, what do you make of it all?" sighed Mrs Longton, plonking herself down in one of the squashy sofas and kicking off her shoes; she wriggled her toes in relief. Lizzie pulled off her sweatshirt and flopped down on the sofa opposite her grandmother.

"It's been the weirdest, most fantastic and totally unbelievable day ever," she breathed; over-awed by everything that had happened to them in such a short space of time.

"But are you alright, darling?" her grandmother asked her, concern etched on her face. "I realise that what's happened today has been a huge shock and totally not what we were expecting when we left the house this morning." Lizzie smiled wanly at her grandmother and nodded slowly. She had so many thoughts and emotions running through her mind and body. Whilst she was being escorted everywhere and carried away with the events of the day, she had been on something of a high – the adrenaline pumping through her body had kept her going. Now in the quiet solitude of this room, with just her grandmother for company, she felt bewildered and suddenly a little low. Her grandmother seemed to sense this and went and sat next to her, placing an arm around her shoulder and pulling Lizzie close to her in a warm hug. Lizzie slumped against the security of her grandmother and they sat quietly together for a while, just resting. After a few moments, Mrs Longton released Lizzie slowly and got up and walked over to the table containing their supper.

"Come on, Lizzie, all this excitement has made me ravenous. Let's tuck in," she said enthusiastically. Then, lifting up the top layer of bread on a selection of sandwiches, said, "It appears that we've got the choice of ham, egg, cheese or jam. What'd ya fancy?"

She placed some sandwiches on a plate and poured herself a steaming cup of tea. Lizzie joined her at the table and picked up a jam sandwich and munched it hungrily. Mrs Longton walked over to the bookcase and took out a book. She sat down and flicked through the book's pages.

"What's the book about, gran?" Lizzie mumbled through a mouthful of sandwich.

"Well, it seems to be some sort of history of trolls; their origins, leaders, behaviours and stuff. It's bizarre reading a *factual* book about trolls," Mrs Longton grinned, making Lizzie laugh at the comical look on her face. They were both soon laughing hysterically, as much from relief than in any real cause for amusement, and when they stopped they looked at each other and slumped back into their chairs exhausted, their arms hanging loosely to their sides.

"Well, I don't know about you, Elizabeth Longton, but I'm shattered," Mrs Longton groaned. "Hey, do you realise we haven't inspected our sleeping quarters yet?" With great effort, she pushed herself off the sofa. They both walked over to the door at the side of the room nearest to where they were sitting and Mrs Longton opened it tentatively. Poking their heads around the door, like two naughty children spying on something they shouldn't, they looked into the room behind it.

The room that confronted them looked as if it had come out of some historical TV drama. A large four-poster bed with deep maroon velvet drapes dominated the room and the curtains at the window appeared to be made of the same fabric. Ornately gilded furniture was placed strategically around the room and the whole effect was extremely grand.

"I think you'd better have this one, gran. I don't think I could sleep in here, I'd be frightened of creasing the sheets," Lizzie said in awe.

Mrs Longton nodded. "I agree with you, Lizzie, but I think I'll cope," she said, and walked over to the bed and pushed down on the mattress with both hands. "Well, the bed's soft enough," she said happily.

Another door led off from the corner of the bedroom and upon opening it, Mrs Longton discovered that it was a bathroom with a huge sunken bath.

"I think I'll have a good long soak in the bath before I retire to bed, but first we ought to check out your billet for the night, Lizzie," Mrs Longton smiled.

Going back through the sitting room, they opened the door on the other side of the room. It was as if their host had known exactly what sort of room Lizzie had always dreamt of. It was a proper girl's room with a huge, round, squashy bed with nets and sashes draped over it. Posters of animals adorned the walls. Lizzie ran across the room and dived onto the bed.

"Wow, *this* is brilliant!" She yelled in delight.

The bathroom leading from Lizzie's room was also beautiful. The walls and floors seemed to be made of marble and there were tall white pillars holding up a vaulted ceiling. Mrs Longton drew in a sharp intake of breath.

"Well, Miss Longton, you will bathe like a princess tonight," she grinned, staring at the grand surroundings as she kissed the top of Lizzie's head.

"I'm off to my bath now, darling, so I shall say goodnight," Mrs Longton yawned. Lizzie kissed her grandmother fondly on the cheek and bade her good night. As her grandmother left the room, Lizzie decided that she too would take advantage of the fantastic bath in front of her.

On a table at the side of the bath, there were some delicate crystal bottles, similar to those in her grandmother's bathroom, filled with different coloured liquids. Lizzie pulled out the stopper of each one in turn and smelled the contents; they were perfumes and oils. As the bath began to fill, she poured a little of one of the bottle's contents into the gushing water.

The most wonderful aromas swirled around the room and the clear water in the bath turned into mounds of sparkling white foam. Lizzie dipped her arm into the water to check its temperature, and found that it was just right. So, quickly stripping off her clothes, she jumped in. The water was bliss as it enveloped her body.

The bath was so deep and long that it was more like a small swimming pool. Dunking her head under the water was like slipping into a cocoon, and a feeling of peace and serenity filled her as she closed her eyes and let the waters soak into her skin. As she lifted her head out of the water, she shook her head like a shaggy dog; it felt as though she were shaking away the cares of the day. Lizzie reached up to turn the taps off and, as she did so, she knocked a small lever

129

with her elbow and suddenly the water around her began to swirl and churn like a massive cauldron.

"Ooh…," thought Lizzie with joy, "my very own Jacuzzi."

Lizzie enjoyed the pleasures of her bath for a while longer until, wrinkly like a prune, she clambered out of the tub. She then realised that she hadn't considered towels, but to her relief she saw a pile of white fluffy bath sheets piled on some shelves nearby. Taking one, she wrapped it around her. It was soft and warm and, as she snuggled herself up in it, she made her way back into the bedroom.

As she walked towards the bed, she saw some soft cotton underwear and a long, shimmering green nightdress lying on it. Lizzie lifted the delicate garment up and held it against her face. It felt wonderful and so she dried herself off quickly and slipped it on. She then noticed a pair of green, gem encrusted slippers on the floor beside the bed and slipped those on too. They fitted like gloves and were so soft and comfortable, she barely felt as though she were wearing anything on her feet at all. She now felt like a princess and went over to a large mirrored dressing table and her face, pink and freshly scrubbed, stared back at her. Well, she thought, I may feel like a princess but I still look the same.

Picking up a pearl encrusted comb lying on the dressing table, she began to pull it through her wet hair. She wished her grandmother would let her grow it long but it was so fine, like silken silver threads, that she had never been allowed to. Maybe now Lizzie had discovered she was a princess, she could demand to be allowed to grow her hair long.

"Yeah, right," she thought again, pulling a face at herself in the mirror. "Like my gran will stand any truck with that!"

Lizzie put down the comb, scrutinised her reflection once more and stroked her ears, just checking that they still looked and felt the same (old habits die hard), and then went and flopped down on the bed. As she lay there spread-eagled, gazing up at the white netting and pink ribbons and sashes tying the nets in elaborate folds, Lizzie went over everything that had happened that day. She thought about the questions she'd asked her grandfather when they were returning to the castle from Elvenholme. She mustn't forget to ask him again tomorrow she thought; particularly about that song Elmara sang. Who was this Elvyth guy? How could a musician have such power over people?

She sat up suddenly and realised that she didn't really feel tired anymore; there was too much going on in her head. She didn't think she would ever get to sleep with so many questions that needed answering, so she got off the bed and paced around the room; nervous energy surging through her.

Eventually, she went to the door leading back into the sitting room and peered out. The supper things had gone; obviously Eldora or another elf had been to take them away. In their place was another tray containing glasses and decanters of different liquids. She poured herself some juice and went over to her grandmother's bedroom door and knocked; there was no reply so she opened the door and peeped in. Mrs Longton's bed was untouched and Lizzie could just about hear the sound of her grandmother singing happily from her bathroom. She'll never make a pop star, grimaced Lizzie and then, smiling to herself, went back into the sitting room.

Replacing her glass on the table, she walked over to the bookcase and looked at the leather bound books on the shelves; they all looked very old. Running her finger along the spines of the books, she found that one of them jutted out further than the others. She decided to pull the book out to see what it was. According to the title on the spine, it appeared to be "A History of the House of Elfron". Well that might prove quite interesting, she thought; especially if had anything to do with her own ancestors.

Lizzie pulled on the book cover but it seemed to be wedged in firmly and so she yanked on it even harder. Nothing happened; the book stayed precisely where it was. She tried again, but the book stood firm and so, in frustration, Lizzie gave it a hard whack with the palm of her hand. As she did so, she felt the book depress like a large button. Slowly and creakily, a whole section of the bookcase swung inwards to reveal a tunnel behind where it had stood. Lizzie was stunned. The tunnel was pitch dark and she could only make out a short part of it from the light emitting from the sitting room.

She considered getting her grandmother to see what she made of it, but then decided against disturbing her. Part of Lizzie wanted this bit of the day to be her adventure and hers alone, so she decided that she would tell her grandmother all about it in the morning. Lizzie was just about to step into the tunnel when she thought about how Mrs Longton would feel if, when she came out of the bath, she popped in to wish Lizzie goodnight and she wasn't there. So, instead of her grandmother calling for someone to look for her and spoiling the adventure, she decided she would wait until she knew her grandmother was in bed and then she'd check out the tunnel. In the meantime, she had to work out how to close the bookcase door. She tried grabbing its edge and pulling but it wouldn't budge. She then felt along for the book she'd pressed to open it to see if she could pull it out again, but when she tried, nothing happened. Lizzie felt along the books on the other shelves, but it wasn't until she reached the end book on the topmost shelf, standing on her tiptoes to reach it, did she find another book that stood out from its neighbours. Pushing on its spine, the door to the tunnel began to slowly but surely swing back into place.

With excitement coursing through every nerve in her body, Lizzie ran back into her room and threw herself on the bed. She could hardly wait until she could go and explore the tunnel. Shortly afterwards, there was a soft tap at the door and Mrs Longton poked her head round it.

"I thought I'd just pop in to check you're okay, darling," she said. Mrs Longton came into the room and sat on the edge of the bed. She leant over and kissed Lizzie on the forehead.

"You must be very tired; you should try to get a good night's sleep," she said softly, ruffling Lizzie's hair. She stood and walked to the door and then, blowing Lizzie a kiss, said good night before closing the door behind her.

For what seemed like an eternity, Lizzie lay there, listening out for any noise. Finally, thinking her grandmother must be asleep, she leapt out of bed. Lizzie knew that the tunnel was very dark and so she would need some source of light, but what could she use? She scanned the room and saw on the mantelpiece an assortment of candles, mainly of the scented variety. She couldn't use one of those as one hint of a draft in the tunnel and she'd be plunged into darkness.

She went round to one of the bedside cabinets and looked in the top drawer and there, lying looking up at her, was a small pink torch. She took the torch out of the drawer and pressed the on switch. A bright beam of light shone across the room. Brilliant, thought Lizzie, impressed; silently she thanked the elves – they really did think of everything.

Lizzie looked down at her night-time attire and decided that it probably wasn't very appropriate for clambering through a dark tunnel. So, she quickly ran back to the bathroom, grabbed up her jeans and tee shirt from the floor and quickly pulled on her clothes and trainers. She then went over to the bedroom door and pressed her ear against it. She couldn't hear anything and so tentatively opened it. The sitting room was empty and dimly lit by a small lamp on a side table. Lizzie ran across the room and held her ear to the door leading to her grandmother's bedroom. The sound of Mrs Longton's snoring permeated through and confirmed that she was fast asleep.

At the bookcase, Lizzie eagerly pressed the History of Elfron's book spine and, once again, the secret door swung open. Switching on the torch and taking a deep breath, she stepped into the tunnel.

"I'd better shut the door behind me," she thought, "or the game's up before it's started." So, she reached up, pressed the book on the top shelf and quickly nipped into the tunnel as the door swung back into place. Lizzie was alone in the tunnel when another thought suddenly occurred to her. "How on earth do I get back out?"

Chapter 13 – The Sorcerer's Apprentice

Lizzie suddenly felt panic creep up on her. She turned on her heels and began pushing against the rear of the bookcase wall in an attempt to get back into the room. If she could just re-open the secret door, she could leave it slightly ajar and so be able to get back through; but the wall stood firm. Lizzie then scanned the walls to see if there were any levers or switches that could be pushed to re-open the door, but she could find nothing. With panic continuing to rise in her chest, she began quickly running her hands over the walls, feeling the rough stone to see if she could find any invisible or hidden buttons that could be pressed to open it; but there were none.

"Oh, will you open?" Lizzie yelled, pushing at the wall with all her might. She tried yelling a number of things whilst pushing and kicking at the wall. "Open up; open for heaven's sake," were just a few, until finally realising that none of them were going to work. Taking a deep breath to steady her nerves, she decided that the only thing to be done was to follow through her madcap idea and see where the tunnel led. So, with a slightly shaky hand, she shone the torch in front of her and followed its beam.

The tunnel floor was well-worn, dry and smooth, as though it had been used often over the years. Sloping slightly downwards, the tunnel went on straight ahead, deviating neither left nor right. Lizzie walked on for what felt like ages, when she suddenly came to a junction in the tunnel where it branched off in five different directions. "Oh no," she thought, "Which way now?"

Lizzie stood and shone her torch down each of the tunnels in turn, hoping that by doing so it would inspire her to take one of them – it didn't. She then shone it on the walls to see if there were any signs or symbols pointing her in any particular direction – there weren't. In the silence of the tunnel, she could hear the sound of her own heart pounding in her ears as panic began raising its ugly head in her chest once again. Oh, well there's nothing else for it, she thought, and began reciting, "Eeny, meeny, miney, mo, catch a tiddler by its toe..." When, above the roaring of her blood coursing through her body, Lizzie thought she could hear singing.

Lizzie took several deep breaths in an attempt to calm herself and slow her rapid heartbeats, then, holding her breath, she listened hard. Her acute hearing could just make out the sound of a voice singing heartily in the distance. She stood at the mouths of each of the tunnel offshoots and cupped her hands to her ears, trying to work out which one would lead to the voice. Having made up her mind that it was the second tunnel to her right, she set off once again. Walking quickly, avoiding the urge to run in case she fell, Lizzie followed the sound of the voice as it gradually rose in volume. Suddenly the singing stopped.

Caught off guard, Lizzie stopped in her tracks and waited. She felt confused; had the person actually stopped singing or, in her eagerness to find its source, had she taken the wrong tunnel and the voice had just faded from her hearing? Standing there with her mind in a quandary, she tried to decide whether she should carry on or turn back and retrace her steps when the singing began again, however, when it continued, it was a little louder. Almost crying with relief, Lizzie walked quickly towards the singing once more, the sound growing louder with every step she took. Suddenly she came to an abrupt halt when she saw that she had reached a dead-end. Lizzie could now make out that the singing was coming from behind the wall of the tunnel end.

"It must be another secret door," she thought to herself. So, as Lizzie had done before, when she had closed the secret door to her sitting room, she began searching for some kind of device that would open the wall; but once again Lizzie found nothing. She kicked the wall in frustration.

"Ouch," Lizzie yelped, grabbing her foot and hopping around in pain.

"Who's that?" shouted an alarmed voice. It sounded like a young boy and came from the other side of the wall.

"Hello, hello, can you hear me?" called Lizzie excitedly, stopping her hopping.

"I can hear you, identify yourself. I warn you; I'm armed," the voice called in reply.

"Oh, I'm not dangerous or anything," Lizzie yelled. "I'm stuck in this tunnel and I don't know how to get out. My name's Lizzie Longton and I'm staying here in Elvedom Castle as a guest of the King."

"Lizzie? Lizzie Longton? What sort of name's that?" said the voice, disdainfully.

"It's my name," said Lizzie indignantly, a little put out by the tone of the voice. "Well, actually I suppose people here know me as Princess Elizabeth."

"Oh dear! Oh dear, oh dear," the voice now sounded agitated and slightly horrified. "I beg your pardon, Your Highness. I didn't know. I, I would never have been so disrespectful had I known it was you. Please forgive me."

Lizzie could almost picture the person on the other side of the wall bowing and scraping dutifully and she smiled at the thought. She would even have laughed had she been a little less frightened at the thought of being stuck in the tunnel for the remainder of her life.

"That's okay, you weren't to know," she managed to say with as much gravitas as she could muster, given the circumstances. "Look, can you help me out here? I'm stuck in a tunnel that led from my rooms to somewhere behind yours. I don't know how to get out and it's getting a bit scary now," she called, trying to keep her voice calm.

"Yes, ma-am, of course I'll help if I can," the voice called. "Now, can you bang on the wall of where you are again, please? Then perhaps I can work out where you are and see if there's some way of reaching you."

Lizzie began to bang her hand on the wall once again, but the cold hard stone was solid and she wasn't sure her hand slapping it would infiltrate its thickness.

"Again," the voice called, when she stopped, "I can't quite make out where you are. The noise is echoing around the room." Lizzie banged hard on the wall again. They went through this routine several more times until her hands hurt.

"We're not really getting anywhere like this," she called out, trying not to sound too annoyed. She flopped her back against the wall; tired and frustrated. Then suddenly she had an idea.

"I've just had a thought," she shouted, leaning back and calling over her shoulder at the wall. "I found the tunnel from my room by opening a secret door behind a bookcase. Is there a bookcase on your side of the wall, by any chance?"

"Yes; yes there is," called the voice excitedly.

"Well, can you see if there are any books jutting out and try pushing them in. That's how my door worked, so mayb…" but before she could finish her sentence, she found herself tumbling backwards into a strange room and ending up flat on her back, staring up into the face of a young skinny boy who was staring back down at her with huge blue eyes. The boy bent down and took Lizzie's outstretched hand as he helped her to her feet.

"Are you alright, ma-am?" he said, his tousled blond fringe hanging in his worried blue eyes. He brushed away

138

the hair with his free hand as Lizzie straightened herself up and brushed herself down.

"I'm fine, thank you," she puffed in relief. "Nice voice by the way," she smiled.

He looked at her quizzically. "Thank you, ma-am," grinned the boy shyly.

"I meant your singing," Lizzie said, scanning the room she'd found herself in. Turning back to him she continued, "So, you know who I am, who are you?"

"I'm Max, Your Highness," said the boy, bowing low. "I am apprentice here."

The room they were standing in was amazing. It appeared to be a cave or dungeon of some sort. There were unusual, intricate instruments of brass and copper on the numerous surfaces of tables and benches. Various gadgets littered the room. Ancient, dusty books lined the wall from behind which she'd just fallen. Globes and models of star systems and planets were dotted around the room at strategic places. There was a huge brass telescope, which seemed a bit pointless as there were no windows visible through which to see the sky.

On a long worktable there were tumblers and specimen jars with tubes full of smoking coloured liquids dripping and bubbling through them. It looked like some complex experiment was going on. Jars of strange looking objects that Lizzie would rather not look at too closely lined more shelves. In one corner of the room, with a fire smouldering beneath it, was an extremely large pewter coloured cauldron. Steam seeped up into the rafters of the room and, looking up at the ceiling, Lizzie could see diagrams of the star constellations of the signs of the zodiac and other astrological bodies. The room was totally bewitching. That's it, Lizzie thought, it's like something out of a film set of

King Arthur and the Knights of the Round Table – it's like Merlin's cave.

"Um, where am I?" asked Lizzie, once again looking at Max – who was standing watching her in awe. He reddened when he realised he was staring and looked at the floor in embarrassment.

"This is my master, Marvin's, room ma-am," he replied softly.

Lizzie was amused. "What, like Marvin the Magician?" she giggled, peering into a glass orb sitting on one of the tables. Max looked shocked.

"Excuse me, ma-am; but my master is not a magician, he is a great sorcerer. Possibly the greatest since our Lord Merlin," he said proudly. Lizzie blushed.

"I'm sorry if I sounded impolite about your master, but from where I come from it sounds like some kind of cartoon character," she said.

"Cartoon?" queried Max, looking puzzled.

"Oh, never mind, it's too complicated to explain right now," she said, realising that of course the boy wouldn't have a clue what a cartoon was. A squawk from the corner of the room drew her attention, where she could see two black and white birds sitting on a perch.

"Magpies!" she exclaimed. "Are they pets?"

"Oh no, ma-am. They work for my master. Magpies are very intelligent birds, Your Highness," Max explained.

"Do they have names then?" Lizzie asked, walking over to the birds' perch and peering up at them. They eyed her warily in return.

"Yes, ma-am, they do. This one," he said, pointing to the one on the right "is Mag, and that is Pi," he indicated Mag's companion. Lizzie chuckled.

"Good names," she said in delight. "Does your master have the pair so he could call them those names?"

Max shook his head vigorously, "Oh no, ma-am. That is their names but also it would be bad luck to just have one living here with us. There is an old saying about magpies which says, 'One for sorrow, two for joy'. Having both Mag and Pi living here brings good luck." Lizzie grinned at the boy's faith in the old superstition. He reminded her of Mary back at home.

"I've heard that saying. So what's the point of them? What can they do for your master?" she asked. Max explained that his master was highly skilled in many languages and was able to talk to most creatures. He explained that magpies were very curious creatures and were known for their love of gathering things, and they were exceptionally good as messengers. They were also helpful at finding unusual or rare ingredients that his master needed whilst preparing a potion or spell.

"Isn't it more usual for a wizard to have an owl?" Lizzie asked; she was finding the whole episode highly bizarre.

"An owl?" Max asked looking confused. "Why would my master have an owl?"

Lizzie stared at him in surprise at the question. "Well, I thought that owls are supposed to be sort of magical and wise," she said uncertainly.

The boy giggled. "Owls, wise?" he exclaimed in disbelief. "Wherever did you hear that? Owls aren't very bright, Your Highness. In fact they're pretty silly creatures most of the time. They'd be no good during the day at all; they'd just want to sleep."

141

Lizzie couldn't believe it. All the old stories of witches and wizards that she'd ever heard or read at home included a clever old owl. "So, they don't deliver messages or anything," she asked, disappointedly.

"Deliver messages," spluttered the boy, clearly choking back a fit of the giggles, as though not wishing to appear rude. "How would we get them to deliver messages? They'd peck your hand off if you tried tying anything to them. No, no, no! If we need to send messages, we use pigeons; they're much more manageable and very reliable." Lizzie nodded in understanding; she knew that pigeons had been used for hundreds of years for the very same purpose at home. She'd even read somewhere that pigeons had carried secret messages for the allies during the Second World War.

As Lizzie continued to look around the room, she noticed a globe revolving on an ornate wooden stand in the corner of the room. As she walked towards it, she could see that it was unlike any globe she'd ever seen before. She recognised it as the Earth but it looked quite different somehow. The globe appeared three-dimensional with what looked like layer upon layer of landmass, as if there were countries lying one on top of another. Lizzie put her hand out to try to stop it revolving so that she could look at the detail more closely.

Max rushed over. "Please, ma-am, I must respectfully request that you do not touch any of my master's things. He is very particular about them as they are very precious and I would be in the most terrible trouble if anything got broken," he said urgently.

Lizzie let her hand drop and, leaving the globe, walked over to peer into the labyrinth of tubes and flasks where coloured liquids bubbled and flowed in some complicated experiment on the workbench. She looked over at the boy who was watching her with a look of trepidation in case she touched anything else that she shouldn't.

"So Max, what is it you do here?" Lizzie asked with interest.

"As apprentice, I help my master in any way I can. I look after his equipment and books and assist in making up potions and spells. I hope to be a great sorcerer myself one day," he said grandly, puffing up his chest with pride.

"Well, good luck. I'm sure you will," Lizzie smiled at him. "Where is your master now, by the way?" she asked.

Max explained that his master had been called away to attend an emergency meeting of the King's Council. He said that his master had mentioned that something had happened to give the King great concern and that all the King's councillors and advisors had been called together to discuss the matter. Max said that his master had left him here to clean and tidy the laboratory.

"My master likes things to be in order. He says that working in chaos leads to catastrophe," he said earnestly. Lizzie was only half listening to what Max was now saying, as her mind was more occupied with what the King's Council were discussing at that very moment. She had a feeling that the meeting that was taking place had no doubt been called because of the incident that afternoon concerning the appearance of the pterotorial. She wanted to know what was being said; after all she was pretty sure that it had only appeared because of her. Perhaps Max could tell her how to find out where the Council was meeting.

"Where does the King's Council meet?" she asked.

"They meet in the Great Council Chamber, ma-am," he explained.

"And where would that be?" she asked casually. Max looked suspicious.

"Excuse me for asking, ma-am, but why would you be asking where it is?"

"Because I want to go and find out what they're discussing," she said. Max looked horrified.

"But, Your Highness, the Council is most secret. Only people specially invited by the King are allowed to attend. You can't just invite yourself. I think that I would be unwise to tell you anything further," he announced and, bowing low, he excused himself and went to pick up a broom, which looked exactly like the type witches were alleged to fly on. He began to sweep the floor energetically and Lizzie got the distinct impression that he probably hoped that she would just disappear, but he wasn't going to get rid of her that easily. Lizzie was determined to find out what was going on. She walked over to the boy, stood in front of him and placed a hand gently on the broom-handle to gain his attention. He looked up at her with worried wide blue eyes.

"Nice broom, does it fly by any chance?" she said sweetly.

Max seemed taken aback by this sudden change of tack. "We don't call it a broom, ma-am, we calls it a besom and I wouldn't fly this one as it's a working besom. As it is, I haven't actually been trained to fly yet," he said, looking at the besom as if longing it to be one he could fly.

"Oh," nodded Lizzie and then, realising that she was getting side tracked, once again pleaded with Max to show her the way to the Great Council Chamber.

"Please Max. Please show me where it is. I really need to find out what's going on. I've had a hell of a day today. I've discovered who I really am because of who my mother was and I've found out that I've been living with secrets being kept about me my whole life. From now on, I want to know about the things that affect me and if the King's discussing stuff about Duke Eldorth then I have to know. After all, I

144

haven't got a mother because of him," she emphasised with passion, her eyes suddenly filling with tears and a huge lump forming painfully in her throat. It was as if all the emotions she'd tried to control all day, maybe even for years, had bubbled up inside of her and were trying to force their way out – like a volcano slowly pushing its contents upwards and outwards. A howl came out of Lizzie's mouth that shook and appalled her and she clamped her hand over it to stifle the noise.

Max took a step backwards in surprise and stared at Lizzie with deep concern. Lizzie removed her hand from her mouth to apologise for her sudden outburst, but her lips trembled so violently she couldn't formulate the words. She replaced her hand quickly and stared at the boy as if horrified by what was happening to her. Her mind was in turmoil. Lizzie Longton didn't cry in front of other children; she never showed her vulnerability, as it would only lead to ridicule and torment. Her years of bullying by the Bray twins and their motley crew had strengthened her resolve to never cry in public – crying was left to when Lizzie was alone, when she would relive every cruel word, every push and pull the other children inflicted upon her. She stared at the boy in despair; willing her tears to suck back down into their tear ducts and her trembling lips to cease their involuntary spasms.

Max took a step forward and said with a worried voice, "Are you all right, Your Highness?"

His kindness was even harder to take than if he'd laughed at her like Regina and Veronica Bray always did. Lizzie nodded her head vigorously and the tears that had been hanging on her lashes splashed down her cheeks. Max could see that she obviously wasn't all right at all. He gently took her by the arm and guided her to a chair by the bookcase and helped lower her onto it. He then ran across to a table and poured some amber liquid from a decanter into a glass and brought it to her. She tentatively lowered her hand and lifted

145

the glass to her mouth and sipped the drink. It was sweet and warming and Lizzie thought she tasted traces of honey. The drink squeezed past the lump in her throat, soothing it a little on the way past so that it no longer felt as though it would choke her at any moment.

After a couple more sips of the delicious drink, the lump seemed to have melted away and she managed to say, trembling, "Thank you. I'm sorry about that. I don't know what came over me."

Max pulled up a wooden stool and sat down in front of Lizzie. Placing his clasped hands between his knees and leaning forward, he gazed earnestly into her eyes.

"I must apologise, ma-am, for not being understanding enough. I've been privy to enough of my master's discussions with His Majesty about you, to know that today must have been very difficult for you. I'll help you as much as I can but if my master finds out, I'll be in deep trouble."

"Oh, I won't tell a soul," promised Lizzie, she felt much calmer now and the feeling of being totally overwhelmed had subsided. The amber drink in her glass was half gone and, taking another small sip, she felt its warmth spread through her and she relaxed a little more. "This drink is very good," she said licking her lips. "What is it?"

"Mead," answered the boy. "My master swears by its medicinal properties." Lizzie suddenly realised why she now felt more relaxed, she'd heard of the drink before. Monks usually made mead and, as well as its so-called medicinal properties, it also contained alcoholic ones. Lizzie thought that if she drank anymore of the stuff, she wouldn't be able to function properly, and the last thing she needed at the moment was to get drunk, so she placed the remainder of the mead to one side and spoke directly to Max.

"So the Great Council Chamber?" she pressed. "How do I get there?"

146

Max stood and walked towards a large wooden door. "This way, ma-am," he beckoned, and opening the door, he peered out into the hallway beyond. Having checked both left and right for signs of anyone approaching, he turned back to Lizzie and stressed that she should be as quiet as possible.

"Okay," she agreed. "Oh, and Max, could you drop the ma-am thing? I'd like to think we could be friends so please call me Lizzie." Max looked dumbstruck.

"Oh, I couldn't do that. It would be disrespectful, ma-am," he said, his eyes wide with disbelief at being asked to be so familiar.

"And I'd take it as being even more disrespectful if you ignored my request," said Lizzie, with as much authority in her voice as she could muster. Max bowed briefly and nodded.

"If you so request, L... Lizzie, then I must obey," he stumbled over the name as if he'd be struck down dead by just uttering the word. It wasn't quite the response Lizzie wanted but at least it was a start. So, following stealthily behind Max, she crept into the deserted hallway.

Chapter 14 – The Great Council

The hallway outside Marvin's rooms was dimly lit. Burning torches in sconces seemed to light automatically as Lizzie and Max approached them, and then extinguished themselves once they had passed. As Lizzie crept along silently behind Max, she felt as though she'd never stop being amazed by the castle. It seemed to be more than just a building but something of a living, breathing entity of its own.

Lizzie's trainers and Max's soft leather shoes made no noise on the flagstone floor as they walked along. Lizzie's ears were primed to pick up any sound that might indicate someone approaching, but she heard nothing. They passed numerous doors and other corridors that led off into further parts of the castle and Lizzie, who was anxiously looking around her, almost bowled Max over when he came to an abrupt stop at the end of the hallway. Max put his hand out behind him and pushed Lizzie back against the wall as he peered around the corner. Stretching away to their right was another hallway; this one was much wider and more brightly lit, and led to a pair of enormous wooden doors, attached to their frame by huge, gold coloured hinges. Standing in front of the doors were two guards. They were tall and the flickering light from torches close by reflected off their silver helmets and metal tipped spears and shields.

"What now?" Lizzie hissed into Max's ear.

"This way," he whispered and, taking her hand, dragged her quickly back the way they had come. A few feet from where they'd stopped was a small door. Max twisted the iron ring handle and they quickly entered the small room beyond. It was dark and cold and Lizzie felt a surge of fear when Max closed the door and plunged them both into complete darkness. Fishing in her pocket, she drew out her torch and switched it on.

As she shone the beam around the room she could see that it was tiny; nothing more than a kind of antechamber. It was sparsely furnished with nothing in it except a bare wooden table with three plain wooden chairs seated around it. Max went to the far wall of the room where there was another small door. He tried to turn the handle but the door was locked. Placing his hand over it and closing his eyes, he muttered some words under his breath and then tried the handle again. This time it turned easily. Taking a step through the door, Max beckoned Lizzie to follow him.

"What did you just do to that handle?" She whispered.

"It's just a simple opening spell my master taught me. I usually use it for opening the stubborn lids of jars or bottles," he replied casually.

"Handy," Lizzie acknowledged.

They found themselves in a short tunnel that ran ahead of them and they could hear the murmur of voices getting louder as they walked along. At the end of the tunnel was another small door and they could see a light coming through a grill in the top half of the door. Max indicated that Lizzie should extinguish the torch in case it should be spotted, and when they looked through the grill, Lizzie could see a huge room beyond, in the middle of which was a massive oval table. Sitting around the table were a great number of men and some women, and presiding over the whole scene sat Lizzie's grandfather. He was sitting on a large, beautifully gilded throne at the far end of the table.

"The Great Council," Max hissed into Lizzie's ear.

She nodded; she'd gathered as much. Lizzie looked around the table at the various individuals sitting there and saw that just a few seats to the right of the King was Elmer, and seated just slightly behind him was, to her great surprise, Elrus. What was he doing there? She thought; he was a child just like Lizzie. Although she was glad to see him, she was also annoyed that he was being included in the Council meeting when she wasn't. But then her attention was drawn to a male elf who was speaking and it sounded as though he was talking about her.

"But if he has discovered her presence we must surely take stringent security measures, Your Majesty," the elf said gravely.

The King nodded. "Of course we have processes in place to ensure her safety, but he is cunning and his use of dark magic and employment of evil creatures knows no bounds. He has the means of creating trouble, the like of which our people have not experienced for thousands of years. Not since the Elthurian wars."

A rumble of concerned chatter ran around the table. A large man with a long, brown beard and a mop of brown, unruly hair sitting to the left of the King suddenly stood up. When standing, Lizzie could see that he was tall and rangy and that he was wearing a long, dark purple cloak that sparkled from what looked like thousands of stars. He put out his hands and waved them slowly up and down asking for quiet, in a gentle but deep and imposing voice.

"We know from our sources that Eldorth has been gathering forces in the North," he said in a low, slow growl. His voice suited his appearance. "We also know that he has gained the services of one of our most dangerous foes - Melificent." The table erupted in a cacophony of discussion this time as worried faces and agitated gestures surrounded the table. The purple-cloaked man raised his hands again in call for quiet. "The fact that we know this puts us at an advantage; I know Melificent and how she works. Do not be fooled by her coarse appearance, we are old acquaintances and she has nothing in her powers that I cannot thwart, but she is clever and cunning. Our spies will continue to keep us informed and we will use the intelligence we gather to our advantage."

An important looking woman elf called out, "But is the Princess adequately guarded?"

"Of course," said the King. "She is protected by various enchantments as well as the protection of her spending her time away from our world and, therefore, out of Eldorth's reach. We know that he's had no idea what she looks like or even her name; until now that is. Because she has now come of age, our own people must further protect her and so we have had to bring her into our world. He will learn her name quickly enough, we are sure, but she will return to the human world soon and will be watched over by an appointed guardian as she always has been."

"Does she understand the danger she is in, Your Majesty?" asked a male elf, wearing what looked like a silver breastplate and a fur trimmed, brown cloak.

"She is beginning to, Elnest. I have not told her everything yet as there has not been time, but her education has only just started and I had hoped to have the opportunity of introducing her to our ways and her heritage before Eldorth became aware of her. Unfortunately, the appearance of the pterotorial would indicate that this will not now be the case. We must work quickly to strengthen the magic around her to keep her out of harms way," the King concluded.

Lizzie, standing in her hiding place, was wide-eyed in horror at what she was hearing. Would Eldorth really try to have her killed? She was trembling at the thought, when suddenly there was a commotion at the doors of the Great Chamber. They suddenly swung open and Elwood rushed in looking highly flustered and very red in the face.

"Please forgive the intrusion, Your Majesty," he blurted out, bowing low in reverence to the King. "But I thought I should advise you that Princess Elizabeth is missing!"

As Lizzie leapt backwards away from the grill like a scalded cat, she heard the clamour of voices and chairs

151

scraping back as people stood up in alarm. She and Max turned and began running back along the tunnel and out into the small antechamber. Just as they were about to open the other door to the hallway and run back along it to Marvin's laboratory, it burst open and the two tall and imposing elf guards they had seen guarding the Council Chamber barred their way.

"If you would like to follow me, ma-am," said one of the guards firmly, bowing his head in respect as he spoke. He then turned and walked back through the doorway with Lizzie and Max following meekly behind, the other guard's hand on Max's shoulder.

The guards led them back to the Great Council Chamber and Lizzie felt that if her legs shook any more than they already were, she'd probably collapse in a heap on the floor. The elves in the chamber were standing facing her as she, Max and the two guards walked in. Lizzie dreaded looking at her grandfather for fear of the disapproval he would show in his face, so she kept her gaze firmly on the floor just in front of her toes.

She waited for the onslaught of being severely told off, but instead she heard him say calmly, "Well, young Miss, did you hear what you expected to hear?" Lizzie looked up cautiously at her grandfather and, although she could see that he had a grave look on his face, she was convinced she saw a twinkle in his eye.

"Not exactly," she replied tentatively; and then more boldly added, "We've only been there a couple of minutes." Almost as an afterthought, she asked, "How did you know we were there?"

Her grandfather tried to stifle a smile; "The light from your torch shining through the grid over there (he pointed at the small door to the side of the chamber) gave you away briefly before you had the good sense to extinguish it." He

152

summoned her to him and, on impulse, Lizzie grabbed Max's hand and pulled him reluctantly along with her as she walked round to stand in front of her grandfather. Max kept staring at the floor as if willing it to open up and swallow him, but much to his regret it failed to do so.

"Ladies and gentlemen of the Council, may I introduce my granddaughter, the Princess Elizabeth," the King announced, standing up and taking Lizzie's shoulders and holding her in front of him. The Council members bowed and curtseyed to Lizzie and Lizzie curtseyed back, being a little unsure of what else she ought to do. She looked over her shoulder and up into her grandfather's face and said, more bravely than she felt, "I just want to say one thing before you tell me off."

"Yes?" said the King, looking at her with interest.

"Don't punish Max. It wasn't his fault. I made him help me." Lizzie insisted, grabbing the boy's trembling hand.

"Really?" said the King, looking at Max who was still staring at the ground, his slim body shaking in fear of what punishment may be in store for him.

"Yes," Lizzie stressed. "He didn't want to help me. He said that he'd get into terrible trouble if he did but I pulled rank so that he couldn't refuse. So if anyone's to be punished it should be me."

The bravado in her voice belied the butterflies that were not only fluttering, but now also cartwheeling, around her stomach. Lizzie heard someone snigger to her left and, swivelling her eyes in that direction, she could see Elrus. He looked away and she saw his shoulders shaking with suppressed mirth. His father, Elmer, was frowning down at him.

"So, you order me not punish Max but to punish you? Very honourable," said the King thoughtfully, rubbing his

153

chin as if contemplating what horrible sentence he could inflict upon her. Lizzie realised that she had perhaps spoken out of turn by telling the King what to do, so she looked down grimacing; awaiting her fate. The King turned to the tall, purple clad man standing next to him.

"Well, Marvin, what do you think? What punishment can I possibly impose that will sufficiently rebuke the Princess's bad behaviour?" he asked, his face unreadable.

Unable to suppress her surprise at the name of the King's companion, Lizzie blurted out, "So you're Max's master, Marvin. Nice to meet you," she thrust out her hand in greeting. Having no friends of her own age meant she'd always been able to talk to most adults around her in almost equal terms. Marvin looked slightly taken aback at the sudden gesture and, looking down at Lizzie's proffered hand with surprise, he smiled broadly and offered his huge hand in return.

"Pleased to meet you too, Your Highness," he said warmly; his rumbling voice sending vibrations through her arm as he spoke. The King watched on in amusement at the exchange, but then asked Marvin for any ideas as to how best treat his granddaughter's misdemeanour.

The Chamber's assembly, along with Lizzie and Max (whose trembling hand was still in hers) were silently watching the King and Marvin with bated breath.

"Well," said Marvin, his eyes now gazing off into the middle distance, as if pondering all the possible types of punishments available to them, "I think, Your Majesty, that the best punishment would be..." he paused again, "for Her Highness to be detained here at Elvedom Castle for at least the next few days, as I think it may be unwise to send her back to her own world at this time."

Lizzie raised her eyes to her grandfather's face in shock. "B.. but, I....," she stuttered.

154

Marvin continued gravely, "I feel that Her Highness should attend lessons with me, and some of your other counsellors, to learn about her heritage and fill in the gaps of the information she's missing from her eavesdropping before she returns to her own world," he peered down at her through big bushy brows.

Marvin's face broke into a wide smile, revealing rows of perfect, shiny white teeth, and his eyes crinkled in the corners in amusement. Lizzie heard Max let out a huge sigh of relief and she looked at him and grinned.

"But that's great, I can…" she began, but was cut off as Marvin turned his attention to Max.

"But, Your Majesty," he continued, now staring down at Max intently, "I feel that, despite Her Highness's defence of my apprentice, he cannot go without some punishment also. He could have led Her Highness into danger," he said gravely, his mouth twitching at the corners as if suppressing a smile. Max looked up at his master in alarm and his grip on Lizzie's hand tightened so that it almost caused her to gasp out loud.

"Indeed," nodded the King, in agreement, not looking at Max but keeping his eyes on Marvin. "What would you suggest?" he asked.

"Well," Marvin said slowly, "As he is obviously keen to serve Her Highness, may I suggest that he joins her in her lessons, then he may be of more valuable assistance to her in the future?" Marvin smiled down at his apprentice and placed a paternal hand on his shoulder. As Max gazed up at his master, Lizzie witnessed the love and respect that he had for Marvin.

The King smiled. "I think that's an excellent idea," he agreed, clapping his hands together. Then, turning to Elmer, he said, "I think it would also be useful if Elrus joined Princess Elizabeth and Max here in their lessons. Perhaps it may instil in him some of the responsibility that he will one day have to display." He smiled at Elrus warmly.

Elmer bowed his head, "As you say, Your Majesty."

The three young people looked at each other and grinned; the elf, the Half-Elf and the sorcerer's apprentice.

Chapter 15 – The Layered Globe

The morning sunshine broke through a chink in the drapes at Lizzie's bedroom window and a beam of light flashed across her eyelids. She lay there with her eyes closed, enjoying the warmth and comfort of her bed and the sensation of the sunlight on her face. Her thoughts were full of the events of the previous day. So much had happened in such a short space of time that it all seemed like some wild and amazing dream. She was almost frightened to open her eyes in case it all had been.

Princess Elizabeth, she said in her head over and over again, as images of the previous day replayed themselves like videotape in her mind. Could it really only be 24 hours since she and her gran had set off on their grand adventure? It seemed impossible that so much had happened in one day.

Lizzie lay back, thinking about the last part of the day.

*

After she and Max had left the Great Council Chamber, Elwood had escorted her back to her rooms where she had found her grandmother sitting anxiously on one of the sofas. Mrs Longton had jumped to her feet and rushed over and clasped Lizzie tightly to her, kissing her in relief. Then she had become cross and had scolded Lizzie for her thoughtlessness and recklessness and all sorts of other 'nesses. After Mrs Longton had got that out of her system, she asked Lizzie about what had happened after she had disappeared from her bedroom; it seemed that, unable to sleep, Mrs Longton had popped in to check that Lizzie was asleep and discovered her gone.

Lizzie explained how she had discovered the tunnel behind the bookcase and decided to see where it led, and then told her grandmother about meeting Max and what had happened at the Grand Council. Lizzie explained to Mrs

157

Longton that the King and his Council had decided that she was to stay in Elvedom for a while to learn more about the elven world before she would be allowed home. Mrs Longton looked surprised and said that she should have been consulted before such a decision had been made and that she would speak to the King about it in the morning.

Finally, exhausted and on the verge of collapse, Lizzie had let her grandmother lead her to her bedroom, tuck her into bed, kiss her on the forehead once more and make her promise to go to sleep and not to disappear off on any more hare-brained schemes. Lizzie had fallen asleep before her grandmother had left the room.

*

As Lizzie slowly opened her eyes and looked around her in the room, she realised with satisfaction that she hadn't been dreaming. She really did have a whole new future ahead of her and she smiled to herself contentedly. Just then, there was a knock at the door.

"Come in," called Lizzie, sitting up in bed. The bedroom door opened and a young female elf entered.

"Good morning, Your Highness," she said, curtseying low and placing some freshly pressed clothes on a chair by the window.

"Good morning," replied Lizzie, happily. The girl elf went to the window and drew back the drapes and sunlight flooded in.

"Your breakfast is in the sitting room, ma-am," said the girl, as she backed slowly out of the room, curtseying once more and disappearing before Lizzie had the chance to ask her name. Lizzie thought she would never get used to all this formal treatment.

She swung her legs out of bed and slipped on the beautiful jewelled slippers that she had so admired the night before. They were just as comfortable as she remembered and, walking lightly across the room, she entered the sitting room that sat between her and her grandmother's bedroom. Mrs Longton was already there, sitting at the small dining table, which was now laden with all sorts of scrumptious breakfast food.

"Come on, sweetheart, tuck in," Mrs Longton said, swallowing a mouthful of hot buttered toast. "These elves are wonderful hosts, I must say," she mumbled, munching contentedly.

Lizzie plonked herself down on a chair opposite her grandmother and surveyed the table. There was so much to choose from that she was spoilt for choice. Eventually, she decided on some warm croissants and raspberry jam. Her grandmother poured herself some coffee and offered Lizzie something to drink.

"There's hot chocolate, tea, juices, cordials; the choice is yours, Madame," Mrs Longton smiled. Lizzie decided on some hot chocolate and tucked into her croissant with gusto. She discovered that she was actually ravenous; it must have been because of all the excitement from the previous day, she thought. Either that or her elvish heritage was kicking in, because elves certainly seemed to like their food.

Mrs Longton told Lizzie that the King had arranged for her to be able to telephone Mary Crowther to let her know that they would be staying on at the castle for a few more days, and let her know that all was well. Mrs Longton expressed her amazement at how intuitive the elves were when it came to being able to provide anything you needed just when you needed it. Even though the elves didn't have telephones in the same way humans did, they seemed able to come up with one on cue. Mrs Longton said that she hadn't elaborated on the details but had told Mary a bit of a white lie. She'd said that Elvedom Castle had indeed turned out to be a luxury hotel and they were booked in for a short stay.

"You'll get a pimple on your tongue for telling fibs, gran," Lizzie laughed; this was something her grandmother had always said to her whenever she'd ever been found out lying.

Mrs Longton laughed and said that if she'd told Mary the truth, she'd have thought that she'd taken a knock to the head. She also told Lizzie that Mary had said that she and Bob would stay at the Hall and take care of Basil and Rathbone, and keep an eye on the place, until they got back. Lizzie smiled; she loved Basil and Rathbone almost as much as she loved her grandmother and knew that they would be in good hands with Mary and Bob looking after them.

After breakfast, Lizzie went back to her bedroom and dressed for the day. In her room, she discovered that the maid elf must have been in again unnoticed whilst she was occupied eating her breakfast. A clean pair of jeans and a tee shirt had been laid out ready for her on her neatly made bed. She washed and dressed quickly and returned to her grandmother in the sitting room. Mrs Longton looked up from a newspaper she was reading.

"This has just been brought in, Lizzie, and it makes fascinating reading," said her grandmother, showing her the front page of the newspaper. It was called the Elvedom Chronicle and it claimed under its title that it had been established in 4500 BC.

"Makes our Times look like a new boy, doesn't it?" Mrs Longton said cheerily. Lizzie nodded in agreement.

The main headline read - ***Rare Sighting of Pterotorial over Elvedom Countryside*** – in large bold typeface. Lizzie peered at the article over her grandmother's shoulder. Scanning the item, she was relieved to see that there was no mention of either her or any other member of the royal party

160

being present. She thought perhaps the newspapers in Elvedom were more strictly controlled than they were in England. The picture supporting the item wasn't a photograph, as she would have imagined, but a beautiful etching of the creature she'd seen the previous afternoon. Mrs Longton looked at one of the smaller headlines that littered the page. *Woodland Elves Report Insubordination Amongst Hobgoblins*, the first line of the report read, "Our correspondent informs us that Hobgoblins in the North are revolting…" Mrs Longton grinned to herself. "They're probably pretty revolting in the South too," she thought sardonically. There was a knock at the door.

"Come in," Mrs Longton called. The door opened and Elwood entered.

"Good morning, Your Highness; Mrs Longton," Elwood bowed his characteristic low bow, his nose nearly touching the floor.

"Good morning Elwood," they replied in unison.

"It's a beautiful morning," he chirped, a huge grin on his pointy little face.

"It most certainly is," agreed Mrs Longton.

"I hope we have recovered from the excitement of yesterday," Elwood continued.

Mrs Longton said that it might take a little time to get over that sort of excitement, but that they had eventually had a good night's sleep and were all set for the day ahead.

"Good, good," said Elwood cheerily. He then announced that he had come to escort Lizzie to her grandfather in readiness to attend her first lesson. He also said that His Majesty had specifically said that Mrs Longton would be most welcome to sit in on the class. She said that she would like that very much. So, taking a last bite of her third

161

croissant, Lizzie followed Mrs Longton and Elwood out of the sitting room and they made their way to the King's rooms.

When they reached the room where they had first met King Elfred, he was already there but he wasn't alone. The King was sitting at his large desk and standing by the enormous fireplace was Marvin, resplendent in his long purple cloak. They had obviously been in some deep discussion before Lizzie and the others entered the room. The King's face was etched with worry but his face lit up in a smile and he seemed to relax a little when he saw them.

"Ah, Elizabeth, Mrs Longton," he said in welcome to them both. He stood and bowed briefly. He then introduced Marvin to Mrs Longton. Turning back to Lizzie he said, "You've already met Marvin, Elizabeth. He will supervise all the lessons and skills you must learn during your time here." Lizzie looked up into the big friendly face of the sorcerer and smiled.

"Well, Your Highness, I trust that you eventually had a good night's rest in order to face the day's lessons," he said to her.

"Oh, yes. I can't wait," she replied enthusiastically. The King suggested that no more time be wasted and that Marvin should begin Lizzie's education in the ways of elves without further ado. So, having bid good day to the King, Lizzie and Mrs Longton followed Marvin out of the room. As they walked, Marvin explained that Lizzie's first lesson would take place in his laboratory.

"I understand that you have already visited my laboratory, Princess," he said.

Lizzie admitted that she had and that it had been fascinating. Then, turning to her grandmother, she began describing the wonderful contents of the room and suddenly remembered the unusual globe she'd seen there.

"Gran, you should see this amazing globe that Marvin has. It's got sort of different layers of countries, one on top of another. It's hard to describe and I don't know what the layers mean but we can ask Marvin when we get to his lab," she whispered. Marvin smiled to himself as he listened to her eagerness to learn.

"Marvin, can I ask you something?" Lizzie asked.

"Of course, Your Highness," Marvin replied, continuing his long legged march towards his laboratory, causing Lizzie and her grandmother to scurry along after him.

"Well, last night, when I found the tunnel that led from the back of our bookcase in our sitting room, once the door had swung closed I couldn't find any way of making it open again. Then when I got to your rooms, I couldn't find a way in. Is there some kind of lever or switch that I should have used?"

"No, ma'am. There are no switches or levers. All you need is to say just one little magic word and that would have done it," Marvin smiled.

"Can you teach it to me?" Lizzie asked.

"I don't need to teach you. I'm sure it's a word that your grandmother would have taught you from when you were a baby. You would have used it your whole life."

Lizzie looked bemused. "But I don't know any magic words," she said, racking her brains. Marvin continued to smile as they walked along.

"Oh, but indeed you do," he said. "Can't you think what it may be?" Lizzie shook her head and looked to her grandmother who just shrugged her shoulders. Marvin stopped and looked down at Lizzie and laughed.

"It's *please*," he grinned. "You just had to say, 'Open please' and the door would have opened. Please, if used correctly, can help you get most things that you require in life. I ought to stress that not just anyone can open the secret doors and passageways around the castle. The building is protected by spells and enchantments and so it will only respond to certain members of the royal household," he reassured her. "But as a royal princess, the secret doors you found would most certainly have opened at your request."

They soon reached the door to Marvin's rooms and, as they entered, Lizzie could see Max was already there, and sitting in an old battered chair by the bookcase was their other companion, Elrus. Both boys stood and bowed to Lizzie as she approached them.

"Good morning," she said brightly, her face blushing pink in embarrassment at being treated with such reverence. The boys returned the greeting and then turned to bow politely to Mrs Longton, who said that there was no need for such formalities.

"Oh, but I'm afraid there is," announced Marvin, his voice serious. "In our world there are certain behaviours and protocols that must be adhered to. Bowing to our elders or betters is one such sign of respect." Mrs Longton was nodding in understanding when Lizzie spotted the unusual globe again.

"Here it is, gran," she called over her shoulder as she ran to the globe. Her grandmother followed her and looked at its surface.

"Well, it's certainly not like any globe I've ever seen," Mrs Longton announced, peering at it closely. The various layers of land seemed to hover and float over and around the globe with no visible means of remaining there. Marvin walked over and picked the globe up by its heavy brass base and looked deep into the gently spinning ball. As Mrs

164

Longton and Lizzie gazed into the globe, the effect was mesmerizing. The various layers seemed to converge and intertwine as they spun around their axis.

"I think this will form the basis of our first lesson," announced Marvin.

He asked his four pupils to each take one of the chairs placed around a long, rectangular table to one side of the room. Beside the table on the wall was a large, old-fashioned blackboard. As they took their seats, Marvin went to the head of the table and placed the globe on its polished, wooden surface. He began by saying that he was not surprised that Lizzie and her grandmother had never seen such a globe before, as it was the only one of its kind.

"Maps and atlases in the human world are nearly always flat or one-dimensional and globes have flat images on their surfaces. This is because they only show the world in which humankind live. What humans can't see with their naked eye, or explain away by scientific means, are pronounced as being imaginary, myth or legend," he explained. Lizzie and her grandmother nodded in agreement.

"This globe," he continued, peering into its depths, "shows all the worlds that surround our mother Earth. In this world, elves are taught from an early age that they are not the only occupants of the universe. They know that their world is only one of many layers that surround the core Earth. In the human world, you sometimes talk about parallel universes but most humans never truly believe in them. However, I assure you that there are parallel worlds. This globe shows you that these parallel worlds co-exist around our one life source – The Earth." Lizzie leant across the table and lost herself in the slowly spinning globe, its layers whirling and shifting hypnotically.

"The layers almost seem to blur into each other in some places. Why is that?" she asked, looking up at Marvin quizzically.

"It's because in some places on the planet, the different worlds and realms are very close. Also, at certain times of year, the layers come so close that they almost converge."

"Like at Halloween?" asked Mrs Longton.

"Exactly," agreed Marvin. Mrs Longton beamed like a little schoolgirl who just won a merit badge for good work.

"What's Halloween?" asked Elrus, looking perplexed.

"Halloween is a celebration held by humans in the late autumn. It originates from an ancient Celtic rite, which was originally known as Samhain," explained Marvin, addressing Elrus and Max, who also looked puzzled. "Halloween or All Hallows takes place at the end of October and is the night when the spirit world comes close to the living or, in this case, human world. People used to hollow out turnips and turn them into faces to scare away evil or mischievous spirits. Sadly, these days the meaning of All Hallows has been all but lost and the evening is now just an excuse for children to dress up in silly costumes and knock on other peoples' house doors asking for sweets. Instead of turnips, people now use pumpkins. But going back to its origins, the ancient Celts got it right because long ago, people were more in tune with the Earth and the worlds surrounding it. The world of spirits and the human world did indeed come close, but so too did other worlds."

"So don't you have anything like Halloween?" Lizzie asked. The two boys shook their heads.

"We have no need for such a celebration because elves are attuned to the other worlds. We revere their existence in all we do," announced Marvin.

166

"Can you explain what these other layers are?" Mrs Longton asked, eagerly.

Marvin beckoned his students closer to the globe and the four keen pupils gathered nearer in order to see. "There, deep under the ever moving layers, you can see the Earth herself, her core and crust; a hotbed of shifting plates and magma: the gases, minerals, metals and rocks that form her moving and changing all the time. There you can see her seas and ice caps." Marvin pointed at the North and South poles as he spoke. "Above her surface float her worlds. Nearest her soul is the world you are now in. This is the world that works closest to her, mending her and caring for her; protecting her from the damage being wrought on her by another world - the human world. This world you are now in is also the world where ancient, magical and, what you would call, mythical creatures now live. Once, they also roamed the human world but, in order to protect themselves from the harm they suffered, and would have continued to suffer, at the hands of man, they left the human world.

Then there is the spirit world. I believe that in the human world you would call it Heaven. According to humans, when a good person dies their spirit goes to Heaven, and when a bad or evil person dies their spirit goes to Hell. In our world, a person would either go to the Spirit world if they are good or the Netherworld if they are not. Each of these different worlds, or realms, are but layers around the Earth and there are certain times, like Halloween, and certain circumstances, when it is possible that you may cross over from one world to another. When you, Your Highness, and you, Mrs Longton, crossed between your world and this, you did so by means of the Diamond Line. As soon as you entered through the door at Paddington station to go down to catch the Diamond Line train, you crossed over into our world."

Lizzie and her companions sat transfixed. Lizzie's brain found it almost impossible to comprehend this multitude of worlds that existed around her. Everything was much

167

simpler when there was only one world to cope with, but what were the implications of having so many to contend with from now on? It was true that she'd been taught that there was Heaven and Hell, but she'd always been a bit dubious about the concept. Now it seemed that they really did exist, of a kind. She looked over at her grandmother sitting opposite and saw that she looked just as stunned by the revelations as she was. Mrs Longton suddenly seemed to find her voice.

"This is incredible," she said, shaking her head in amazement. "So there really are other worlds. They're not just some tall story that was cooked up by the ancients years ago to fool people into thinking that there's life after death." Marvin nodded.

"But, of course, spirits are not alive," he stressed. Mrs Longton clapped her hands together and let out a loud laugh.

"Ha, if I wasn't afraid that I'd be locked up for being nuts, it would be great to tell the world, I mean my world, that there are all these other dimensions around us. It would give people such greater understanding and appreciation of the Earth."

Marvin looked at her sadly and shook his head.

"I agree that it would be wonderful, if by telling human kind that there are these other worlds they would have a greater appreciation of the Earth, but unfortunately, as you say, people would just think you had gone mad. Also, should you be believed, history shows that humans are a destructive and exploitative race and it is best that the majority of them be kept in the dark. If they knew about this world, they would probably try to seek a way of moving between the worlds in order to enter each one and exploit it. I would sincerely beseech you to keep any knowledge you gain in this world to yourselves."

Mrs Longton nodded sadly. She knew that Marvin was speaking the truth and wished it were different. She agreed that it would be best all round if she and Lizzie kept this fantastic information to themselves.

*

After a light lunch of sandwiches, cake and fruit, brought to Marvin's rooms, the lesson was concluded. It had been a fascinating morning; not only had they learnt about the multi-layered worlds they lived in, but Marvin had explained something about the stars and other planets in the universe. Unlike most humans, the elves were under no illusions that they were the only living creatures in the universe. Marvin said it defied logic to believe that, considering there were hundreds of thousands of solar systems. He told them that Earth was the only planet to contain life in our own solar system because of its unique position in relation to the sun. He described some of the star constellations and touched on the subject of astronomy, a subject that he promised they would learn more of as time went on.

"I think that you should all now go and take some air and think about what you have been told. I expect you to come back tomorrow with more questions for me so that we may deepen your learning," and with that, Marvin waved them out of his rooms.

With their heads spinning with all that they had learned that day, the four students bade farewell to their teacher and made their way out of the castle.

Chapter 16 – Our Friends from the West

Lizzie sat alone on a log by the side of a large lake in the castle grounds, watching swans and other water birds glide, swim and dive upon it. She felt like she'd somehow slipped through one of the Earth's layers and arrived in Heaven. She had never felt happier in her whole life and finally felt like she'd actually found a place in which she fitted. She still couldn't really believe that she had discovered a family she never knew she had and had even made some friends. There was so much to take in, so much to learn, that Lizzie thought she'd never come to terms with it all. Lost in her own thoughts, she didn't hear the approach of someone behind her and almost jumped out of her skin when that someone said, "Hey."

Lizzie swung round and found Elrus standing there, grinning down at her. He sat down next to her.

"Sorry, did I scare you?" he apologised, not looking in the least bit sorry.

"No," she lied sharply, but she smiled inwardly because she didn't want to give him the satisfaction of knowing that he had, in fact, given her a bit of scare.

"How'd you creep up so quietly?"

"That's what we elves do, have you never heard of stelf," he laughed, nudging her with his shoulder.

"It's pronounced stealth; with a th, you idiot," Lizzie laughed, nudging him back.

"So, what'd you make of this morning's lesson?" he asked breezily, picking up a pebble and lobbing it into the lake.

"It was amazing," Lizzie replied, watching the ripples from the pebble, each one reminding her of the Earth's

170

layers. She turned to him and said earnestly, "You know, I can't really take all of this in. I mean, it's all totally unbelievable: all these worlds floating around one planet. In my world we're taught that there is just the one; the one that we live in. Some people believe in Heaven and Hell and all that, but no one really believes in elves and magic. In my world they're just imaginary, you know, legends and myths and stuff. I kind of always knew there was something different about me, from other kids at my school, like I've never really fit it; but this is mega."

"Mega?" queried Elrus.

"Eh, huge?" explained Lizzie. "I can't wait to see the Brays' faces when they find out I'm part elf, let alone a royal one," she grinned widely in satisfaction and picking up a pebble herself, threw it hard and long into the waters.

"Is that a good idea?" cautioned Elrus, looking at her uncertainly. "I mean, I don't know who these Bray people are, but won't it be difficult explaining all this to someone in your world, someone that hasn't been to this place for themselves; particularly if no-one in your world knows that this place exists and think that elves and fairies are imaginary. Won't they think you're, well, a bit mad?"

Lizzie nodded slowly. He was right, of course. She couldn't tell anyone at home about this. No-one would believe her if she did, and it would just give them more ammunition to use against her. But there must be something positive to be gained out of this that she could take home with her. Perhaps some of the skills her grandfather had mentioned that she'd be taught could come in useful.

Elrus watched her face as she thought about what he'd said. "I'm sure by the time you go home, you'll know how best to deal with what you've learnt here," he assured her, as if reading her mind.

"Yes, you're right. I'll just see how things go over the next couple of days," she agreed.

"Princess Elizabeth, Princess!" Lizzie and Elrus could see Max running at full pelt across the grounds, shouting to Lizzie as he ran towards them. Breathless and panting, he skidded to a halt in front of them. Lizzie stood up and looked at him in concern as he fought to catch his breath.

"What is it, Max?" she asked him. "What's wrong; what's happened?"

Max looked at her with worried eyes, "I... (gasp), I was with (gasp), with my master (gasp), when His Majesty came into see him (gasp). There's another Great Council meeting being held," he spluttered.

"And?" Elrus asked impatiently.

Max glared at him, "And," he repeated, straightening his shoulders, "the Princess is requested to attend and we are instructed to accompany her." So, without missing a beat, the three of them began to walk briskly back to the Castle.

"Is it usual to have two Great Council meetings so soon?" asked Lizzie.

"No it's not usual, Your Highness," said Max. "But just as I was running out of the room to find you, I did hear the King say that new information has been received about Duke Eldorth."

Lizzie stopped in her tracks, stared at Max and grabbed him by the arm. "Did you hear anything else?" she asked impatiently.

"No, ma-am. As I said, I had to run as quickly as I could to find you. His Majesty was very clear in his instructions," he said.

172

"Well, come on then, we'd better hurry," urged Elrus, and the three of them set off at a run across the grounds.

As they entered the castle, they could see a number of other elves milling around the main entrance hall. Most of the elves were dressed grandly, as though for a great state occasion. They stood in small groups, many deep in discussion, and a few voices were raised in heated debate, but Lizzie and her companions were unable to make out what was being said in the general hubbub of conversation. As the three of them watched, the tall figure of Marvin walked up several steps of the huge marble staircase in the centre of the hall and stopped and faced the throng. He was once again dressed in his deep purple robes, embroidered with the gold stars and symbols, and he was carrying a long, gnarled wooden staff. He held up one hand and banged the staff with a resounding crack on the stair three times with the other. The silence was instant.

"Members of the Great Council," his deep resonant voice boomed out, reverberating around the large space, "please prepare to enter the Council Chamber."

The elves quickly and silently organised themselves into a long orderly procession. They each seemed to know precisely their place in ranking, because there was no arguing or jostling for position. They formed themselves into two columns, and each pair in the procession then strode grandly through the entrance hall and along the long, high corridor leading towards the two enormous wooden doors, guarded by two elven soldiers that Lizzie and Max had been escorted through the previous night; the Great Council Chamber.

Lizzie, Elrus and Max followed behind the procession as it filed into the chamber. Marvin walked along behind, his long staff hitting the floor with a sharp rap at each step they took. Lizzie wanted to keep turning around to look at Marvin but the solemnity of the occasion meant she kept her eyes focused forwards. As the elves entered the Great Chamber, the two columns split and each one walked around opposite sides of the long oval table, at the top of which sat King Elfred in the beautiful gilded chair that he had occupied the night before. As Lizzie and her companions entered the chamber, with Marvin close behind, the great doors slammed close with a thunderous crash.

Marvin indicated that they should stand in front of three empty seats that had been positioned at the opposite end of the oval table to the King's. He then strode towards the King and stood at his right hand side. Marvin banged his staff one last time on the ground and the whole assembly sat. As Lizzie, Elrus and Max followed suit, Lizzie took a quick look around at her surroundings. They were much as they had been when she and Max had been discovered the previous evening and brought before the assembly. However, there was one small change. An ornate chair had been placed against the wall just behind and to left of the King, and there, sitting observing the events unfolding before her, was Mrs Longton. She gave Lizzie a quick wink and smiled. Her grandfather standing and addressing the Council quelled Lizzie's surprise.

"Good and noble brethren, welcome. Thank you for coming at such short notice. You are no doubt wondering why I have reconvened the Council so soon after our only meeting yesterday. We have received intelligence concerning Eldorth and the whereabouts of the four sacred relics that he stole from us. This is important news and it is necessary for us to discuss the way forward. I have called upon our great friend and ally from the West, Elroy of Elcarib, and he has been good enough to come to our aid and support us in our quest against Eldorth."

Lizzie had been so engrossed in the formalities of the meeting that she hadn't really noticed a black skinned man sitting next to the King. He stood and bowed to the congregation who applauded him loudly. He was tall with broad shoulders and was athletically built, his powerful face with its strong, handsome features looked out at those present, almost in challenge. Lizzie could sense he was a force to be reckoned with.

As Elroy sat back down, the King turned to an elf sitting a few seats from him on his left. "I request that we begin with Elnest, my Chief of Secret Surveillance, reporting his finding to us."

A short stout elf, with cropped grey hair and a matching large moustache covering his top lip, stood up and bowed to the King and the rest of the assembly.

"Your Majesty, my good and noble brethren, I bring news of the latest situation with regard to our most dreaded enemy, Duke Eldorth. After many months, my spies in the North have managed to breach the barriers of protection surrounding Duke Eldorth and infiltrate his most inner circle. One of my spies, who has privy to the most inner sanctum of Duke Eldorth's stronghold, has reported back that for some time now he has been gathering forces. Some of the most vile and vicious creatures from the dregs of society have been joining the Duke from the many corners of our world. My brethren, he is planning to wage war on our people in order to take over the Kingdom. This comes as no great surprise to any of us; it was always known that he was likely to plan an attack at some time, but we believe that that time may come sooner than we'd anticipated. Duke Eldorth has employed the dark witch, Melificent, to try and break down the old magic protecting the Harp of Elvyth, so that he may use its powers to raise an even greater army and bring forward his attack on our people. One piece of good news is that she has not yet had any success, but we need to find and retrieve the Harp before that situation changes."

The members of the Council took a sharp intake of breath at this grave announcement and there were mutterings between the various groups of elves sitting around the table. Lizzie looked at Elrus in horror.

"What does it mean? What's going to happen?" she hissed under her breath. Elrus placed a quietening hand on her arm and put a finger to his lips to signal that she shouldn't speak. There was a sudden rap on the floor from Marvin's staff, and the chamber fell silent once more. Elnest continued with his report.

"As we are all aware, since Duke Eldorth and his followers stole four of the sacred relics, the powers of our monarchy have been diminished. My people have been working to discover where Duke Eldorth has secreted the sacred relics for some time now, and we have discovered that the Duke has had each one of the relics hidden in four different worlds; one in this world, one in the world of men, one in the spirit world and one in the netherworld."

The muttering in the hall began again with elves expressing disbelief and anger. Lizzie turned to Elrus again and whispered, "What are these relics? Why is everyone so upset about them?"

Elrus whispered out of the corner of his mouth that he'd explain later because the King was staring straight at them and he didn't look pleased. Once more, Marvin rapped his staff on the floor of the chamber and the mutterings subsided. The King nodded at Elnest again to continue.

"Although we know that the relics have been crossed over to these other worlds, we do not know which relic is hidden in which world. My spies are still working to discover more. However, we do have some positive news with regards to the relic hidden in our own world. We know that it is the Harp of Elvyth and we also know where it is. There is a small reconnaissance party working in the area with the sole purpose of preparing the way for the Harp's retrieval. Once retrieved, it will be returned to a safe place." Elnest bowed once more to the King and sat down.

The King thanked him. "Thank you, Elnest; and please send The Council's grateful thanks to your spies. They have done well, especially your spy in Eldorth's inner circle. I will wish for their continued safety and anonymity."

The King then turned to the Council and said, "Well my brethren, we are at last making some headway in discovering what our most dreaded enemy is planning. I think it comes as no surprise to any of us that he has always intended laying claim to Elvedom, but we have never been able to find out at what stage that may happen.

From what we now know, he has gathered quite some considerable forces together: some are with him in the North but we have yet to discover where the others are deployed. We have also yet to discover what he has promised them in reward for their allegiance, but what we do know is that whatever it is, Duke Eldorth will no doubt renege on it. He cannot be trusted. But then that is not our concern, as we must concentrate our efforts on recovering the Harp of Elvyth and the other sacred relics. As we are well aware, Eldorth is clever in the dark ways and growing ever more so. We have no doubt that he, together with the witch Melificent, will have devised dark magic to prevent their retrieval." The King then turned and faced Marvin and asked him to explain to the Council what kinds of protection were likely to have been used.

Marvin turned to the assembly and solemnly explained the difficulties that anyone attempting to find and retrieve the Harp would face.

"We know that Eldorth has been employing the skills of my dear sister in magic, the Witch Melificent, for some considerable time. Her knowledge of dark magic is extensive and she will no doubt have placed protective spells and enchantments that may disguise the relics in such a way in that they are difficult to find, or if found will harm the person retrieving them in some way. Some of these enchantments may take the form of curses and if this is the case, and I suspect that it is, it would be very unwise for anyone to attempt to remove the relic from its hiding place unless they themselves are protected by very powerful white magic. White magic, as you know, is magic that works for good.

There is no disputing that we must rescue the relics from Eldorth if we are to return the power of them to their rightful master and thereby weaken Eldorth's position. We believe that Eldorth will not allow the Harp to be kept far from him; this is logical because the Harp must be played in his presence for it to call his allies to him. So, with that assumption then, it is hidden somewhere in the North." At this point, he turned and bowed to the King. The King bowed his head in return and Marvin sat down once again.

A tall elf with jet-black hair and a black pointed goatee beard stood up. He looked fierce and proud and was wearing light armour over what looked like a crocodile skin jerkin and trousers. Lizzie thought he looked like a soldier.

The King nodded to him in acknowledgment, "Yes, General Eldron?" Lizzie smiled to herself in satisfaction; she'd guessed correctly.

The elf spoke with an authority that was in keeping with his appearance.

"Sire, with all due respect, everyone in this room knows the importance of returning the relics to their rightful place." There was a general noise of assent and lots of nodding of the heads of the elves around the Council table. "But as it stands, the information we have at this point in time does not bring us any nearer to retrieving the relics. Why do we not raise an army now and attack Eldorth before we ourselves

178

are attacked? Surely there is strength in a surprise attack, then we can seek out the relics in our own time." General Eldron bowed to the King and sat down again.

"I appreciate your reasoning Eldron, but our strength must be in our resolve to achieve our ends by peaceful means. We do not want war. In war there are no real winners: our people will suffer and our lands will be laid waste. We have to continue our work in protecting the Earth. She has suffered enough at the hands of our neighbours, the humans. If we go to war, we will be assisting Eldorth to destroy all the hard work we have done over thousands of years. Of course, we cannot allow him to take control of this world; for if he did, the future of our planet would be bleak.

For now we will play to our strengths by achieving our ends through stealth and intelligence. If we are unable to achieve what we must peacefully then we will have to reconsider our position, but war is an absolute last resort. If Eldorth attacks before then, well, we must respond in kind. As you well know, Eldron, when required we can call on our people to do what is necessary. You, above all others here, know the strength and readiness of our armies when rallied, but for now we must concentrate on finding Elvyth's Harp to reduce Eldorth's capacity to unite evil forces against us. With the Harp in our possession, I will be able to summon, not only our own people, but all the good peoples of the magical world. With an army such as that, we would be invincible; Eldorth would know he was beaten before he began any war against us. War could then be averted, for he would be foolish to attack us in such circumstances.

As you have already heard, because of the information gathered by Elnest's spy in Eldorth's camp, we have arranged for a small group of our allies to go and retrieve the Harp and return it here. Elnest is right when he says that we must retrieve the Harp before Melificent breaks down the defences protecting it, but the Harp is protected by very powerful old magic and Melificent will find it difficult to break it fully. For now, the magic protecting the Harp will not allow Eldorth use it to its full potential. Only the Monarch and direct heirs to the throne can do that. As Eldorth is neither, he cannot use the full powers of the Harp."

Lizzie watched the proceedings with fascination. She was beginning to at least understand what one of the relics was and why it was of such importance. What the others were exactly, she didn't yet know, but she thought that she was likely to discover that before too long. What she didn't understand though, was why she, Elrus and Max had been included in the Council meeting. As if reading her thoughts, the King turned to her.

"Elizabeth, I invited you and your friends to attend this meeting today because it is important that you all understand what is happening and what we, in this world, are facing. You must appreciate the dangers you face as you undertake your journey towards becoming Monarch of this realm. Your friends are important as they will accompany and protect you throughout this journey. They need to be as informed as you about the dangers ahead of you, so that they are well armed to face the responsibility of friendship and loyalty. It is also important that you were invited here, rather than have a repetition of last night's events." A hint of a smile flickered across his lips.

Lizzie turned and looked at each of the two boys sitting either side of her. Elrus had drawn himself up in his seat, his head held high. He looked as if he had always known that this would be his role in life. When she turned to Max, however, his face had gone as white as his hair, his mouth gaped and his eyes were wide in alarm. He had obviously not expected this. Lizzie knew how he felt. Part of her just wanted to slink away back to the anonymity of Chislewick and just be little Lizzie Longton that the local kids thought of as being a bit odd. The other part of her and, when she thought about it, probably the bigger part, was glowing with

180

excited anticipation. Was it really only a few days earlier that she was wishing for some excitement as she looked out of her classroom window at the rainy playground? Well, now she was getting it in bucket loads.

As all eyes in the room watched the three young people sitting facing the King, he continued, "Friends and family are the most important things in life. Wealth and power are nothing if you do not have the love, respect and support of those around you. Life is fragile and can be gone in an instant; you must relish the time you are together. If you are loved and respected, and you love and respect others in return, then you are richer than the wealthiest person on the planet. Eldorth cannot understand that, as he has never felt love or respect for anyone. Your friendship, Elizabeth, will form a strong magical bond that will protect you from Eldorth and his vile accomplices. In that light, I should like to introduce you to another who I hope will also be a good friend and ally to you."

The King then turned to the black skinned man next to him and smiled. Elroy stood and held out his arm to the rear of him, and rising from a chair in the shadows towards the back of the room was a young girl. She walked quickly towards Elroy.

Holding the girl by the shoulders, he introduced her in his deep, rich voice, "Princess Elizabeth, may I introduce my daughter, Eloise."

Eloise curtseyed to Lizzie, who dipped her head in return. She was very pretty, with large dark eyes and bouncing black curls. Her round friendly face smiled broadly at Lizzie and it made her feel good to think that, maybe, at last she'd found a girl friend to share all those thoughts and feelings that girls do. Boys were good as mates, but she'd always longed for the friendship that girls share.

The King turned to Lizzie. "Now Elizabeth, I pass Eloise over to your care. Go, have fun and explore whilst the Council continues with its business. We must now discuss the plans for the retrieval of Elvyth's Harp."

Their dismissal had come so abruptly that they continued to sit there, staring at the King for a moment until Elrus seemed to snap to his senses and jump to his feet. The noise of his scraping chair jolted both Lizzie and Max into action, and they rose to their feet too. The four children then bowed to the King and turned and walked from the room, hotly pursued by Mrs Longton, bowing and curtseying as she went. As the Chamber doors opened to allow them to exit, the King called out, "Oh, and Elizabeth."

Lizzie turned to look at her Grandfather.

"Stay out of trouble," he said sternly, with a knowing look.

Lizzie grinned back at him. "I'll try," she quipped cheekily.

Outside the Chamber doors, which banged shut with a heavy clunk behind them, they all stopped and looked at each other. The two guards standing either side of the doors peered down at them without moving their heads.

"Well," sighed Mrs Longton, shaking her head as if she couldn't believe what she had just witnessed. She turned to Eloise and said, "It's very nice to meet you, dear."

'Thank you, it's nice to meet you too," Eloise replied, grinning at Mrs Longton and the others. "I thought it was going to be really boring coming to some old Council Meeting. My father never mentioned that there'd be other kids here too." Eloise had a bright and open personality.

"Have you had to come far?" asked Lizzie.

"We come from Elcarib," explained Eloise and, seeing Lizzie's baffled look, said, "Surely you've heard of it; it's a group of islands in the Western Seas."

"Oh," said Lizzie, still bemused. Then looking to her grandmother, Mrs Longton said, "I think it's Elvedom's version of the Caribbean."

Lizzie then turned back to the subject of the Great Council. "I wish we hadn't had to leave just as it was about to get really interesting," said Lizzie, indignantly. "Now we only know half the story."

Elrus indicated the two guards with a jerk of his head and, taking Lizzie's arm, led her further along the corridor, the others following in their wake.

"We don't want to say too much in front of them. Don't forget, we elves have sharp hearing," he hissed. Lizzie nodded in understanding.

"Look, perhaps the King wants the mission to be kept secret, so the fewer people who know about it, the less likely it is that Eldorth will find out about it," Elrus suggested wisely. But Lizzie still wasn't happy. If she was really the heir apparent, then she felt she should be included in all the discussions and decision-making. The fact that she was still only eleven didn't occur to her. She suddenly had an idea.

"Let's see if we can listen in again. Come on, Max, get us into that little room again," she said, and started to run towards the corner, around which the door to the little anti-chamber that she and Max had hidden in the night before was located. Max followed her, still looking a bit like a rabbit caught in a car's headlights, but doing what he was trained to do which was to obey orders unquestioningly. Elrus strolled along behind them with Mrs Longton and Eloise in tow; he was in no hurry, as he knew what they were likely to find when they got there.

"Where are we going?" asked Eloise.

"Nowhere fast," smiled Elrus, knowingly.

As Lizzie turned the corner, she saw that her plan had been thwarted. Standing to one side of the door to the small ante-chamber that she and Max had entered the previous night, was another tall guard. Lizzie stopped short.

"Well, it's nice to know you're trusted," she complained. Elrus looked at Max and raised his eyebrows in a look of resignation.

"He has a point, don't you think?" he whispered to Max, with a wry grin. Max nodded in agreement and looked a little relieved at not having to go through with Lizzie's plan.

"So, what now?" Lizzie asked; her face eager with excitement at the next stage of the adventure.

Mrs Longton looked at her granddaughter and smiled. She'd never seen such a change in someone over such a short space of time. What had happened to the timid little girl who wouldn't have said boo to a goose just a few days ago? Mrs Longton watched with satisfaction as Lizzie and her two companions discussed their next course of action.

"Well, we're not going to find out much standing around out here," stated Elrus.

"Perhaps," began Max hesitantly, "we should go back to my master's rooms and see if we can find any information that might give us some clues as to what is being planned to rescue Elvyth's harp," he suggested.

"Brilliant idea, Max," enthused Lizzie, clapping her hands together. "As Elrus said, we're getting nowhere standing here. Come on." She looked at her grandmother and told her that she didn't need to go along with them if she wanted to go back to her rooms and rest. Mrs Longton

184

looked sternly at her granddaughter and said that there was no way she was going to miss out on the adventure.

"I'm coming with you, young lady, and that's final. I'll be there to make sure you don't overstep the mark," she said emphatically. Lizzie gave her grandmother a brief hug and then turned to Eloise.

"Come on, Eloise, let me bring you up to date on what's been going on," she said, taking Eloise by the arm and striding confidently along the corridor. Mrs Longton followed on, listening to Lizzie explaining to Eloise about how she'd only arrived the previous day having known nothing about where her mother had come from. The two boys stayed where they were and Mrs Longton stopped, looked from the boys to Lizzie's retreating back, when Elrus put his fingers to his mouth and blew a sharp whistle in Lizzie's direction. She swung around and glared at him.

"Yes? What's the problem?" she asked irritably.

"You're going the wrong way," Elrus grinned at her. He and Max then turned on their heels and strode away towards Marvin's rooms, with Lizzie and Eloise running after them in hot pursuit and Mrs Longton scurrying along behind.

Chapter 17 – Through the Threshold

As the five companions entered Marvin's room, Mag and Pi each opened a lazy eye to see who had disturbed their slumber. Having seen that it was only Max and his friends, they nestled back down together on their perch and continued with their nap.

Mrs Longton walked over to the layered globe and, sitting down, gazed into its depths. She was worried. Things were beginning to take a turn in the wrong direction. When the truth about Lizzie's origins had finally sunk in, she had started to enjoy the whole experience. Watching Lizzie grow in confidence, having at last found somewhere she felt she belonged, was a joy to behold. It was as if a light had suddenly been switched on in Lizzie and she glowed with this newfound confidence. The pleasure of the thought welled up in Mrs Longton's chest but now, as she sat and thought about what they'd just discovered at the Grand Council, and the dangers Lizzie faced, frightened her.

The enthusiastic discussions going on between her four young companions brought her out of her reverie. She looked up and watched as they excitedly chatted about what they'd found out at the Council and what they were now looking for in Marvin's room.

"I haven't a clue where to go from here," Lizzie was saying, as she looked rapidly around the room trying to decide where clues might be hidden. Elrus was at the large bookcase against the wall, through which Lizzie had fallen the previous evening. He was peering at the spines of the numerous books that filled it. Max was standing behind Marvin's huge oak desk, pouring over various bits of parchment and papers that seemed to be strewn higgledy-piggledy all over it. Eloise just stood and watched them all with interest.

"My master keeps reminding me to tidy up his desk and file his papers away, but I keep putting it off. I wish I'd done as he'd told me now because I can't find anything useful amongst this mess," Max complained, rummaging through another pile of scrolls. "I'm not even sure I know what I'm looking for, even if I find it."

Lizzie joined him at the desk and started picking up papers and reading them too, which was a complete waste of time because most of them were written in a variety of different languages – none of which Lizzie understood. Symbols and squiggles sprawled across the pages and they could have been written in double-dutch for all the sense they made. Elrus had just walked across and joined Lizzie and Max when Max suddenly let out a yelp.

"Look!" he cried. "Look at this!"

The sudden sound of his voice woke Mag and Pi and they looked up at him with looks of disdain, and then of interest. Mag flew across the room, landed on Max's shoulder and cast an eye at the paper he was reading. Being a female magpie, she was by far the more curious of the two birds and had always been a little closer to Max, watching out for him and trying to keep him out of trouble.

As Mrs Longton and Eloise joined them, it seemed that Max had found a document that mentioned Duke Eldorth. Lizzie, Elrus and Eloise peered over his free shoulder and attempted to decipher the writing on the scroll that Max had just unrolled.

"Look, just here it says Eldorth is holed up in his castle in Maladorth," Max read, his finger pointing to a series of squiggles written on the page. Lizzie thought she'd have to just take Max's word for it because the writing was illegible to her. Elrus pointed to one of the symbols and asked Max if he was right in thinking that it meant magic. Max said he was.

"It says that the castle is protected by magic that keeps it concealed from spies," explained Max.

"What language is that?" inquired Lizzie, staring at the swirls that supposedly constituted writing.

"It's old Elvish," said Max knowledgeably. "Most of the ancient books of learning and history in our world are written in it. I had to learn to read and write it before I learnt any other language. My master uses it when he wants to write secretly. Most elves don't use it these days. I think the King and some of his closest advisors are now amongst the few people who understand it."

"My father has some old books written in it," Eloise said. "He knows something of the language and taught me some of the words, but it's really hard to learn and I didn't think it was worth worrying about too much. I just thought that 'old elvish' was a dying language, only used by people needing to read law or medicine or something. I wish I'd concentrated harder now," she frowned, perusing the writing on the scroll.

"Do you think I'll have to learn it?" Lizzie asked, thinking that it looked really complicated. Her lack of knowledge and ignorance of this new world she belonged to was starting to weigh heavily on her mind. The realisation was beginning to dawn on her of the enormous task ahead; not just having to learn about whom she was and what she was to become, but the whole history that had gone before her. She was scared that she wouldn't live up to role that she'd unwittingly been born to.

"'I think it's very likely that you will have to learn it at some point," Max nodded, still pouring over the scroll in front of him. "It takes quite a long time to learn. I've been studying it for a few years and I still have so much to learn. From what I can see here, though," he continued slowly, running a finger along a row of more squiggles, "it would seem that Duke Eldorth and the Witch Melificent have shrouded his castle with dark magic to protect it from intruders. It says something about the land thereabouts being laid to waste by the, erm..., poison, that's it – poison – of the dark magic. It goes on to say that any approach by anyone opposing Duke Eldorth would be difficult as there are many of his, um… I think that says henchmen, yes henchmen, guarding the land." The four young people looked at each other.

"Does it say who these henchmen are?" asked Lizzie warily, staring at Max in wide-eyed horror. Max scanned the page further and told her that there were no specific names, but it did list a number of different creatures, including trolls, ogres, renegade hobgoblins and something called creatures of the night - whatever they are!

"Does it say where Maladorth is?" asked Elrus.

"No," replied Max, "but I know it's somewhere to the North of the realm because I've heard my master speak of it."

Mag suddenly let out a loud screech and began hopping about on Max's shoulder and flapping her wings frantically. Pi joined in the fracas from his place on his perch. Their outburst made everyone jump and they looked at the birds in surprise.

"Ouch, that hurt Mag, get off," complained Max, trying to push Mag from his shoulder. "Shh…," he hissed, attempting to quieten Mag and Pi, as they continued to screech. Elrus suddenly grabbed Max's arm.

"Quiet!" he hissed. Everyone went silent; even the two birds snapped their beaks shut. Elrus cupped a hand to his ear; his sharp hearing listened out for any noises. "Quick," he said urgently. "Someone's coming, we've got to hide." Lizzie and her four companions scanned the room desperately to find a hiding place.

"Here, behind this curtain, quickly," urged Mrs Longton, beckoning the children over to a long, deep blue velvet drape that hung in a recess of the room. She quickly stepped behind the curtain and Lizzie, Elrus, Max and Eloise ran over to join her; Mag flying in their wake. They could hear a number of footsteps in the corridor outside the room rapidly approaching; a mumble of voices in urgent discussion accompanied the footsteps.

"Perhaps we'll get to hear where Maladorth is," Lizzie breathed hopefully as she swiftly followed her grandmother behind the curtain. In their haste to hide, Elrus and Max stumbled and fell against each other just at the moment Mrs Longton turned the knob of a large, old wooden door that was hidden behind the curtain. "Don't ope...," cried Max as, tumbling and falling over each other, the five companions, together with Mag flapping wildly behind them, fell through the door just as the King, Marvin, Elnest, Elroy, and General Eldron entered the room.

The five men fell silent as they watched the curtain in the corner of the room billow out from the draft, caused by the closing of the door behind it. Marvin ran to the curtain and pulled it aside just as the door slammed shut. The King looked at him in dismay when he saw the look on Marvin's face.

"What's just happened, Marvin? What's wrong?" he asked concernedly.

"I fear, my Lord, that Her Highness, Princess Elizabeth, and her companions have crossed over the Threshold" Marvin replied slowly.

"The Threshold? The Threshold to where?" queried Elroy, a hint of panic in his voice. His brow furrowed with worry.

"That, My Lord Elroy, I do not know. Whatever was the last place they spoke of before crossing the Threshold will be where they have ended up," Marvin said earnestly.

The elves looked at each other anxiously.

"We must discover where they've gone and follow after them. Begin searching the room; there must be a clue somewhere of what they may have been discussing prior to going through that door," ordered the King.

Standing at his desk, Marvin picked up a piece of parchment that had been carelessly thrown down on its surface in the previous reader's haste to hide.

"Sire, I think I may have discovered where they've gone but I hope, with all hope, that I am wrong," announced Marvin, holding up a scroll of parchment.

Chapter 18 – A Terrible Terrain

"Where on Earth are we?" panted Mrs Longton, picking herself up and dusting herself down. She looked down at her four young companions, still sprawled out on the ground around her feet. Mag flapped about, complaining bitterly in her rasping voice, and then landed a few feet away. She stared back at them with her beady black eyes, as if accusing them of causing her great inconvenience by luring her away from her comfortable perch in Marvin's room.

Lizzie, Eloise, Elrus and Max scrambled up and surveyed their surroundings. They appeared to be in some kind of barren landscape. There were no blossoms or young leaves on the trees here as there were at Elvedom Castle. In the dry, dusty soil were only a few scrubby looking tufts of gorse and brush. Everywhere looked parched and lifeless, as if the moisture had been sucked out of the place. It wasn't as though the sun could have burnt the land, as it wasn't hot at all; in fact the air felt quite cold. The whole place appeared as if some terrible weather pattern had left it dead or dying.

"What a grim place," shuddered Eloise, rubbing her elbow; it had taken quite a knock when Elrus had fallen on top of her as they had fallen through the door.

Elrus was brushing down his knees as Lizzie looked over at Max, who had the appearance of someone in severe shock. He stood and stared around wide-eyed, unshed tears glistening on his eye-lashes and his mouth squeezed tight as though he was about to cry. Lizzie grasped his shoulder and shook him gently.

"What is it, Max? What just happened? Where are we?" she asked him encouragingly.

"Oh dear, oh dear, oh dear," babbled Max, turning his head this way and that, taking in his surroundings and looking like he wanted to run and hide. "This is terrible, just terrible."

"What's terrible?" asked Elrus, he was intrigued with what had just happened but not particularly concerned. "Surely we've just fallen into some secret part of the castle," he said.

"No, no, no," stammered Max. "We've just crossed over a Threshold and I don't know how to get us back." He looked at Lizzie, his blue eyes filling up further. "The King told us to protect you, Princess, and I don't think we're ready to do that yet. I don't think we have enough power to do that."

"What do you need to protect me from, Max? I don't understand what's going on. Please tell me where you think we are," urged Lizzie; she was beginning to feel very frightened. Mrs Longton had now walked over and put a reassuring arm around Max's shoulders.

"Max, dear, you're getting upset. Perhaps we can decide what we should do if you can explain what's just happened. What do you mean by we've crossed over a Threshold?" she prompted him gently. Max took a deep breath and began to explain.

"The door you opened, the one we fell through, well, that was a Threshold. Thresholds are special magical devices for crossing over to other worlds or places within a world. A Threshold will take you to the place you desire to be. You just have to say the name of the place and step through and you'll find yourself there."

His four companions looked at each other in bemusement. "But Max, we didn't ask it to take us anywhere," said Lizzie, smiling reassuringly.

Max shook his head. "I beg to disagree, Princess. You see, you don't need to specifically ask it to take you to a place, you merely have to say that place's name."

"But that's a bit dangerous isn't it?" asked Eloise. "After all, anyone could then go to a Threshold, open it and turn up anywhere. I mean, what if you were taking a bath or something and someone just popped in," she said, grimacing and widening her large brown eyes in horror.

Max didn't look amused, but Lizzie and Elrus grinned at her. "They don't work quite that easily," Max huffed.

A look of realisation suddenly spread across Mrs Longton's face. "Oh dear," she whispered. Max nodded his head at her as she rubbed her hand across her mouth in dismay. Taking her hand from her mouth, she asked quietly, "So we've arrived near Maladorth?"

"Yes, my lady," Max nodded slowly. "Very near, if I'm not much mistaken." The grins on Lizzie, Elrus and Eloise's faces disappeared in an instant and they looked at Mrs Longton in surprise.

"But that's impossible," cried Lizzie. "How did that happen? Who mentioned Maladorth?" She looked around at each of them accusingly. Elrus turned to her, with a wry look on his face.

"You did, *Your Highness*, just before we fell through the door. Well done." he said sarcastically, shaking his head.

"Bu., bu.., but...," blustered Lizzie in confusion.

"The Princess wasn't to know," said Max, rising up in indignation, outraged at Elrus's disrespect towards Lizzie. "Thresholds, and what they do, were to be covered in a later lesson of my master's."

194

"Oh, this is great!" snapped Elrus. "We couldn't have come to a nicer place for our first trip over a Threshold," he said, cuttingly.

"My father's going to go mad," swallowed Eloise; her father in a temper was not something she liked to witness too often.

"It isn't my fault. I didn't know what would happen," Lizzie snapped back at Elrus.

"Trouble seems to follow you wherever you go," Elrus snarled at her.

"Well, excuse me, but you're..." she began indignantly, when Mrs Longton stepped between them.

"Now, now, children. Turning on each other is not going to get us anywhere. This unfortunate situation has occurred through no-one's fault. We have to work together now to try and extricate ourselves from our present predicament," she said firmly, looking around as if a door might suddenly appear through which they could return to Elvedom Castle.

"Uh, pardon?" asked Elrus, unsure of what Mrs Longton's long words meant.

"She means, we need to get ourselves outta here," snapped Lizzie, glaring at him irritably.

"Oh," Elrus replied, glaring back at her.

Mrs Longton walked around the spot where they had just appeared with her hands outstretched, palms facing forward. She looked like a mime artist pretending to be stuck in an invisible box.

"What's she doing?" Eloise whispered in Lizzie's ear. Lizzie shrugged. Eloise was trembling and Lizzie took her hand and gripped it tightly, smiling at her reassuringly. She wasn't feeling all that brave herself but she could see that Eloise was feeling worse.

'It's got to be here somewhere," murmured Mrs Longton, continuing her mime performance.

"What has, gran?" asked Lizzie, peering quizzically at her grandmother.

"That Threshold thing," replied Mrs Longton, feeling the air in front of her. "We fell about here when we came through the door, so it's got to be here." She bent down and patted the floor where the children had lain just a few minutes previously. Max stood watching her in fascination, and then suddenly seemed to come to his senses.

"It's no good doing that, my lady," he said, his voice quavering slightly with nerves. "A Threshold doesn't work like that. It doesn't necessarily stay in one place. We must find another one. There are not many around and not everyone can find them. If they could, it would be as you said, people crossing over and appearing all over the place. It would be chaos. There is a spell to summon one but it's powerful magic and I'm only an apprentice," he concluded.

The five companions looked around as they considered their next move. Mag hopped on the ground, peering at it and pecking around for anything edible. She didn't seem to be having much luck.

Elrus spoke first. "Well, I don't think we should stand around out here in the open for too long. We could be seen, and not by anyone who we'd want to see us. I suggest we look for some kind of cover, away from spying eyes," he said. They all agreed that this was probably the best thing to do, and then once they'd found some cover they'd decide what to do from there. They scanned the landscape for any sign of somewhere suitable.

"There are some trees over that way," Lizzie called from the top of a small boulder she'd clambered up onto to get a better view. She pointed away to their left where a small wood was located. Elrus scrabbled up beside her to take a look and agreed that the wood looked as good a shelter as any.

The five companions began walking towards the woods and Mag flapped along just ahead of them, keeping a keen look out for any sign of life with her sharp eyes, but saw nothing. In fact, there was no sign of life at all. Not a rabbit scurrying back to its hole, not a bird, other than herself, flying in the white sky above. The absence of anything living and the silence was eerie.

"Don't you think it's a bit odd that there doesn't seem to be any animals or birds around," Lizzie said in lowered tones, as if afraid she may be overheard in the unnerving silence of the deserted landscape.

"Maybe it's because there's no food about here," said Elrus, stopping and bending down, taking some of the dry, dusty earth in his hand. It trickled through his fingers like sand. He stood up and looked ahead at the wood. "Those trees look pretty green, so maybe there's a source of water over there."

They continued walking towards the wood, watching and listening for any signs of movement that might indicate life; every one of their nerves tightly strung, in fear of one of Eldorth's henchman or supporters appearing at any moment. Suddenly Mag let out a loud rasping call and flapped around their heads frantically.

"Get off!" yelled Elrus, waving his arms at the bird in an attempt to shoo her away.

"Look," cried Lizzie, pointing up in the sky above the woods. Some distance away they could see two black blobs on the horizon heading their way. At first the creatures

197

looked like a couple of crows with large, black wings, but as they drew closer it was obvious that they were an awful lot bigger than crows.

"Pterotorials! Run!" screamed Max, and he began running like mad towards the shelter of the woods, the others in hot pursuit. Mag flew alongside them, screeching as she urged them on. Mrs Longton straggled along behind, her skirt flying out behind her and a look of terror on her face as she looked up to see the creatures gaining on them quickly, their huge leathery wings beating powerfully. Her legs felt like lead and it seemed to take an eternity to reach the shelter of the woods.

With fear giving them an extra spurt of speed in their haste to hide from the pterotorials, they eventually plunged under the canopy of the woods, stumbling and falling over the roots of trees and other plants as they went. They could only hope that the trees would shield them from the sharp eyes of the creatures overhead. Peering out from their hiding place, Lizzie and her companions could see the huge creatures wheeling and soaring around in the sky just above where they had been moments earlier.

"Do you think they saw us?" Lizzie panted, bending over and gripping her side, trying to ease the stitch that pinched her painfully.

"You can bet on it," said Elrus, looking with concern at Mrs Longton who had slumped down on a fallen tree that was covered in vines. She was panting hard and was holding her forehead in her hand, her elbow resting on her knee. Her hair and clothes dishevelled by the race to hide. Max sat down next to her and was looking up at her with interest.

"Are you okay, Mrs Longton?" he asked. Eloise went over and laid a gentle hand on Mrs Longton's shoulder, looking at down at her with worried eyes.

"I'm just a bit out of breath, dear, but I'll be fine. I think I may be getting a bit too old for this kind of thing," Mrs Longton gasped, her face red with the exertion of running. Running was something she tried not to do too often at her time of life. As she began trying to pat her hair back into some semblance of a style, a sudden loud screaming call, that sent a shiver like iced water trickling down her spine, caused her and the children's eyes to snap open in horror and peer up through the trees.

"Those horrible creatures!" Mrs Longton whispered breathlessly.

Elrus joined Lizzie and Max, who were standing behind a tree at the edge of the wood, peering up at the sky through the leaves of the trees' low hanging branches. They could see the two pterotorials still circling the area, letting out their piercing screeches as they did. Then suddenly the creatures turned and flew off back in the direction from whence they'd come.

"What do you think they'll do now?" asked Lizzie in a small voice. The incident had shaken her badly and she could feel herself trembling all over. Her legs felt distinctly wobbly.

"Go back and report to Eldorth, I should imagine," said Elrus. "What do you think, Max?"

"I agree." Max nodded, looking grave. "This is not good."

The five companions looked around them. Compared to the bright, parched landscape around it, the wood was dark and foreboding as they peered into its depths.

"Well, I think we should move on and see if we can find any sign of life around that might be of a friendly nature," said Elrus.

"I can't see that being very likely, can you?" said Lizzie, sceptically.

"Elrus is right about one thing and that's that we can't stay here. We need to see if we can find any source of food or water than can keep us going for a while," said Mrs Longton, standing up from her log and still breathing hard. "We're bound to be missed back at the castle. I mean, someone was coming in as we went through that Threshold. They may have heard us and be trying to find us. Is it possible that Marvin will be able to trace us, Max?" she asked.

Max looked unsure. "My master is a very powerful sorcerer, Mrs Longton. I'm sure he will do everything he can to help us," he said earnestly. He sounded and looked as though he was trying to reassure himself as much as anyone else. "The only problem is that Thresholds aren't always an exact science. Even if he has deduced that we are in Maladorth, he won't know exactly where, so anyone trying to find us could end up miles from here."

The little party looked at one another hopelessly and Eloise looked close to tears. Mrs Longton put a comforting arm around her shoulders.

"Come on then. Let's go this way; it's as good a way as any," urged Elrus, as confidently as he could. He picked up a sturdy piece of branch lying close by and began to stride off further into the woods, beating and crashing through bracken and brambles as he went. Lizzie, Eloise and Mrs Longton looked at each other and then followed the rough path that Elrus had beaten; Mag flew from tree to tree in their wake.

Max stood watching them; his pale face seemed even paler and he didn't feel good about this. He had the uneasy feeling that something sinister was going on in there, although he acknowledged that it wasn't really very surprising, given that the wood was situated right in the middle of Duke Eldorth's lands.

Elrus, taking the role of self-appointed group leader, checked that the others were following. Seeing that their party was one person short, he turned back and saw Max standing rooted to the spot, fear etched on his face. "Come on, mate," he called. "There's safety in numbers."

Max looked at Elrus and swallowed hard, trying to quell the feeling of panic rising in his chest. He took a few tentative steps over the broken bracken and followed Elrus, Lizzie, Eloise and Mrs Longton further into the woods.

Chapter 19 – Witch Brew?

A foul smell emanated from the cauldron sitting over the brazier in the middle of a dark, dingy dungeon somewhere in the bowels of Duke Eldorth's castle. The fire beneath the cauldron blazed brightly and sparks spat and flared angrily.

Melificent, sitting at a large table nearby, was chopping up the remains of some poor small creature that was now totally unrecognisable. A mangy, moth-eaten old cat sat on the table close by, watching her hungrily with its one remaining eye. A large black crow flew across from the top of a battered old cupboard that was standing in the corner of the room and landed on the handle of the cauldron. He squinted down through the steam rising up from the bubbling liquid below.

"Ge' offa there, you," Melificent screeched, at the bird. "I don't want you bloomin' poopin' in my soup!" she yelled; her coarse voice slicing the air like a cheese grater. The crow gave a loud rasping caw and flapped back to his perch on the cupboard, eyeing Melificent malevolently with his hard black eyes.

Melificent carried on with her chore, humming tunelessly as she did so. Suddenly the door to her dungeon crashed open and Duke Eldorth strode in, his dark blue velvet robe billowing out behind him. His entrance sent the cat leaping from the table, whereupon it settled itself on a comfy, but smelly and stained, old padded chintz armchair nearby.

"Good gods woman, what's that disgusting stench!" Eldorth boomed

"It's me dinner, me Lawd," said Melificent, jumping to her feet and curtseying briefly, knocking her chair over with her large, fat bottom in the process. She went over to the steaming cauldron, took a large wooden paddle hanging nearby and began to slowly stir the soup. Stronger smells drifted up from it, almost choking Eldorth in the process. He coughed and retched as Melificent sniffed the air in ecstasy. "It's good old cabbage soup, just the way me ol' muvver used to make. Mm..., luvverly," she purred as she removed the paddle from the soup and licked it with her fat wet tongue.

Eldorth looked away; the sight of her repulsed him. He dabbed his watering eyes with a white handkerchief he'd taken from the recess of his robe, then put it over his mouth and nose to shield them from the revolting smell of the soup.

"Do you think you could be so kind as to do something about that dreadful smell?" he pleaded, sarcastically, having regained his composure. "I can't think straight, it's so revolting."

"Oh, all right," grumbled Melificent reluctantly, and withdrawing a long, thin gnarled piece of wood from a deep pocket in her brown robe, she waved the wand over the cauldron. "Aromagon!" she said and the awful smell disappeared instantly. Eldorth took a deep gulp of air in relief. Melificent, however, was not so pleased - she loved the smell of cooking cabbage.

"Right, perhaps *now* we can talk business," said Eldorth, flicking a nearby chair with his handkerchief to brush away the dust and dirt that had accumulated there. Melificent's general household hygiene was pretty much like her personal one, non-existent. He sat down and watched Melificent as she shuffled over to her chair at the table and plonked herself down on it.

"So, I trust that you've been working on what needs to be done about this child of Elethria's?" Eldorth said, expectantly.

"I 'ave, Lawd," nodded Melificent, her blotchy face breaking out in an uncomfortable sweat. For some reason, the discovery that one of her most powerful curses had failed had discombobulated her. It had never happened before and she was unused to the feeling of failure. But the thing that bothered her most was that it had taken eleven years for the discovery to be made. How had she never been made aware of the child's existence?

When Eldorth had berated her just a few days earlier, when the news had broken that the child was in Elvedom, she had scurried back to her dungeon and called upon her sources of information. A number of her cronies had slunk away, nursing sore ears and backsides, because when Melificent got angry, her raised voice could cut glass and a few choice spells hadn't gone amiss either. She had sent out spies to discover where the girl was and what she was doing but, so far, she had heard nothing. The girl must be under some kind of protection that prevented hostile forces from finding her, she thought.

Melificent had not wasted her time whilst she had been waiting, though. She had poured over her various volumes of books to try to get to the root of the curse's failure and how it could be overcome.

"I've been studyin' me aynshant (ancient) books to try and figure out what 'appened to stop the curse from bein' completed," she explained. Melificent then told Eldorth that she believed it was as she'd suspected; that together with Marvin's magic, the fact that the King still possessed a number of the sacred relics at the time of the birth had meant that his power had remained significant enough for the curse to be only partially successful. It had destroyed the mother, but only after the child was born alive. King Elfred's power, even with Marvin's help, could not protect them both. However, their combined powers had been strong enough not only to save the child, but to keep her hidden for the past eleven years. Melificent was seething about that and said that she was still, "gonna find out 'ow that could 'ave 'appened."

204

Eldorth smiled coldly. "Well, at least I was avenged in some part. Elethria never got away with her rejection of me. Good." he said bitterly, leaning back in satisfaction. "Go on," he waved his hand impatiently at Melificent for her to continue. As Melificent opened her wide mouth to speak, there was a loud bang on the door of her dungeon and crashing through it came a large, lumbering ogre.

He had to bend almost double as he entered through the doorway, as he was about two and a half metres tall. His massive arms and legs looked as if they'd been hewn from boulders picked off a mountainside and were roughly the same colour. He had a huge barrel chest that was decorated with tattoos and on his shoulders he had reinforced leather pads that were studded with metal spikes. On his legs he had similar looking pads to those on his shoulders that protected his shins, and he wore wide copper-coloured metal wristbands on his arms. Covering his lower torso he wore an animal skin loincloth that protected his modesty; the loincloth seemed to be held in place by a deep leather belt, once more studded with spikes that went around his broad girth. He was a grizzly sight.

"SIRE," roared the Ogre, and attempted a slight bow, which was difficult given that the width of the belt he was wearing restricted any bending at the waist, if indeed you could describe him as having a waist.

Eldorth winced at the loud rumbling roar that assaulted his ears. There were distinct drawbacks in recruiting these barbarians to his ranks, he thought.

"Could we try that a little quieter next time, Orfwit," Eldorth grimaced, in reply. "What is it?"

The ogre's slow, booming voice continued. "WE'VE... HAD A RE...PORT," he began, but Eldorth made a downwards movement with his hands in an attempt to quieten him down a little. The ogre stopped and looked

205

confused about what Eldorth meant but, as the realisation that he needed to lower his voice dawned, Orfwit crinkled up his big jowly face in concentration, and began again, only this time with slightly less decibels, "WE'VE HAD A RE...PORT THAT STRAN...GERS HAVE BEEN SEEN IN THE VINC.. IN...,VIC... IN...,ERR, ..."

Eldorth rolled hiseyes in exasperation. "Are you trying to say vicinity?" he said irritably.

Orfwit nodded his massive head vigorously.

"That's better," sighed Eldorth in relief at not having his eardrums perforated. Then suddenly the realisation of what the ogre had just said seemed to hit Eldorth and jumped to his feet.

"What!" he yelled.

"I SAID...," boomed Orfwit.

"I know what you said," interrupted Eldorth, agitatedly. "It was a rhetorical question, you idiot."

"UH?" boomed the Ogre, who had absolutely no idea what Eldorth was talking about. These elves were a mystery to him, he was just happy that he didn't have to deal with too many of them. Orfwit just wanted Eldorth to tell him to go and bash somebody. That's what he was good at, not all this running around giving messages. Ogres were built for beating people up, he thought to himself. He watched Eldorth and Melificent with his broad forehead furrowed in confusion. Too much thinking hurt his head.

"Explain, Melificent," demanded Eldorth. "Who are these strangers? There's no use asking this halfwit, apart from the fact that he's practically illiterate, he'll deafen us before he gets his report out. You're supposed to be on top of the situation," he accused, jabbing a finger at her. "I thought you

206

had ways and means of knowing what's going on when and where." He sat down on his chair and glared at her.

"Well, I am, but I can't be in all places at bloomin' once can I? I mean you wan' me to find out 'ow this kid survived and got 'idden away," she mumbled, moaning to herself as she made her way over to the old cupboard standing in the corner of her dungeon.

Still muttering cusses under her breath, she opened the cupboard's doors and began rummaging in its depths. Eventually, she pulled out a large wooden basin. It's surface was carved with intertwined creatures such as snakes and spiders, mice and bats, and other creatures and animals that were used in her dark magic, and it looked very old and battered. Pushing the remnants of her chopped up animal to one side, she placed the bowl on the table.

Melificent then went over to some shelves at one side of her dungeon that held a hodgepodge of jars and bottles, books and other strange implements, and took down three small containers from a rack that contained several more. She placed the containers on the table next to the bowl and then, from a large jug standing nearby, she poured water into the bowl, followed by a few drops of liquid from each one of the three vials.

The water in the bowl began to bubble and churn, and a lime green vapour rose from its surface. Melificent closed her eyes and wafted her hands over the bowl, murmuring incantations as she did so. Eldorth watched on with interest.

Slowly, Melificent opened her eyes and looked down into the concoction in the bowl that had now settled into a clear green liquid; the vapour having evaporated into thin air. She seemed to be in a trance-like state.

"I see a dry parched land," she said in a voice quite unlike her usual one. It sounded dreamy, almost soft - not the harsh common brogue she normally spoke in. Eldorth leaned forward eagerly. Good; that's obviously here in Maladorth, he thought.

"I see five travellers. No. Wait. There are six - one is flying," she said, and a quizzical look passed across her face. Then she continued. "They travel on foot across the dry barren plain - towards shelter. They seek shelter but I cannot see them clearly - their faces and bodies are distorted - they are fading, fading, fading. I, I, I am losing, losing, losing sight of them," she said breathlessly, her voice sounding like an echo losing itself in some deep cavern. "I don't understand - why can I not follow them?" Melificent was sweating profusely, as if the effort to see what was in the waters was too much for her. She suddenly slumped forward, as if unconscious, knocking the bowl as she did so, so that the liquid it contained slopped over its sides and spilled on the table.

Eldorth watched her with narrowed eyes and a look of utter contempt on his face. She was losing it. Whatever powers she had were not what they once were. Something or someone was sapping her energy and she was of no use to Eldorth if she could not fulfil her purpose of sorceress. He rose slowly from his chair and walked towards her. The ogre watched on in interest, a sense of excitement beginning to grow and swell in his huge belly. He sensed the evil emanating from the elf in front of him; this was more like it – this, the ogre understood.

As Eldorth reached the witch sitting slumped in her chair the anger and loathing he was beginning to feel towards her intensified. Suddenly, he grabbed her hair and yanked her head backward. She opened her eyes in shock and stared up at him. Until now, he had always kept an element of respect for her, but she could see in his eyes that this was rapidly disappearing. The fact that he'd laid hands on her was evidence of that. She was a little afraid and it was not a feeling she was used to.

"What's happening? Why can't you see?" Eldorth snarled through gritted teeth.

"I'm not sure, Lawd. I fink it's 'coz I'm a bit tired. You know I've been working 'ard tryin' to find out where this grandkid of Elfred's is and it must 'ave sapped me energy a bit. Maybe if I get a good night's kip I'll do better tomorra'," she lied; Melificent had a very good idea why her powers were waning. She looked up into the darkly handsome face of Eldorth; he was still holding a large chunk of her wispy hair in his hand. As he let go, he shoved her head forward so that it nearly hit the table in front of her.

Melificent watched as Eldorth walked towards the door of the dungeon, her eyes burning with hatred in his back. She had once loved this man, he was her pupil and her protégé and she had taught him so much, but it had been to her own disadvantage. She had taken pleasure in seeing him grow into the elf he was today. She had hardly been able to wait to put one over that pompous prig, Marvin. But what she had not realised at the time was that the powers she was instilling in Eldorth would be at her own expense. Never having had an apprentice before, she had not known that it would mean that her own powers would gradually transfer to him, unless she had taken better care. Luckily for Melificent, Eldorth did not yet realise that, due to this, her weakness was ever-growing, and she was determined that she would not let him know. If she did then she was dead. At the moment the powers they shared together were sufficient but individually they were not. As Eldorth grew stronger with the dark magic, Melificent grew weaker. She had to find a way of redressing the balance before Eldorth realised what was happening.

At the door, Eldorth turned and, with his voice dripping with disdain, said, "Get your sleep, if you must, but tomorrow you had better perform Melificent. My patience will not hold out much longer. I want answers. I want this child found and destroyed before too long. Or else..." He left the threat unsaid and then, turning to the ogre, instructed him to get a search party to find the trespassers in his lands.

"YES SIRE!" bellowed the creature; and as he followed Eldorth out of the dungeon, he turned and gave the white-faced Melificent a malicious grin.

Melificent glared at their departing backs and, as the ogre slammed shut the door to her dungeon, she poked out her tongue and let out a loud raspberry. She tipped the contents of the wooden bowl away into the plughole of a grimy old sink in the corner of the room, muttering curses to herself as she did so. She put the bowl back into the cupboard from where she'd got it, and then walked over to her books piled haphazardly on some shelves close by. "Now, where is it?" she muttered, rummaging through the books and scattering them around in her haste to find the book she was looking for. "Ha, ha! 'ere it is," she crowed gleefully, feeling a little more like her old self at her discovery.

She began rifling through the book's pages. It was very old and had been well thumbed over in its many years, but this didn't prevent Melificent from turning its pages roughly in her urge to discover the spell she sought. The mangy old cat leapt onto the top shelf of the bookcase and peered down at her curiously with his one slanted green eye.

"Now it's in 'ere somewhere, Lucifer me ol' mate, I know it is," she mumbled, addressing the cat. "If me mem'ry serves me righ', I'm gonna need the blood of some young wizard or witch to make ..., ahh, 'ere it is!" she yelled suddenly, causing the cat leap to off the bookcase and the crow to flap his wings and let out his rasping caw in surprise.

Melificent plonked herself down into her battered old armchair and read the spell greedily.

Chapter 20 – If You Go Into the Woods Today

The light filtering through the canopy of leaves above their heads sent shadows flickering and dancing across the ground of the wood. Lizzie, Eloise, Elrus, Max and Mrs Longton's nerves were on edge as their eyes flitted around them watching for any signs of life; their ears listening out for any noise that might indicate that someone or something was near at hand.

They had been walking for a little while and the silence around them was eerily oppressive. They had hoped to find some bush or tree that might contain something edible, such as berries or fruits or nuts, but so far most of the trees seemed to be great tall scots pine or other types of fir tree. As they all knew, pine cones didn't make for the tastiest of snacks. Although there were plenty of brambles about, it was too early in the year for them to bear any berries. They needed to be able to sustain themselves until they either found a way out of their situation or someone rescued them. The trees around them were quite green, given the lack of any sign of water thereabouts so far, but they hadn't yet given up hope of finding a stream or spring of some sort.

They came across a large open space, a sort of woodland glade, where the trees had formed a circle around a flat mossed-over piece of ground. Above them, they could see a patch of the white burnt out sky, and the light from it shone down onto the ground beneath their feet. There were a number of severed stumps of trees dotted around the glade, and it looked as if someone had been there a long time before and chopped several trees.

"Well, someone's been here before," said Elrus, running over and standing on the largest of the stumps. "I wonder who chopped these down." The group looked around them at the other stumps, there were seven of them.

"Hundreds of years ago, in our world, people created places like these for worshipping gods and the likes. They created shrines that they could come to in order carry out their religious ceremonies. Maybe this is something like that," Mrs Longton suggested.

"Oh yes, I remember seeing something about that on the telly, gran," said Lizzie, nodding in agreement, turning her head to gaze at her surroundings.

"Telly?" asked Max. Elrus and Eloise also looked at Lizzie equally puzzled.

"Yes telly, well, television actually. It's a special type of box we have in our world that shows us moving pictures and spoken words that we call programmes. These programmes can be about things that are happening in the world or they may be just things to entertain or amuse us. Most homes have one," she explained.

"Sounds fascinating," said Elrus, getting down from his tree stump and sitting on it, staring at Lizzie intently.

"I'd like to see a telly," said Eloise, breathlessly. Elrus nodded in agreement, he too would like to see a telly.

"Well, if we ever get back to Elvedom Castle perhaps Marvin can organise us a Threshold, and then maybe you can visit us one day in our home and see our television," smiled Mrs Longton, and then she suddenly became serious. It was as if, for a moment, they had all forgotten the seriousness of their situation, but they were brought back to reality by Mrs Longton's words - "If we ever get back to Elvedom Castle" and they all looked at each with worried eyes.

Suddenly Max's eyes sprang wide open and he put a finger quickly to his lips. "Shh," he hissed.

"What?" mouthed Lizzie, silently.

Max cupped a hand to his ear and then beckoned them all over to him. As they huddled around, he whispered, "I just heard something. I thought I heard it a few times before as we've been walking along but I'm absolutely sure I heard it just then."

"What did you hear? My hearing's pretty good and I've not noticed anything," whispered Elrus.

"That's because you've been walking up front and making a racket with all that crashing through the undergrowth," Max hissed back at him.

"I've not been crashing," said Elrus, petulantly.

"Now, now, boys," whispered Mrs Longton. "This is not the time for squabbling. What did you hear, Max?"

"A kind of fluttering noise, like a bird's wings beating very fast," he said nervously, glowering at Elrus. "I've heard it a few times but this time it sounded a lot closer."

The five of them stood in a circle with their backs to each other, peering through the trees looking for whatever might be making the fluttering noise, but they could see nothing. Mag flew up and sat on the branch of a nearby tree, looking around with jerky head movements, her beady eyes looking out intently. Listening closely for any sounds, everyone's eyes flitted from tree to tree and branch to branch when suddenly they each heard the noise that Max had obviously been hearing for a while. It sounded, as Max had said, like the beating of very fast wings; a shimmering flutter, like an enormous butterfly. What could it be? Lizzie thought, her nerves jangling.

Stepping forward nervously, and sounding more confident than he felt, Elrus said in a loud voice, "Come out, whoever you are."

The fluttering sound increased, as if there were more than one of the creatures lurking somewhere behind the trees. Annoyed now, Elrus tried again in an even more confident voice, "I said come out and show yourself."

Lizzie reached over and grabbed his arm fearfully. "Are you sure about this?" she asked, urgently. "It might be dangerous."

Elrus turned to her. "Look, if it was dangerous it wouldn't be so scared of us and it's got to be scared because it's hiding. If it was one of Duke Eldorth's cronies we'd have been grabbed and dragged off long before now. That's if Max is right in saying that he's been hearing that noise for some time." He looked at Max, who glared in return at Elrus's evident lack of faith in him.

Mrs Longton agreed. "Elrus is quite right, Lizzie. It makes sense. Perhaps whatever it is that's hiding thinks we have something to do with Eldorth." Lizzie nodded; what Elrus and her grandmother were saying did make sense.

"Well, let me try talking to it then," said Lizzie and, looking at Elrus who didn't look convinced, went on, "You sound a bit scary challenging whatever it is like that. I'll try a different approach." So, stepping towards the direction from where the sound seemed to be coming, Lizzie spoke to the creature.

"Hello. My name's Lizzie and this is my grandmother, and these are my friends, Elrus, Max and Eloise," she said gently, pointing to her three companions in turn. "Perhaps you can help us. We're a bit lost you see, and..." but before she could say anything further, a small sharp but beautiful face peered out from behind the nearest tree. Its large startlingly hazel eyes stared nervously at Lizzie and its mop of golden curls shone in the rays of sunlight that filtered down through the branches above. Lizzie took a step back in surprise. As she did so, several more similar looking faces

214

began appearing from behind the surrounding trees and stared at the little group of companions.

Lizzie, Elrus, Max, Eloise and Mrs Longton stood closer together for protection. The creatures didn't look particularly dangerous but there were obviously a number of them and so they had to tread carefully.

Eventually, the creature that had first looked out at them became bold enough to step out from behind its tree and there, in front of Lizzie, was one of the most beautiful creatures she had ever set eyes on. Dressed in shades of green, brown and mauve that camouflaged well with its surroundings, it was small in stature, no more than about three feet tall with small slim arms and legs. Its beautiful skin was almost transparent in its delicacy but its most amazing feature was the pair of delicate multi-coloured wings that were fluttering agitatedly on its back.

"Oh! A fairy!" exclaimed Lizzie, in delight. Eloise's face broke out in a broad smile as she looked at the fairy. The fairy cocked its head to one side and looked at Lizzie suspiciously.

"What are you doing here?" it asked in a clear, musical voice. Spurred on by the boldness of their companion, other fairies hiding behind the trees came out from their hiding places and stood in support behind her. Their small faces with their bright eyes watching Lizzie and her friends closely, their radiantly coloured wings fluttering behind them. A little flustered by the intensity of the attention of the fairies, Lizzie tried to explain.

"As I was saying, we're lost and we're trying to find a way to get back home. We came into these woods for shelter and provisions. We're so glad we found you, are you able to help us?" she asked.

"Why would we help you? You are strangers here. We don't like strangers coming into our woods; they always

215

cause trouble. Duke Eldorth sends bad creatures into the woods and they try to hurt the few creatures that are left living here. Many are gone now, in fear, or are dead. We don't want strangers here," said the fairy, narrowing her eyes and crossing her arms defiantly.

Mrs Longton spoke to the fairy, saying softly, "We know of Duke Eldorth and we know that he has treated people badly, but we are not his followers; in fact we're quite the opposite. We are against Duke Eldorth. We follow the elf, King Elfred," she said, as way of explanation.

At the sound of King Elfred's name, the fairies began whispering together excitedly. The first fairy who had appeared, and who seemed to be the group's leader, then spoke again.

"Is this true? You are followers of King Elfred?" she asked, directing the question at Lizzie.

Lizzie nodded emphatically. "Oh yes. Absolutely," she stressed, smiling broadly, as way of proof. She decided against telling the fairies that she was actually his granddaughter in case unfriendly ears should hear.

The fairy turned back to her associates and, once again, they whispered urgently to each other, obviously discussing what should be done. Lizzie and her companions looked on in anticipation. Eventually, the leader turned and addressed them.

Bowing low she said, "I am sorry that we seemed hostile to you, but we must be sure that you mean neither us nor any other creature harm before we can be of help to you. My name is Fionnella and these are my compatriots, Fiodrick, Forianne, Fabion and Fimley." Fionnella pointed to each of the fairies in introduction. "We are woodland fairies and have been sent here to try and help protect those creatures that have survived Duke Eldorth's slaughter of innocent ones. I am the leader of this small band of scouts. We keep watch for intruders into these woods and report back."

"Report back? Report back to who?" asked Elrus, intrigued. "Who are you working for?" Fionnella chose to ignore the question and continued speaking as though Elrus hadn't spoken.

"We choose to believe that you are who you say you are. You seem to have honest faces," she peered deeply into each one of them, "and your manners are fine. We will help you. Follow us," said Fionnella, turning and walking away. With Fionnella leading the way, and the other fairies following behind, the group walked further on into the woods, Mag flying from branch to branch beside them.

They walked for some time. Max trudged along, watching the back of Fionnella's head; he looked like he was in some sort of trance. Mag had seemed to have decided that she was tired of flying from tree to tree and so had settled herself comfortably on Max's shoulder. Eloise and Mrs Longton looked as though they were quite enjoying the experience, considering the seriousness of their predicament, chatting animatedly in hushed tones about what was happening. Mrs Longton also smiled gently at each of the fairies in turn, none of whom seemed to notice as they were more intent on keeping watch all around them.

Elrus kept looking around suspiciously at the four fairies walking behind them, trying to work out if they were being led into a trap. Lizzie, walking just behind Fionnella, watched the fairy's wings with rapt fascination, a multitude of questions spinning around her brain. After a short while of walking in silence, Lizzie couldn't wait any longer to ask some of her more burning questions.

"Excuse me, Fionnella," she said, as politely as possible. "May I just ask you a couple of things?" The fairy turned her head back towards Lizzie, not letting up on the pace of their march through the woods. The fairy inclined her head in agreement.

"Where are you taking us?" asked Lizzie.

"Yeah, and who are you working for?" Elrus asked, slightly aggressively. Lizzie glared at him for his rudeness; they weren't going to get any answers that way. Elrus just looked at Lizzie and shrugged but Fionnella hadn't seemed to notice his rudeness and didn't seem at all put out by his interruption.

"I cannot say at this time where we are going, or whom we are meeting. You will find out soon enough," Fionnella said, calmly.

"Can you fly?" asked Lizzie, enthusiastically.

"Of course, these are not just for show," answered Fionnella, fluttering her wings and looking at Lizzie as if it was a bit of a stupid question. "But we are not flying at the moment as you cannot and it would be both impolite of us to do so, but more importantly you would not be able to keep up with us."

As the fairies continued leading the way, Lizzie went back to thinking about where they were going and how on earth they were possibly going to get back to the castle. Elrus just continued following along suspiciously eyeing each of the fairies in turn. He didn't feel particularly threatened by them, or that the others and he were in any real danger from them, but he didn't like the way they weren't being told what was happening. After all, they were in enemy territory so they needed to be on their guard.

After what seemed like several minutes, the party was confronted by the trunk of an enormous gnarled old oak tree. Its trunk was several metres in diameter and its huge branches stretched up far above them. Fionnella stopped in front of it. The fairies looked around anxiously, as if checking that they weren't being watched and, when satisfied that there was no one else around, Fionnella approached the tree. Standing very close to it, she placed the palms of her hands flat against its bark and, caressing it gently, she murmured words that none of the rest of the company could make out. A slight rumbling noise began emanating from the tree and then its bark seemed to begin to peel away revealing an opening in the body of the trunk. Leaning forward, Lizzie peered into the gap that had been created and could see a tunnel leading away down under the roots of the tree.

Turning to face them, Fionnella invited Lizzie, Mrs Longton, Eloise, Max, Elrus and Mag to follow her. She then turned and began descending down into the darkness of the passageway.

Chapter 21 – The Underground Unit

As the small party descended into the depths of the tunnel beneath the tree, they discovered that it wasn't dark at all. The walls seemed to shimmer with an iridescent glow; as if small particles of some metal that radiated light were coating the tunnel surface. It wasn't bright, but it was light enough to allow them to see where they were going.

A short way down the tunnel, three passages branched off in different directions, but Fionnella led the way determinedly forward through the one leading straight ahead. At the end of the tunnel were several doors and, choosing the largest of them, she rapped on it sharply. Lizzie's heart was in her mouth by now. She could only guess what her grandmother was feeling, but then felt reassured when she felt Mrs Longton grab her hand for support. The small party stood and waited until a female voice called out, "Enter!"

Fionnella opened the door and walked through, then, having bowed low to the occupants of the room, she stood to one side beckoning Lizzie and her companions inside. As they entered they could see a large table, covered with what looked like maps and other documents, with several people standing around it. Standing at the back of the table, leaning over the documents, was a tall young woman with the most amazing long, thick, blond wavy hair that was tucked behind her pointed ears and held back from her face with a circlet of gold. There was no doubt at all that this was a She-Elf, and a noble one at that.

The woman stared at them with deep-set brown eyes. An energy force seemed to radiate from her that was quite tangible, and Lizzie thought she was the most beautiful woman she had ever seen, but there was also something very familiar about her. Lizzie felt that she had seen her or, someone like her, somewhere before. She was snapped out of pondering the matter further when the woman spoke with a strong, confident voice.

"Well, Madam? What do you think you are doing coming to this neck of the woods?" she asked sternly, her eyes twinkling.

Lizzie was taken aback at the familiarity with which she was spoken to. "Well, I er...," began Lizzie, stuttering and stumbling for an explanation. She was taken unawares by the question; it wasn't the greeting she was expecting. The woman spoke to her as if she knew her.

"And you boys were supposed to be keeping an eye on her," said the woman, turning on Max and Elrus. Lizzie turned to look at them and was shaken to see that both boys were down on one knee with their head bowed in the direction of the woman. Next to them, Eloise was in a deep curtsey, her head bowed. Still clutching her grandmother's hand, Lizzie looked up at her grandmother in confusion, but Mrs Longton was obviously as nonplussed as Lizzie.

"We're sorry, Your Highness," said Elrus in a small voice. "But it was an accident..." he tried to explain, but the woman spoke over him.

"You could have been captured, for goodness sake. Or even worse killed," she continued, leaning on the table for emphasis. She walked around the table towards Lizzie and her friends, moving with incredible grace, like some sort of dancer or athlete. She was wearing clothes in similar colours to those of the fairies who had brought Lizzie and her companions to her. Her long legs were covered in what looked like the lightest and softest of brown suede trousers and they were tucked into a pair of soft brown buckskin boots. Her jerkin, of leaf green, clung to her torso like a second skin. Lizzie was so surprised by the events unfolding before her that she was stunned into silence. Mrs Longton seemed to find her voice first and, looking up from Eloise and the boys still kneeling in front of the woman, she turned to face her.

"I'm sorry, but we haven't been introduced," she said, extending a hand to shake that of the woman. "My name's Amelia Longton and this is my granddaughter, Elizabeth."

"Yes, I know who you are," said the woman, and looking at Mrs Longton's hand as if unsure of what it meant, then took it in hers and shook it heartily. "It's great to meet you but it just shouldn't have been right now," she said, placing a hand under Eloise's elbow to raise her out of her curtsey. She then turned to the boys and told them to stand up or they'd get sore knees. Elrus and Max quickly scrabbled to their feet and stood still as if to attention.

The woman then turned to Lizzie and grabbed her by both shoulders and looked deep into her face. As she did so, her eyes seemed to fill with tears.

"Well, you really do look like your mum," she said, with a slight catch in her voice. A single tear escaped her lashes and ran in a little rivulet down her cheek, dropping off her chin. Lizzie looked up at her face in bewilderment when suddenly the woman crushed Lizzie to her in a tight embrace.

"And you are?" asked Mrs Longton, peering round at the woman's face.

"Oh, I'm sorry. I'm forgetting myself, she said, letting go of Lizzie and extending her hand once more to Mrs Longton. "I'm so used to people knowing who I am I take it for granted that everyone should know me," she said, smiling brightly; her shining white teeth sparkled in the light cast by the lamps burning around the edges of the room.

"I'm Elenya," she announced. And, turning back to Lizzie, said, "I'm your aunt."

Lizzie's mouth gaped open in shock. Well that explained Eloise, Elrus and Max's behaviour; they were in the

222

presence of a princess. Mrs Longton let out a little whoop of delight.

"Oh my goodness; this is wonderful! Lizzie and I've heard all about you from your father but I thought he said that you were out at the coast somewhere working with some of your people."

"Yes. Well, I was, but I move around constantly," Elenya explained. "Moving about is useful for two main purposes. Firstly, for security - by not staying in the same place for too long I'm harder to get hold of. Secondly, and most importantly, I have to be where I'm most needed. The royal family give a lot of hope and support to those people living in difficult circumstances and we have to get stuck in and help where we can. We motivate people to do more for themselves and their communities by giving them something of ourselves. My father isn't able to do too much travelling as he's needed back at base to run the Grand Council where important decisions need to be made, although he does travel out to see the people when he can."

Mrs Longton nodded in understanding. "So, what are you doing here; in Maladorth? Isn't it very dangerous for you being in the middle of Eldorth's lands?" asked Mrs Longton, with concern.

"Yes, it's dangerous, of course, but I'm running a small reconnaissance unit here, working to gather information about Eldorth's movements. We've got the assistance of some of our nearest allies working with us, some of whom are the woodland fairies who found you here in the woods," said Elenya, glancing over and smiling in the direction of Fionnella and her companions, still standing at the door. The fairies bowed to Elenya and Lizzie and then backed respectfully out of the room, closing the door behind them.

Elenya then turned back towards the table at the other people standing around it and indicated another fairy standing there. He was a little taller and stronger in build than the fairies who had escorted Lizzie and her friends, and his wings appeared less delicate but more robust with more vibrant colours.

"This is Prince Finnion," introduced Elenya. "He and his people have given us their support in trying to retrieve the Harp of Elvyth which we know is being held somewhere here in Maladorth. Prince Finnion and his people are very important and trusted allies to us elves. Their magic is invaluable to our cause. Theirs is very old and powerful magic; even great wizards or witches find it difficult to deal with," she said, with a smile at the Prince.

Prince Finnion bowed his head at Lizzie and her companions and they bowed theirs in return.

Lizzie looked across at the other individuals standing around the table; they were an eclectic bunch. Apart from the fairy - Prince Finnion - there was a dwarf; a short creature with big pointed ears and nose and a warty complexion; a tall thin creature with green skin; another with goat-like ears; and another elf, this time a male. Upon seeing him, Lizzie gasped in surprise.

"Elwood! What are you doing here?" she exclaimed. Elrus, Max and Mrs Longton seemed surprised too as they stared at the elf.

Elenya laughed and the elf smiled as he bowed his head in respect to Lizzie.

"Begging your pardon, ma'am," said the elf. "But I am not Elwood. My name is Elwind. Elwood is my twin brother."

"Oh, I'm sorry but you look so like Elwood," Lizzie apologised.

"So I am told, ma'am," grinned Elwind. "It is said that we are identical but may I say that this is only in looks," he continued, looking up at Elenya as if sharing a secret joke.

Elenya then introduced Lizzie and her friends to the rest of the company around the table. "Gentlemen, as you will already have gathered, this is my niece, Princess Elizabeth," said Elenya, sweeping her arm towards Lizzie by way of introduction. She then introduced Mrs Longton, Elrus and Max. "And this is?" she said, suddenly realising that she hadn't actually been introduced to Eloise.

"I am Eloise, Your Highness, daughter of Elroy of Elcarib," Eloise explained, curtseying once more.

"Pleased to meet you Eloise, I've heard much of your father. He is a good and brave ally. Now, may I introduce you to the rest of my brave band of comrades," Elenya said grandly, bowing her head in respect to the young elf. "You've already been introduced to Prince Finnion and Elwind," she announced. "Now may I introduce, Gorin of Goblin folk," she said, bowing in the direction of the short warty creature, with a big nose and ears.

"Your Highness," bowed the Goblin, his ears flapping as he bent forward. He had a strange high-pitched voice with a gruff edge to it. He then bowed to each of Lizzie's companions in turn and they bowed their heads at him in reply. This process continued with the others around the table as Elenya introduced, Digby the dwarf, who was a chief excavator (something to do with digging mines and tunnels) for the dwarf King; Willo the green-skinned wood sprite, and, last but not least - as Elenya put it - Flaxon the faun. As the faun stepped out from behind the table to bow to Lizzie and the others, she saw that as well as his goat-like ears, the creature also had the distinctive legs to match and tucked in a belt around his middle where she could see a set of wooden pan-pipes.

Tearing her eyes away from the unusual creature before her, Lizzie asked, "How did you know we were here?"

"Ahh!" grinned Elenya. "That's a little bit of our own magic," she laughed. "Come and see." Then, putting an arm around Lizzie's shoulder, she pulled her towards her. Elenya then took out a long silver chain hanging around her neck from under her jerkin. Hanging from the chain was a large silver locket, richly engraved with swirling and intricate patterns. It was beautiful and Lizzie had seen one exactly like it before.

"I've got a locket like that," she cried, looking closely at it. Then, looking up Elenya, she said in a small voice, "It used to be my mother's but I've never been able to open it."

Elenya nodded and smiled sadly. "Our father gave them to us when our mother left us. It was only right that you received your mother's when she left you. There's a special technique to opening it, I'll show you," she explained.

"But my mother didn't leave. She died," Lizzie said, almost matter of factly. Elenya seemed to wince at the word and seeing the pained look on her aunt's face suddenly made Lizzie feel acutely sad. She didn't remember ever having such an overwhelming feeling of sadness about her mother before. Of course Lizzie had missed her mother, or at least the thought of her, but she had never known Ria, other than being told about her by her grandmother or seeing photos of her in old albums. Because of that, Lizzie never really felt nor thought about the loss of a mother she had never known. Lizzie's grandmother had always been like her mother anyway.

Maybe now because she was in the presence of her mother's sister, who was looking down at her with such sad eyes, Lizzie suddenly felt as though a huge hole had opened up in her chest and exposed her heart to the reality of her situation. A great sob threatened to escape her throat and she swallowed it back down.

Elenya smiled at her gently. "We never say die," she said softly. "We just say that our loved ones have left us for a while. They've travelled on to another place and one day we'll be reunited with them. In time you'll come to understand that."

Mrs Longton watched the two of them with a surge of emotion. She was overwhelmed by what was unfolding before her. Elenya was closer to Lizzie's mother than anyone else because she shared the same blood. However, the eyes were different. Elenya's were a deep brown compared to Ria's blue, and there was a slightly different tilt to Elenya's nose and she seemed more confident and in control, whereas Ria had always been more gentle and vulnerable. But this young woman's likeness to Ria was unmistakable.

"Come, let me show you that magic of ours," grinned Elenya, squeezing Lizzie's shoulder tight and bringing both Lizzie and Mrs Longton back to the present. She took the silver locket in her hand and, showing Lizzie the clasp on the locket, rubbed her thumb over it three times and flipped it open with her thumb nail.

On one side of the locket, Lizzie could see a picture of her own mother. In the frame on the opposite side of the locket was a picture of King Elfred; his warm and friendly face smiled out at them. Elenya lifted the locket to her lips and kissed the picture of her father. When she lowered the locket for Lizzie to see, the picture had faded and all that could be seen was a blank frame. Gradually, something began to appear; like one those instant polaroid photographs where the image slowly comes into view, and she could see her grandfather's face once more. But this time, it wasn't just a picture because it was moving. Lizzie looked at the locket in surprise. She wasn't sure she could take many more surprises today. That was until the moving picture spoke to her.

"Hello there, Elizabeth," said King Elfred.

"Grandfather!" exclaimed Lizzie, her eyes flying wide open.

"Yes, it's me," he announced unnecessarily, looking out at her in evident relief. Then his face became more serious.

"I've been very worried about you all. When Marvin and I came back to his rooms and discovered that you had all travelled over the Threshold, we had grave concerns for your safety. Really, Elizabeth, you have got to be more careful. Your reckless curiosity is going to land you in real trouble. What did I tell you as you left the Grand Council?" he scolded.

"I'm sorry grandfather, but it was an accident. We didn't know what was behind Marvin's curtain. We just thought the door would lead to another room; we'd no idea it'd bring us here. It wasn't until Max explained about the Threshold that we realised what had happened," she gabbled in way of explanation.

Her grandfather's expression softened a little. "Well, be that as it may, it was fortunate that you arrived where you did. I was able to contact Elenya so that she could send out a party of our good friends, the woodland fairies, to find you. I don't want to think about what would have happened if Eldorth's people had found you first," he shuddered.

Mrs Longton leant over the locket to speak to the King. "Hello there, Your Majesty," she said, smiling at the man in the locket.

The King inclined his head in acknowledgement. "Mrs Longton."

"We're very sorry for the trouble we've caused. It was my fault for opening the door and then we all sort of tripped over ourselves and fell through it and found ourselves here. I should really have stopped the children from searching through Marvin's papers in the first instance. I can only apologise, but I have to say I was as curious as them to find out more," she said, apologetically.

"Well, fortunately there's been no harm done as far as we know but we need to arrange for you to get to the nearest Threshold and returned here as soon as possible," said the King. Mrs Longton decided this wasn't the time to tell him that they had had another close encounter with a pterotorial. The King asked to speak to his daughter and Elenya took the locket once more and looked at her father.

"Yes, dad?" she said cheerily.

"I trust you to take care of Elizabeth and her companions. Eloise's father is most concerned about her safety. You need to get them all back here and out of Eldorth's reach immediately. Do you understand Elenya?" he said firmly.

"Yes dad, you've made your point. We'll get them back a.s.a.p.," she said, winking at Lizzie and making a sharp salute with her hand to her father. Lizzie grinned. She liked Elenya already, she was sure that they were going to be good friends.

King Elfred made his goodbyes and his image faded from the locket to be replaced by the original portrait that had been there. Lizzie was impressed with the locket and said so to Elenya.

"Yep, it's pretty neat. It means that I can speak to my dad whenever I need to," she said cheerfully.

"How do you know when he wants to speak to you?" Lizzie asked.

"When you usually feel the locket it is cold to the touch, see," explained Elenya, offering the locket for Lizzie to feel. "If the King's trying to get in contact, then the locket glows warm and vibrates. I always keep it close to my skin so that I know when I'm needed by my dad," she said, closing her hand around the locket lovingly.

"Does my locket have any pictures in it, do you think?" asked Lizzie, thoughtfully.

"Oh yes, there should be pictures of the King and myself in it," nodded Elenya.

"Does he have a locket too then?" asked Lizzie, who thought that lockets were a bit girly.

Elenya laughed. "No, he doesn't have a locket. He has a ring that he can open the front of and it has a picture of me and one of Elethria, that does the same thing," she explained. "Anyway, as he said we should set about getting you home to him as soon as possible," she said, quickly changing the subject. The thought of Elethria not being there to use her locket made her sad.

Lizzie felt her heart sink a little. "Can we just stay for a bit and find out what you're doing?" she asked, trying to hide her disappointment. She had only just met Elenya and wanted to spend more time with her. Elrus nodded enthusiastically in agreement.

"Well, okay," said Elenya, hesitantly, looking at them both. "Just a short time then or I'll be getting into trouble," she smiled.

Mrs Longton whispered urgently in Lizzie's ear. "I'm not sure that staying longer is a good idea, Lizzie," she hissed. "I think we should get as far away as possible from Eldorth." Her brow was furrowed in concern for her own and the children's safety.

"Oh gran! Come on, where's your sense of adventure gone?" Lizzie whispered excitedly.

"It disappeared when I discovered that we have an evil elf bent on harming you, miss," Mrs Longton replied with a worried look.

Back at the table, Elenya invited the company to continue their perusal of the documents spread out before them.

"This is a map of Maladorth," she explained, bending over and pointing to a diagram on a huge sheet of parchment. Then, indicating a large square block, she said, "this is Eldorth's castle and we're over here," she said, pointing to what was evidently the woods that they were currently underneath. Standing up straight, Elenya went on.

"This line here," she said, pointing to a dotted line leading from the woods towards the castle, "is a tunnel that Digby and his brethren have been digging over the past few months. We've managed to reach under the castle and are waiting the opportunity to enter it when Eldorth and his henchmen are distracted. We know that the Harp of Elvyth is secreted away somewhere in a dungeon deep in the castle."

"How do you know that?" asked Elrus, looking Elenya in the eye.

"Let's just say we have, what you might call, a mole in the castle," and seeing the quizzical look on the children's faces, grinned and explained, "One of our people is posing as a recruit to Eldorth's cause." Elrus looked impressed; Max less so.

"Isn't that very dangerous for that person," said Max, shuddering at the thought. He was only here by accident, the thought of volunteering to go into the enemy's den was terrifying to him.

"Yes, so the sooner we get on with the task in hand, that is to rescue the Harp, the sooner we can get our agent out," Elenya said, briskly.

Digby then spoke for the first time. He had a deep resonant voice that seemed to reflect the fact that he dug deep resonant tunnels. "We've managed to tunnel through some pretty tough granite and rock to reach the castle. Due to my men being some of the best engineering miners on the planet, we've done that undetected," he rumbled proudly.

"We've also created an entrance through the castle floor which is protected from detection by fairy magic," interjected Prince Finnion, as if he wanted to ensure that the contribution of his own people didn't go unrecognised. "After we've breached the castle, all being well, we should be able to reseal the entrance so that our enemy cannot enter our base."

"May I just ask something," asked Max, shyly. Elenya nodded her assent.

"What about Melificent? We know that she's working with Duke Eldorth and I guess she's in the castle, so won't her magic be able to counteract that of the fairies?" Max suggested. Prince Finnion looked at Max sternly, his wings shivering in slight indignation at such impertinence. Questioning fairy magic indeed!

Elenya answered, "Our intelligence is such that we are given to understand that Melificent is experiencing, shall we say - a slight malfunction in the magic department. There have, apparently, been a number of instances where Melificent's magic has let her down and Eldorth is not best pleased." Elenya and her colleagues smiled in satisfaction. "She and Eldorth are totally unaware that their enemies are just beneath them," she laughed.

"Duke Eldorth has been throwing a few tantrums because of it. Oh, I'd have loved to have been a fly on the wall at those altercations," cackled Gorin, gleefully.

"So there's discord in the enemy camp," crowed Mrs Longton, clapping her hands together. "Wonderful. That's how you bring them to their knees." The company looked at her with interest.

"My dad was a Colonel in the army. He used to talk strategy over the dinner table. Divide and fall, he always said," she explained. Elenya smiled and nodded in agreement.

"We're just waiting to create a diversion in order to entice some of Eldorth's troops out of the castle so as to weaken his defences. We know that the Harp is guarded, but we understand that it's only by a couple of stupid hill-trolls. Eldorth will not believe anyone could possibly enter his castle undetected and under his very nose," Elenya continued, smiling widely.

"Hill-trolls?" queried Lizzie. She'd never heard of such things.

"They're smaller than mountain-trolls," explained Elenya. "Hill-trolls should be a bit easier to handle. Mountain-trolls on the other hand would have been much more difficult to deal with. They may be stupid but, as their name suggests, they're big and lumbering and can cause serious damage if they tread or fall on you. Anyway, if we can cause a diversion then hopefully we can penetrate the castle and retrieve the Harp with as little fuss as possible." Just as Elenya said this, there was an urgent rap on the door and, before Elenya could call enter, Fionnella had entered the room at a run.

"Your Highness," she said slightly breathlessly, as if she'd been running, and quickly bowed her head. "It would seem that Duke Eldorth has received news of our visitors. He

233

has sent out bands of his men to search the vicinity for them. There are groups of ogres and hobgoblins and the likes thumping and crashing around the woods and countryside hereabouts," she went on. The company standing around the table looked at each other quickly and then grinned with satisfaction.

"Well my comrades in arms, this appears to be our golden opportunity. Thanks to our guest here, a suitable diversion appears to be in place," announced Elenya; and without further ado, said, "Let's go!"

Elenya and her five companions began running towards the door. Lizzie turned to her grandmother, Eloise, Elrus and Max and, with excitement etched on her face, said in almost a whisper, "Come on!"

Lizzie and Elrus began following the others but as she turned to run her grandmother grabbed her arm. "No, Lizzie," she hissed. "It's too dangerous. You're going to do as you're told this time and I'm not letting you go." Lizzie pulled her arm away sharply.

"I have to gran," she said, determinedly. "I just have to. I feel it in my bones that this is something I must do."

Mrs Longton looked at her with a mixture of uncertainty and pride. In the few days that they had spent in this world of elves and fairies, goblins and dwarfs, Lizzie had changed. It was as if she had suddenly found her place in life - she fitted in with these people - Mrs Longton could see that now. She looked at Lizzie resignedly and realised that she had to let this new Lizzie go a little. Lizzie had a destiny in this new world and part of it was for her to follow her instincts. Mrs Longton smiled at her sadly, "Okay, darling. If you really feel this is what you must do; I'll wait here for you. I'm too old and slow and I'll only hold you up. Please be careful, though. Make sure you do as you're told and don't do anything silly."

Lizzie looked at her grandmother and smiled and then threw herself in Mrs Longton's arms. "Don't worry gran, I'll be fine, honest," she said reassuringly. Mrs Longton kissed the top of Lizzie's head and let her go.

Lizzie looked at Eloise, sadly. "I guess you ought to stay here too, Eloise, where it's safe. Like my grandfather said, your dad's really worried about you. He'd go nuts if anything happened to you." Eloise looked at Lizzie and raised herself up to her full height in indignation.

"If you think you're going to get all the excitement and leave me out then you're very much mistaken," she said and strode across the room to join Elrus at the door. Lizzie then turned to Max who was hanging back, next to Mrs Longton, looking very unsure of himself.

"Well, Max. Are you coming?" Lizzie urged. Max looked from Lizzie, to Elrus, to Mrs Longton, and back to Lizzie again. Every fibre in his body wanted to avoid this but every one of those fibres knew that he could not. He had promised the King that he, along with Elrus, would protect Lizzie to the best of his ability. Taking a deep breath, he stepped forward, taking a little wooden wand out of his pocket as he did so.

"Well, here goes then," Max said swallowing hard. Then, with shaky legs, he joined the raiding party.

Chapter 22 – Unto the Breach

Following close behind, Lizzie, Elrus, Eloise and Max saw Elenya and her companions run into a room further back along the corridor, through which they had come earlier. They could hear the commotion of people running about and instructions being called. As the children reached the door to the room that Elenya had just entered, they could see that she and the others were putting on various bits of protection and weapons. There were also others in the room, compatriots of Elenya and her colleagues.

Lizzie watched as Elenya slung a quiver of arrows across her back and a short-bow over her shoulder. Prince Finnion had fastened a scabbard around his waist and was holding a long silver sword, the pommel of which seemed to be encrusted with glittering stones; in his other hand he held a round silver-coloured shield. Digby had armed himself with a pretty impressive looking axe, that seemed almost bigger than himself, and he was swinging it with aplomb, narrowly missing Gorin who was passing a long, deadly-looking spear from one hand to the other, as if judging its weight and balance. Elwind, on the other hand, was spinning a pair of daggers in his hands and looked as if he would be most at home performing in a ninja movie. Only Flaxon was unequipped with a weapon and seemed to be satisfied with just covering up his bare chest with ornate body-armour. Preoccupied, as the comrades were with their preparations for the foray into Eldorth's castle, they didn't appear to notice Lizzie and her companions watching them. It was Elwind who finally spotted them and whispered something to Elenya, nodding in their direction.

"Oh, no young lady," admonished Elenya, shaking her head. "I can see in your face what you're thinking and you and your friends are to stay here. Go back to your grandmother." She pointed back through the door to emphasise her point.

"Please let us come, Elenya," Lizzie begged, looking at Elenya imploringly. "I know that we can be of use. Anyway, I'm as much a princess as you are; I've just as much right to protect my country as you," she said, proudly. It didn't hurt to push home the point, she thought.

"Oh, really?" said Elenya, suppressing a smile. "As much a princess as me are you? And are you the daughter of a King?" she asked, haughtily, tongue firmly in cheek.

Lizzie flushed but stood her ground. "Well, no, but ..." she started.

"And are you used to wielding weapons and fighting battles?" Elenya continued, hands on hips.

Lizzie blushed, her cheeks burning even redder. She couldn't believe that she'd had the nerve to speak up for herself in that way. Her confidence was beginning to dwindle and she mumbled, "No, but ..."

Elenya laughed and then walked over to Lizzie and placed a hand gently on her shoulder.

"Look, Elizabeth," she began. "It's more than my life's worth to let you come with us. For one thing, my dad will kill me if anything happens to you, and secondly, Elroy will probably join him in tearing me limb from limb if anything happens to Eloise. I can't be responsible for you and your friends. I can't be distracted by looking over my shoulder for you while we're preoccupied with finding the Harp," she said kindly but firmly.

"We cannot be sure of what awaits us when we get into the castle and I can't be watching out for you four. We want to be able to get in and out of there as quickly and quietly as possible. Stealth is our strength but if that doesn't work, there may be some combat with our enemies."

"I'm good at stealth," chipped in Elrus. Max looked at him dubiously - if Elrus's crashing through the woods on the way here was his idea of stealth, they were in big trouble. Prince Finnion stepped forward.

"They could be useful, Princess," he said. Elenya looked at him sharply. He continued, "We may, as you say, be occupied with a conflict with whatever is guarding the Harp. Whilst we distract any guards, these four are small and insignificant enough to slip past unnoticed."

The children began nodding their heads enthusiastically in agreement; all except Max whose head seemed to be prevented from doing so by the large knot of fear forming in his brain and chest. Lizzie turned to Elenya and said, "Prince Finnion's right, we could maybe slip by unnoticed. I've heard that the Harp only responds to the monarch or rightful heir to the throne of Elvedom. Well, that's me isn't it? Maybe I'm meant to get the Harp back?"

Elenya looked uncertain. Flaxon was standing close by and was nodding in support of Lizzie. He then spoke for the first time and in a soft, almost soporific, voice said, "Her Highness may have a point, Princess Elenya. As Prince Finnion has suggested, the children are more likely to slip by unnoticed than any of us. Who would feel threatened by children?" Lizzie and her friends looked from him back to Elenya to see what she would say.

Then Elwind spoke. "Princess, we need to get a move on," he urged. "We're wasting time."

Elizabeth and her friends shouldn't even be there and if Elenya allowed them to go with her and her party, she knew that it would be totally against what her father would want. But there was something in the argument for letting Lizzie and her friends go with them - her common-sense told her that it was too dangerous, but in her heart she felt that somehow that it was the right thing to do. Then, seemingly having come to a decision, she straightened her shoulders, took a deep breath, and announced, "Okay."

Lizzie clapped her hands and Elrus punched the air. "Yes!" he crowed, beaming at Lizzie and Eloise in turn. Max seemed a little deflated, part of him still hoped that Elenya would see sense and send them back to Mrs Longton and then safely home.

Elenya then turned to Flaxon and said, "Well, Flaxon, you seem to be on their side so I'm placing them in your charge." Then, turning to the children, "Do you hear that? You do exactly as Flaxon says. If he says retreat, you get away on your little legs as fast as they'll go, and get yourself back down here. Do you understand?" Her brown eyes flashed as she scolded them with a wagging finger. Lizzie and her friends nodded emphatically. Max had no argument with that.

"Well, we'd better get you kitted out with some protection," Elenya announced, running a hand through her hair, and, turning to Elwind, instructed him to find the four some pieces of light armour to protect their "vital bits" as she called them.

In no time at all, Lizzie was wearing some very light metal armour that covered her upper body, leaving her arms free. She also had on a strangely shaped helmet that looked a bit like an upside-down tulip. Eloise wore something similar on her body but her helmet looked more like a pudding basin with a pair of horns sticking out of the top; it was the only one that would fit over her thick black curls. Elrus pointed at her and laughed but soon shut up as Prince Finnion plonked a conical shaped one with some sort of ear-flaps on his head. Elrus then picked up a small lethal-looking knife from a pile to one side of the room; its blade sparkled in the light from the torches on the walls. Max declined another helmet, or any weapon, but took a small, brightly painted shield and strapped it to his arm.

"I need my wand arm free," he said weakly.

Duly prepared for possible battle, the party then made their way out of the room and along the tunnel towards the point where it branched into three directions. Those at the front and the rear of the group carried torches as they went. However, Prince Finnion didn't need any artificial light as his wings seemed to glow, as if lit by some magical light from within. Lizzie thought they were beautiful and turned to see that the other fairies in the group also had luminous wings. As they reached the three way junction in the tunnel, Elenya, who was leading the group, turned and placed a finger to her lips.

"Now, remember; we're to be as quiet as possible. You're only to talk when absolutely necessary. What did I tell you?" she asked. Everyone looked at her blankly.

"Oh, come on," she sighed, impatiently. "Stealth is our strength."

A look of understanding spread across all their faces and they looked at one another, nodding. Elenya shook her head, these people were meant to be the cream of their society when it came to combat, heavens help her she thought and then, turning on her heels, she beckoned them after her.

Taking the tunnel to their left, they made their way quickly and silently along its length. The tension in the air was palpable. Lizzie felt as if all the nerve endings in her body were on edge and sending electric shocks down her arms and legs - it was not a nice feeling. She walked behind Flaxon whose goat-like feet seemed to clip-clop on the compacted earth beneath them, and she could hear Max behind her breathing heavily as he tried to gain control of his fear. She then looked at Eloise walking beside her who seemed to be concentrating on the back of Flaxon's head. Elrus seemed to be the only one thoroughly enjoying the experience; as Lizzie glanced around at him she saw him behaving like some cartoon-like spy. He was holding the small knife out in front of him, creeping and crouching along as he went.

A couple of male fairies following on behind Elrus watched him with interest, nudging each other and smirking in amusement.

Before long, the tunnel floor began to slope upwards. Although it was a gradual slope, Lizzie could feel the pull on her calf muscles as they began their slight ascent. She was beginning to wonder if perhaps she had been a little rash in pushing for herself and her friends to join the group. She was having slight difficulty breathing because of her jangling nerves and racing heart.

Suddenly Elenya raised her arm, her hand outspread as sign that they should stop. Elrus who had been too busy creeping and glancing all around for, who only knew what, hadn't noticed and crashed into Lizzie and Max, nearly bowling them over.

Lizzie reached a hand back towards Max, to steady herself, and placed it on his arm. She felt him jump at her touch and saw him look down sharply at her hand to see what it was. She smiled at him reassuringly; his body was quivering with fear. Bolstered by the fact that he was just as scared as she was, probably even more so, she took a deep breath and whispered to him.

"It's alright. We'll be okay." She wasn't sure she sounded convincing but it helped her just to voice the words. Max looked at her with his big, blue, frightened eyes. She obviously hadn't convinced him; he was still trembling like a leaf.

"What's happened? Why've we stopped?" hissed Elrus.

"Well, if you stopped messing around playing spies, you'd have seen that Elenya's called us to a halt. I guess we must be at the entrance to the castle," whispered Lizzie, over her shoulder.

As she said this she could see Prince Finnion move ahead of Elenya and reach up and place the palms of his hands on the ceiling of the tunnel. Lizzie assumed he must be hovering off the floor in order to touch the ceiling, as he wasn't that tall, but because of the others of the reconnaissance party in front of them, she was unable to see for sure.

A grating noise reverberated around the tunnel and a sliver of light began to filter through a crack that had appeared just where the Prince's hands had been. Lizzie held her breath as a large square gap in the ceiling gradually materialised. She watched as Prince Finnion seemed to hover above them, putting his head slowly through the gap.

Looking back down at them, he called in hushed tones, "It's all clear. Let's go." And with that, he disappeared up through the hole. Elenya quickly followed, deftly hoisting herself up, then she and Prince Finnion reached down and helped pull up the others; Elwind, Gorin and Digby disappeared in quick succession, followed by a couple of fairies who didn't need their help, and then Flaxon. As Lizzie reached the gap, she raised her arms above her head and felt her hands grabbed by Elenya and Prince Finnion and she was swiftly lifted out of the tunnel only to find herself in yet another one. She had the fleeting thought that she seemed to have spent a lot of the past few days in one tunnel or another.

In quick succession, the remainder of the reconnaissance party hauled, flew or hoisted themselves through the gap in the tunnel floor. Elenya ran and Prince Finnion flew quickly along the tunnel until they reached a corner that turned off at 90 degrees to their right. At the corner they pushed themselves flat against the wall, and beckoned the rest of the group to follow. As the others reached them, Elenya put her finger to her lips to ensure that everyone stayed silent and then whispered urgently.

"Quiet," she hushed, cupping a hand to her ear. "I can hear someone approaching."

Prince Finnion withdrew his sword from its scabbard and the others held their weapons in readiness for any fight that might ensue. Lizzie could hear the soft padding of footsteps coming quickly along the tunnel to their right. It didn't sound much like what she imagined a troll to sound like; that would surely sound more like an elephant, she thought. Elenya suddenly smiled, she seemed to realise who it probably was, just as a young elven girl appeared from out of the shadows.

"Ella," Elenya greeted the girl warmly and Ella dipped in a deep curtsey.

"Your Highness," she said in reply. She had a sheet of white blond hair that fell down her back and her young pointed face was pale. She was neither pretty nor plain; in fact her face had no discernible features to make her memorable. Even her hair, which would be a striking feature in the human-world, would have been common place in this world. It occurred to Lizzie that Ella was probably ideal for spying as she would likely go almost unnoticed, or at least be difficult to remember, wherever she went in this Kingdom.

"Are you all right? Are you still safe?" Elenya asked the girl; concern etched on her face.

"Yes, ma'am. I am fine but I must be quick before I am missed," whispered the girl, quickly. "You got the message that Duke Eldorth has sent out hunting parties for someone who has trespassed into his lands. His heavies are thundering around the place looking for them. No-one knows who they are. I've heard that Melificent cannot identify them and this has made Duke Eldorth very angry. He is much pre-occupied

243

with this at present and so you must act quickly before he becomes aware of what is happening. If you go along the passageway here to the end it goes in two directions." She pointed back along the tunnel from whence she had come.

"Go left and then down the first passage to your right. There you will find doors to a number of dungeons; the Harp is in the third dungeon on the left. The Harp is guarded by two hill-trolls but I do not know what else protects it. I've heard that Melificent may have used some enchantments but that has been kept a closely guarded secret and I have been unable to discover what those enchantments may be. I am sorry for that." The girl finished and bowed her head to Elenya.

"You have done well, Ella, and for that I thank you on behalf of us all. You have taken great risks and you will be well rewarded. Now get yourself down the gap there," Elenya said, indicating the hole in the tunnel floor that they had all just come out of, "and keep safe."

The girl curtsied again but shook her head. "Thank you, ma'am," she began, "but if you will permit me, I will stay longer. I can still find out things that may be of use regarding the other sacred relics. Duke Eldorth does not suspect me and if I suddenly disappear he'll realise it was me that gave you the information to retrieve the Harp. It will then be difficult to get another spy to infiltrate his castle, as he will distrust anyone new who comes here. At the moment he seems not to notice me, as I appear no threat. I would like to think that my acting skills are such that he thinks I adore him." She smiled, shyly.

Elenya and the others grinned. "You are a brave and valued subject, Ella, and we owe you a huge debt of gratitude," Elenya said with feeling. She was concerned for the girl's safety but what she said made a lot of sense; Ella would still be a valuable asset to have in Eldorth's inner-circle.

"You have my permission to stay," Elenya continued. "But if at any time you believe yourself to be in danger of discovery, you must leave and leave quickly. Do I have your word?"

"Of course, ma'am," beamed Ella, proudly. "I will not fail you."

"Then you must get back before we go any further. Go quick," Elenya urged the girl, and with another brief curtsey, the girl hurried lightly back along the passageway and out of sight.

When the sound of Ella's footsteps could no longer be heard, the group proceeded to run quickly and silently along the passageway that Ella had disappeared from. At each corner of the route to the dungeons the little band stopped and listened for any signs of Eldorth's henchmen, but they were met with nothing but an eerie silence. Finally, they approached the passage that Ella had described. They crept towards it quickly and silently; even Max was impressed at how quiet Elrus could be when the need arose.

Elenya raised an arm to call the group to a halt. With her back to the passage wall, she peered gingerly around the corner into the passageway with the dungeon holding the Harp. To her surprise, there was no sign of the hill-troll guards that Ella had warned them of. Elenya turned back to the group.

"There's no-one here," she hissed, over her shoulder. "I'm not sure what's going on. Trolls aren't the brightest of creatures, so it's unlikely they will have been allowed to control their own movements. Maybe they've been deployed to one of Eldorth's search parties or maybe they're inside the dungeon to heighten the security of the Harp," she said uncertainly.

Prince Finnion suggested that Elenya and he approach the dungeon alone and if it looked safe enough, the others

245

should follow. Elenya nodded in agreement. So, the two of them ran forward and threw themselves either side of the door to the third dungeon on the left. Peering through a small grill in the door, Elenya thought at first that the cell was empty, but then she saw at the back of it a slight glow and swirling greenish purple mist. Through the mist she could just make out the shape of a small wooden object sitting on a plinth – it was the Harp! Her heart pounded with excitement, it was within their reach.

The noise of Elenya's heart beating in her ears was suddenly drowned out by another pounding. The sounds of several pairs of heavy feet, thumping along the tunnel, were coming in their direction. Before either Elenya or Prince Finnion could react, a group of about half a dozen or so assorted hill-trolls, ogres and hobgoblins came around the corner to their left. They stopped and looked at the intruders with blank expressions, as if the sight of them hadn't quite registered, and then they suddenly seemed to realise that Elenya and Prince Finnion shouldn't be there.

As quick as lightening, Elenya had loaded and drawn her bow and let fly a volley of arrows. A hobgoblin running at the front of the pack took an arrow straight in the throat and fell to the ground, dead before he hit it. Prince Finnion had drawn his sword and was wielding it with expert ease. Hearing the kerfuffle going on around the corner to where they were hiding, Digby stuck his head around and saw what was happening.

"Fight!" he yelled, swinging his axe over his head dangerously, and charged around the corner, pushing Lizzie and her friends to one side. He was immediately followed by Gorin and the rest of the group, all wielding their various weapons ahead of them.

Lizzie had been pushed to the other side of the passageway and Eloise had been knocked over in the rush. A shocked looking Max helped Eloise to her feet and helped her brush herself down. Elrus peered around the corner to see the skirmish that was ensuing there. It was difficult to see exactly what was happening but he could see a number of the fairies buzzing around, beating what looked like an ogre around the head with small maces, whilst the troll swatted at them as if they were irritating flies. The fighting was fierce. Elrus's face looked white when he turned back to Lizzie, Eloise and Max.

"Well, this isn't fun," Max said, quietly.

"These things never are," said a quiet voice, and the children turned to see Flaxon was standing just behind them. He was looking at them with his gentle brown eyes, his pan-pipes in his hand.

"What shall we do?" asked a frightened Lizzie, turning to Flaxon.

"We should wait until our comrades have either killed the group of guards or beaten them back sufficiently enough for us to safely make our way to the dungeon," he said. Then he poked his head around the corner to view the fight that was going on there. He told the children that their group appeared to be beating the guards back and away from the dungeon.

"Come," he suddenly said, urgently. "We must go now, whilst everyone is distracted."

As the children followed the faun, they could see the fight continuing further along the passageway. There was a lot of yelling and roaring, and Lizzie thought that either Eldorth or Melificent should surely hear what was happening. Lizzie didn't have too long to dwell on the thought before they reached the dungeon containing the Harp.

Flaxon tried to turn the large iron ring catch that secured the door of the dungeon, but it would not budge. Elrus grabbed it and started rattling it furiously in an attempt to get it to open.

"There's no point doing that. It must be sealed by magic," said Flaxon.

"Oh, where's a fairy when you need one?" pouted Eloise.

"I think they're a bit pre-occupied at the moment," said Elrus, sarcastically.

Lizzie turned to Max who was standing back a little mesmerised by the fight that was still in full flow along the passageway.

"Max, can you help? You said you've been learning magic. You opened that door to the secret anti-room near the Grand Council Chamber," she said, shaking him by the arm. He tore his eyes away from the fight scene and looked at her.

"I don't know if my magic's strong enough here; I mean, I am still an apprentice," he said, hesitantly.

"Well, it's worth a go, isn't it?" pushed Lizzie. "We've really got to hurry. The quicker we retrieve the Harp, the sooner our friends up there can beat a retreat." The others all looked at Max expectantly.

"Her Highness is quite right, Master Max," said Flaxon. "It is better to have tried and failed than not to try at all."

Max took out his small wooden wand and, taking a deep breath, pointed it shakily at the lock on the door. Closing his eyes, he muttered something under his breath whilst Lizzie, Eloise and Elrus watched on with bated breath, casting the odd fleeting glimpse at the fight to make sure the enemy hadn't broken through.

Max opened his eyes and looked at the lock on the door. Nothing seemed to have happened. There had been no clunking of catches springing back or any other evidence that the spell he had just said had worked. Elrus tried turning the ringed handle again but it didn't shift. The children

248

looked deflated with disappointment. Then Flaxon said softly, "You are too tense, Master Max."

"Well, it's not really surprising, given the circumstances," snapped Elrus, irritably.

"Elrus!" reproached Lizzie, at Elrus's rudeness to Flaxon.

Flaxon looked at Elrus with gentle eyes; he seemed to have taken no offence at having been spoken to so abruptly. "It is alright, Your Highness, these are indeed difficult circumstances."

"Sorry, Flaxon but I'm just a teensy bit tense myself," Elrus apologised, and then turning to Max said, "Come on mate. Have another go. Just take a couple of deep breaths."

Flaxon spoke gently to Max and looked deep into the boy's blue eyes with his own hazel ones.

"Your magic cannot flow through you if you are too tense. Your brain and muscles will fight against the magic, and you need them to loosen if the magic you wield is to be released. You are a channel for magic so you must relax and feel it within you. I'm sure your master has told you this," Flaxon said softly. Max nodded.

"Maybe I can help you a little," Flaxon continued. With that, he took his pan-pipes from his belt and placed them to his lips.

A beautiful, haunting melody flowed from the pipes and Max seemed to visibly relax. His shoulders, which had been hunched up around his ears most of the time that they'd been in Maladorth, began to loosen and lower. His face took on a less pained look and his breath, that had been going in and out in short sharp pants, began to slow and deepen. He loosened his arms and gave them a little shake as the tension in them released. The other children also felt more relaxed and a little less terrified of their situation.

"So what if there are big scary ogres and hill-trolls fighting our friends," thought Lizzie, as she watched Max loosen up. She was feeling less worried about their situation with every note Flaxon played. The thoughts suddenly disappeared as the music stopped.

Flaxon turned to Max and said, "Now, try again, Master Max."

Max raised his wand to the catch of the door and repeated the spell as before. This time, however, he felt a tingle as the spell left his body and was channelled along the thin piece of hazel wood in his hand. It seemed to vibrate slightly with the energy of the spell, and then he heard the clunk of the catches holding the door fast, fly back. He looked up at Flaxon and grinned broadly. Lizzie had never seen him smile like that before, as he always seemed to be wearing a worried frown; the smile transformed his face.

"Thanks Flaxon," Max whispered.

"You are welcome but quickly now," Flaxon urged, bowing his head slightly to Max in acknowledgment of his gratitude. The little group pushed open the dungeon door and found themselves in a cell, about five metres by five, and sitting on a plinth at the back of it was a small wooden harp. They all stopped and stared at it in awe.

Chapter 23 – The Harp of Elvyth

Lizzie had expected the Harp to be much more ornate; gold or silver or some other precious metal at least and encrusted with diamonds or something. Not this shabby, ancient, insignificant looking wooden object. The Harp was also quite small, which she supposed she should have realised it would be; if the Ode to Elvyth was right he would have had to carry it from one place to another. A glowing greenish-purplish mist swirled like smoke around the Harp and through its strings.

"It's a bit of a let-down, isn't it? I mean look at it." Elrus nodded towards the sacred object. He had voiced Lizzie's own thoughts and she suddenly felt guilty at feeling slightly disappointed.

"We should not always go by appearances. Even the most insignificant looking things can have hidden depths and qualities," said Flaxon wisely.

"Well, standing here looking at it isn't going to get it out of here is it?" Lizzie whispered, hastily. "It looks like we might need your help again, Max," she said. Max nodded. As Lizzie watched him, she saw that Max seemed to be considering his next step.

Flaxon made a suggestion. "The Harp is under a protection enchantment. You will probably need to counteract that with some protection enchantment of your own," he said. Max's eyes widened as a look of sudden inspiration appeared to have dawned in him.

"You're right!" he said, then turned to Lizzie. "Your Highness, as the rightful heir to the throne of Elvedom, only you should rescue the Harp. Something bad might happen if one us tries to touch it. I believe that if I place a protection spell upon you, you may be able to enter the enchanted area surrounding the Harp." He then turned to the others.

251

"I remember that one of the first lessons my master taught me was the importance of friendship and its protective values. Do you remember the King saying something about it at the Grand Council that time?" Lizzie, Elrus and Eloise nodded in unison; they had all thought that what the King had said had sounded a bit obscure at the time, but it must have meant something for him to have said it all.

"Well, to put the protection spell on Her Highness, she must stand in the middle of us with us all linking hands around her, and we must channel thoughts of our friendship and care of her towards her," Max explained. "This will strengthen the spell tenfold and should, hopefully, last long enough for her to enter the mist and retrieve the harp. Now, I just hope that I can remember the spell. I've only used it once or twice when I was trying to protect the odd piece of fruit I'd taken for a snack so that Mag or Pi didn't steal it."

Lizzie's eyes snapped up to his face, in horror. "I'm a bit bigger than a banana!" she cried. "I hope this works. What'll happen if the spell hasn't worked and I step into that mist? My grandparents won't be happy if I get shrivelled up into a prune or something." A trickle of fear ran through her, sending a shiver down her spine, and she wasn't sure she really wanted to go through with the plan now.

"You must have faith, my lady," Flaxon, interjected with his soft voice. "As before, you must all relax so that the magic can flow. I shall do my best to help you again."

Lizzie decided that she had got them into this situation by her impetuousness, and so there was nothing to do now but go through with it. She could still hear the fight going on in the passageway outside the dungeon and it felt that they had been in there for hours, although, in reality, it was only minutes.

"Well," she said, taking a deep breath, "let's get on with it."

The three friends, Elrus, Max and Eloise, linked hands around Lizzie, who stood in the middle of the little group looking like a frightened rabbit. "What am I doing?" she kept thinking to herself. Then Flaxon began to play his pipes again; the soft and haunting music flowed over them like a warm blanket, relaxing the children's muscles and slowing their breathing. Lizzie felt herself becoming calm and her doubts ebbing away. Max began murmuring the words of the spell under his breath; his words were indistinct to Lizzie's ears and seemed to blur into each another - it must be old elvish or something, she thought to herself dreamily.

A tingling sensation began to surge through Lizzie's body and she felt almost as if she were floating above herself, looking down on the scene below. She closed her eyes for a moment; it was a very strange feeling. Then suddenly she was back down inside herself and feeling immensely strong, as if nothing could ever physically hurt her again. Her eyes snapped open and she looked at her three friends, who seemed to have become slightly faint in appearance, as if some of their energy had been sapped from them. They looked at her with tired but almost adoring eyes, and she was surprised to feel an intense feeling of love for each of them. She smiled reassuringly at them.

"I think it's worked," she announced; her voice sounding strange and distant. Elrus, Max and Eloise, released their hands and grinned weakly back at her. The experience for them had been draining, and they needed her to do what she had to do quickly so that they could get out of that dungeon and back to safety.

Flaxon seemed to understand that Lizzie needed to work fast and, turning to her, said, "You must go now, Princess. When you enter the mists you must call the Harp to you. You must assert your power over it - it should respond. Go, and good luck!"

Lizzie walked towards the Harp and watched as the mist that protected it snaked its way around it. Then turning once more to take a final look at her friends Lizzie took a step into the swirling unknown.

The last thought Lizzie had as she stepped into the mist was; if gran and grandfather knew what I was doing right now, they'd have a fit. Any further thoughts of her grandparents were squeezed from her mind by the mist pressing in upon her body. Lizzie felt as if she were trying to walk through dense, sticky treacle that clung to every part of her, making walking and breathing difficult. She looked through the swirling vapours at the Harp and it seemed much further away than it had before she'd entered the mist; it was like looking through churning water.

Lizzie concentrated her mind on the Harp and took slow, deep breaths as she moved slowly forward, her hands outstretched. Oxygen was obviously getting through to her lungs because she still felt strong and clear minded. Staring at the Harp, she thought she saw it shudder a little; its strings seemed to be vibrating, but she could hear no noise coming from it. As she ploughed her way through the mist, she kept her hands outstretched towards it. Wondering if telepathy would work, she began to call to the Harp with her mind. Should she say the words out loud, she thought, or was the Harp magical enough to respond to her thoughts. The Harp continued to stubbornly sit on its plinth; telepathy didn't seem to be working.

Lizzie then decided that she should try calling to it out loud. "Harp," she called, quietly. Then, a little louder, she called again, "Harp; Harp of Elvyth." The Harp seemed to vibrate more and she could hear a humming noise coming through the thick, soupy mist. What should she say to make it come to her? Flaxon had told her to summon it to her.

"Harp of Elvyth, come to me," she called, beckoning it with her hands, as if it would suddenly fly through the mist and into her arms. Would it do that? she wondered. She tried again.

"Harp of Elvyth, come to me, Elizabeth, the rightful heir of Elvedom." She tried to make her voice as commanding as possible. It seemed to have an effect as the Harp began to vibrate quite violently; the humming sound intensified. As it did so, Lizzie felt as if the mist that was holding her back was beginning to thin and she could move more freely. The humming noise seemed to form itself into a tune of sorts.

She repeated the words and the Harp responded again, only even more vigorously. Lizzie felt a huge sense of satisfaction. She felt confident that the Harp would allow her to take it. She kept repeating the words and each time the mist became clearer and thinner, until she found herself standing right in front of the Harp looking down at it. It was humming and vibrating, as if in a state of excitement, and Lizzie's own body seemed to be responding in kind. She felt as though every nerve in her body was buzzing.

Lizzie took a deep breath and steadied herself, "Well it's now or never." Then, reaching out, she touched the Harp. She wasn't sure what to expect when she lifted the Harp from its plinth. Would the walls come crashing in? Would terrible monsters fly out of the dungeon walls and attack her and her friends? Would she suddenly be turned to stone? As it was, none of those things happened. The Harp just stopped its humming and vibrating and sat still in her hands as if it felt safe there.

With the Harp's protective enchantment broken, Lizzie turned and ran back through the evaporating mist where, standing near the door to the dungeon, she could see Elrus, Eloise, Max and Flaxon watching her with awed looks on their faces. Lizzie felt a strength that she had never felt before and ran towards them, shouting, "Let's go!"

The five companions hurried out of the dungeon with the Harp tucked firmly under Lizzie's arm. As they entered the passage, they could see the fight was still in full-flow and there were a number of bodies strewn on the passage floor. It was difficult to see who they belonged to, but one certainly looked big enough to be that of a troll.

Lizzie screamed out at the top of her voice, "ELENYA!"

From the fight, faces turned towards Lizzie and her friends, as if the unexpectedness of the scream had brought them out of the frenzied attack, and everyone stopped and stared. Lizzie could see Elenya's tall frame above some of the smaller bodies between them. Elenya turned her head towards Lizzie and, seeing the Harp in her arms, yelled at her comrades.

"Retreat; retreat!" Elenya yelled.

The raiding party turned as one and ran back towards Lizzie, and the whole group ran like crazy back along the passages towards the entrance to their escape tunnel. Eldorth's guards seemed confused by the suddenness of the retreat and stood still for a moment before realising what had happened. An ogre, that seemed to be in charge, then took control and yelled for one of his men to go and get more back-up before lumbering after the intruders, calling his few remaining few troops with him.

As they ran, Lizzie felt as though her feet barely touched the floor. She never knew she could run that fast and the others around her seemed to carry her and her friends along. They could hear the thundering of heavy feet behind them, and the shouts and roars of frustration as the guards tried to catch them. Before long, they were back at the gap in the floor of the passage and everyone almost fell through it, pushing Lizzie through first, quickly followed by Eloise, Max and Elrus. The others followed in rapid succession and just as Prince Finnion, the last to go through, dropped

256

through the gap, Eldorth's guards turned the corner to see his head disappear through the floor.

The first guard stood and looked confused at what was happening; his slow brain unable to make sense of what he was seeing. It gave the Prince time to close the tunnel entrance and seal it once more.

Above in the passage, the ogre seemed to come to his senses and he ran to the spot where Prince Finnion's head had been, but there was nothing there, just a solid stone-flagged floor. The ogre scrabbled at the floor trying to find something to get hold of that could prove to be a secret opening, but there was nothing. As he struggled to discover the entrance, with his companions standing watching eagerly, he didn't notice that he had other company. That was until someone said in a cold, clear voice, "What in hades name is happening here?" Eldorth stood at the corner of the tunnel, his face dark with anger and malevolence. At his side were his henchman, Orfwit, and the guard who had been sent to find backup.

"WE 'AD IN-TROO-DERS!" bellowed the ogre, still on his knees; his voice reverberated around the confines of the passageway.

Eldorth winced. "The gods, why can these creatures not lower their voices?" he thought, before seeming to realise what the ogre had said. Almost stupidly, he asked slowly, "Intruders?"

"YES LAWD! IN-TROO-DERS. THEY WAS TRYIN' TO GET INTA THE HARP!" the ogre roared.

"What!?" screamed Eldorth, finally seeming to lose his cool. Without even stopping to ask the ogre why he was scrabbling around the floor, he ran back along the passage towards to the dungeons and the precious harp, closely followed by the Orfwit and his men. As they reached the door to the dungeon, he could see it flung wide. Looking in

257

at the plinth standing empty against the far end of the cell, Eldorth dropped to his knees.

"NOOOOOOO!!!" he wailed, in despair, placing his hands over his face. Then, dropping his hands to his sides, he got slowly to his feet. His back to the dungeon, his handsome face distorted with rage, he let out a blood-curdling yell.

"MELIFICENT!"

Chapter 24 – Back Through the Threshold

Down in the tunnel beneath Eldorth's castle, the raiding party ran swiftly back to their headquarters. The fairies followed behind the group, destroying the tunnel as they went, zapping the walls with detonating spells in the unlikely event that someone should break through into it.

Lizzie and her friends almost fell through the door of the room that Mrs Longton and Mag were still occupying. The magpie, who had been sitting patiently on the back of a chair for the duration of their absence, actually seemed pleased to see them and let out a rasping caw at their reappearance and flew across the room, landing happily on Max's shoulder and nipping gently at his ear. Mrs Longton spread her arms wide to take Lizzie and the other children into an embrace.

Breaking away from Mrs Longton's hold, Elrus began jumping around the room in delight, whooping with the joy of their success and the relief at being back in the safety of their underground bolt-hole. Eloise grabbed Max's hands and started to dance a jig around the room with him, laughing and singing, Mag squawking and flapping around their heads, "We did it, we did it," as she sang. Max looked embarrassed but didn't want to spoil her fun and so let himself be dragged around the space. Lizzie watched them all, her heart fit to bursting with the pleasure of being with real friends at last.

"Oh, Lizzie, I've been so worried," said Mrs Longton, squeezing Lizzie in a tight bear hug once again. She quickly released her granddaughter as something hard and lumpy stuck into her ribs. "Ouch, what the...?" she began.

Lizzie stood back and grinned up at her. "I did it gran. I got it," she said, holding out the Harp for her grandmother to see. Mrs Longton took the small wooden object in her hands and looked at it in sharp surprise. The euphoria of the moment was short-lived as a solemn Elenya, Prince Finnion and Elwind entered the room. Elenya's face told them that something terrible must have happened and the smiles fell from their faces.

"I am sad to tell you that tragically we have lost two of our dear and brave comrades," Elenya announced.

"Oh no, that's terrible," said Mrs Longton, sadly, slumping down onto a nearby seat. Lizzie's heart leapt and her stomach turned as the reality of the conflict crashed down upon her. She had thought nothing about the deaths of Eldorth's people. They were the enemy; trolls and ogres and the like were the baddies of fairy stories she'd heard as a small child, but suddenly all killing seemed wrong. This wasn't a fairy story, this was real life, and good people as well as bad ones died when weapons were used.

"Who were they?" Lizzie asked, her voice wavering.

"Sadly, there wasn't time to introduce them to you personally before the foray," said Elenya, her voice full of emotion. "However, they were Galin of Goblin Folk, who was one of Gorin's closest aides, and also Forness, a dear and trusted kinsman of Prince Finnion."

Lizzie looked at Prince Finnion and saw the pained look on his face. He smiled sadly at her and said proudly, "Forness was a good and brave fairy. He gave his life for a great cause and we will honour him in his passing. He would not wish us to be sad, but to remember him as he was a good and honest soldier."

Together the little company bowed their heads briefly in respect. Elenya then walked towards Lizzie, who was now clasping the Harp tightly to her chest. The sadness etched in her face eased away as it broke into a dazzling smile. Like any true warrior, Elenya believed that the fallen had gone on to another place and would not be forgotten, but the living must go on.

Taking the precious harp from Lizzie, Elenya beamed down at her niece. "Well, look what you did! There will be celebrations back at Elvedom Castle tonight I think. I bet old Eldorth's having a blue fit right now. I can't wait to receive our spy Ella's report on the consequences of our little visit to his castle." She let out a loud chuckle that was so infectious that everyone laughed with her, and the ever ebullient Elrus began jumping around and whooping again.

Mrs Longton turned to Elenya. "I don't wish to be a kill-joy, Princess," she said. "But do you think it might be a good idea to get to that Threshold your father spoke of and get these children, and that harp, back to the safety of Elvedom Castle."

Elenya nodded in agreement. "You are quite right, Mrs Longton. I'm afraid I was caught up in the moment." She then turned to Lizzie and her friends and said, "It's time to get you all home, kids." Then, turning to Elwind, instructed him to go and rally the troops in order to get ready for a return to Elvedom Castle.

"Will you be coming with us?" Lizzie asked Elenya.

Elenya smiled and nodded. "Yes, I will. There's nothing more that I can do here at the moment. The Harp is retrieved and once back at Elvedom Castle, it'll be safe as Marvin has plans in place for it to be safeguarded once more. I think I could do with some rest before I go off on another of my travels," she grinned, winking knowingly at Lizzie. "But before we return, I think I ought to just let my father know what's happened. He's going to be pretty upset at how we got the Harp back, but he'll get over it. If I tell him now, he'll hopefully have got over the worst of it before we get back." She took out her locket and began walking towards the door, Prince Finnion following closely in her wake.

"So come on now, how did you manage to rescue the Harp?" asked Mrs Longton, looking quizzically at each of the children in turn.

"Well..." began Lizzie, and the four children excitedly recounted their part in the rescue of the precious object.

*

As they prepared to leave the underground headquarters, Elenya had returned and said that her discussion with her father had gone slightly better than anticipated. She said that when his shouting had reached the point where he had become almost unintelligible, she had just closed the locket.

Elenya and Elwind led the small party returning to Elvedom Castle, followed closely by Prince Finnion, Gorin, Digby and Flaxon, down the long tunnel back towards the junction where it had originally divided into three. The tunnel that had led to Eldorth's castle was now filled in and it would take anyone trying to follow several months to dig through, even if they were able to breach the secret entrance in the passage floor of the castle. No-one digs tunnels like dwarfs.

The tunnel straight ahead of them led to the entrance to the small wood through which Lizzie and her companions had originally entered the underground unit. Taking the last remaining passageway on their left, they saw that there were several doors that led off the tunnel at intervals. Entering a room to their right, they found it was empty except for a pair of deep green velvet curtains hanging against the rear wall. Elenya walked over to the curtains and drew them back, revealing a battered wooden door.

Prince Finnion, Gorin, Digby and Flaxon watched as the elves prepared to depart. Lizzie looked at each of them in turn and marvelled at the scene before her. She would never have believed, only days earlier, that she would be standing there in the company of a fairy prince, a goblin, a dwarf and a faun. She asked if they would be accompanying them back to the castle.

Flaxon spoke on their behalf. "No, Princess," he said softly. "There are things to finish here and then we will each return to our own people for a while so that we may be rested for the next phase of our battle against Duke Eldorth." Lizzie nodded in understanding and then turned to Prince Finnion and spoke to him.

"Thank you for everything," she said, shyly. "I'm so pleased to have met you and some of your people. I think fairies are wonderful." The Prince looked taken aback.

"I am glad to have met you also, Princess Elizabeth. I feel sure we will meet again one day," he said, bowing his head to her.

"Oh, I do hope so," Lizzie smiled. She then spoke briefly to Gorin telling him how sorry she was about his friend, Galin. With a straight back, the goblin thanked her for her kindness and Lizzie put out her hand to shake his. The goblin looked at it in confusion but followed suit and stuck out his gnarled, mottled hand in return; it felt warm and leathery in her palm.

Digby bowed low and said he hoped he could be of service to her in the future; Lizzie stuck out her hand to shake his. Having seen the encounter with Gorin, the little dwarf put out his hand and shook Lizzie's hand heartily, a large grin breaking out on his rugged face.

Finally, Lizzie turned to Flaxon. "Thank you so much, Flaxon, for giving us the courage to go through with our part of this adventure," she smiled up at him. Flaxon bowed his head briefly in reply.

"You are most welcome, Highness," he said in his gentle soothing voice; his soft brown eyes looking deeply into her own. "I hope I may be of assistance to you again." Then, turning towards Max, he smiled.

Max went over to the faun and put out a hand. Well, he thought, humans shook hands and it seemed as good a gesture as any to offer a friend. Flaxon smiled and took the boy's hand warmly in both of his.

"I can't thank you enough for helping me when you did, Flaxon," Max said. His voice sounded quietly confident, not as shaky and as unsure of itself as when they had first met.

"There is no need to thank me, Master Max," said Flaxon. "Just remember to always have the courage of your convictions. 'Nothing ventured, nothing gained' is a saying you would do well to remember. One day you will be a great sorcerer, just like your master, I feel sure," he smiled down at the young apprentice.

"Thanks," said Max, smiling shyly.

Elenya spoke to those being left behind. "I take my leave of you, dear friends and comrades. Thank you for your help and support in our struggle to keep this a safe and better world for all our peoples. Until we meet again," she said, and swept a low bow to them. They each bowed in return and Elenya then walked and put a hand on the handle of the battered door.

"Well, here we go," she said cheerily to Lizzie, as Mrs Longton and the children said their last goodbyes. Then, saying the words of their destination, Elenya opened the door and one by one they passed through it, with Lizzie clasping the Harp tightly as if her life depended on it.

Chapter 25 – The Heroes Return

As Lizzie, Elenya and their little group walked back over the Threshold, they found themselves once again in Marvin's rooms and there to greet them were the thunderous faces of King Elfred, Marvin, Elroy, Elmer and the King's Head of Security, Elnest. Hovering at the back of the group was Elwood, wringing his hands and looking more agitated than all the others put together.

Standing with his hands on his hips and legs apart, like an aging Peter Pan, King Elfred looked furious and Lizzie cast her eyes to the ground so as avoid to his glare. His gaze travelled over her head and fixed upon his daughter.

"Hi dad!" chirped Elenya, cheerfully. Lizzie wondered if her chirpy mood was going to be enough to throw the King off his stride. It appeared that it wasn't…

"Elenya!" he barked.

"Oh dear; are you still cross with us?" the princess asked in a babyish sounding voice, pouting her lips dramatically and looking puppy-eyed at her father. Lizzie and her friends peeked at her with sidelong glances and grinned whilst Mrs Longton's face was a picture of contrition.

"You may well all grin now that you're home and safe," stormed the King, looking at each of the children in turn. "Have you any idea how worried we've all been about you? Elizabeth you really have got to stop this reckless and troublesome behaviour. You placed yourself, and your friends here, in terrible danger. And Mrs Longton, what were you thinking?" His finger which had been wagging emphatically at Lizzie was then pointed in the direction of her grandmother. Then he turned on his daughter.

"And you, lady, were given a direct instruction to get these children back here as soon as possible."

265

"But dad, it was as I told you, Lizzie here, and not to mention some of our other friends and allies, put up a good argument for her being included in the retrieval of the Harp," she said, dropping the baby voice, and becoming much more the Elenya that Lizzie and her companions had observed during their adventure in Eldorth's castle.

"King Elfred ...," began Mrs Longton, in an attempt to calm the situation, but then seeing the thunderous look on his face, clamped her mouth tight shut.

Lizzie stepped forward into the firing line.

"Grandfather," she said, softly. "I don't know how and I don't know why, but I somehow knew I had to get the Harp myself. It was like a voice in my head told me it was the right thing to do. So, that's why I did it. And look," she said, holding out the Harp to him. "I was right."

The King's shoulders seemed to sag a little and he sighed deeply.

"Elizabeth," he said; his exasperation filled the single word. Then, smiling gently at her, he held out his arms. Lizzie walked over to him and placed the Harp in his hands. He took it from her with barely a glance at it and passed it to Elnest, and then drew her into a tight embrace. Looking over her head at his Head of Security, he said, "You know what to do with it Elnest."

"Yes, Sire," said Elnest, taking the Harp from the King and bowing low. He then hurried from the room.

"Grandfather, you're cr-ush-ing me," Lizzie said, her groan turning to giggles as he released her a little. Laughing now more in relief than mirth, the King held her away at arms-length and peered intently into her face; how much she seems to have grown in the short time that she'd been in this world, he thought. He then put a hand out to Elenya to join them and, as the three of them embraced Lizzie, she suddenly felt a surge of finally belonging.

Wriggling free, Lizzie asked the King what would happen to the Harp now that it was back in his possession. The King explained that it would once again be hidden away and protected from any possible attempt to steal it again.

The others in the room, who had been standing in frozen silence watching the scene before them, took this as a signal that they could finally move. Everyone began talking at once as the other children ran to their loved ones. The twins, Elwood and Elwind, hugged each other in greeting whilst Elroy lifted Eloise off her feet and swung her round as he held her in his arms. Elrus's father took him into a huge bear hug and Marvin placed a fatherly hand on Max's shoulder and smiled kindly down at his young apprentice.

"So Max," Marvin said. "Come tell me what happened."

As each of the children excitedly told the part they had played in the adventure, with Elenya filling in any gaps in the story, Mrs Longton stood back and watched the scene with satisfaction.

"Well," she thought. "This has certainly turned out to be one hell of an adventure."

*

That night, by order of the King, there was a huge banquet held in honour of the returning heroes.

Before the feast began, Lizzie and her grandmother returned to their rooms to prepare for the festivities. Once again, Lizzie bathed in her elaborate bathroom and soaked away the dirt and grime from the woods and tunnels that she and her friends had navigated through that day. As she lay back in the warm soapy waters, she closed her eyes and let her mind drift. So many unbelievable things had happened to

267

her during the short time since she and her grandmother had set off on their journey to Elvedom Castle.

She felt like a totally different girl to the one who'd set out on their journey just days before. Was she really the same girl who had been so timid, friendless – and apart from her grandmother – family-less? The uncomfortable memory of that last day of term, when she ran home from school to hide from the taunts and teasing of the other children from the village school, made her squirm. So maybe she was weird little Lizzie Long Ears, but look at her now; no longer scared and timid, but brave and determined with wonderful new friends and a loving new family. Perhaps she and her grandmother could stay here forever, she thought, opening her eyes and grinning at the idea. She climbed out of the bath and wrapped herself in a big, soft towel.

As she entered her bedroom, she could see that someone had once again laid out clothes for her to wear. She dried herself off and brushed her hair until it shone like spun silver. She then slipped on the most beautiful dress she'd ever seen. The dress was made of dark green velvet and flattered Lizzie's small, thin body as its soft folds fell in ripples to her ankles. The neckline and cuffs of the dress's long sleeves were intricately embroidered with silver thread and tiny sparkling stones, which glittered in the room's light. She smoothed her hands over it and, slipping on a pair of soft, dark green leather pumps that were also there for her to use, she walked over to look at herself in the large mirror hanging on the wall.

"Well," she said to herself, "the colour seems to suit me."

Grinning at her reflection, Lizzie began to twirl and dance around in front of the mirror. It was like watching a stranger. She had hated looking in mirrors in the past because then she'd have to look at her horrid ears and strange features staring back at her. Now she loved the image dancing before her because here, in this world, she wasn't strange looking with weird shaped ears. Here, she was just like everyone else.

Satisfied that she was presentable for the banquet, Lizzie left her bedroom and went into the sitting room between her and her grandmother's rooms. Mrs Longton was already there and was standing pouring herself a goblet of red wine from a beautiful crystal decanter. She was wearing a long flowing dress in the same colour as the wine she was pouring and she looked radiant.

"Well, don't we look posh," smiled Mrs Longton, looking across at Lizzie who was standing admiring her grandmother. Lizzie grinned.

"You look beautiful, gran," she said wistfully. It was true; it looked as though years of strain and worry had fallen away from Mrs Longton's face. Her greying hair, with its traces of its original red, was piled up on her head and was secured by an array of jewel encrusted combs and pins. The society beauty she had once been was back again for all to see.

"Thank you, my darling," smiled Mrs Longton, brimming with pleasure and doing a brief twirl.

At that moment, there was a knock on the door and Eldora Cherrytree entered the room. She curtseyed low and told them that the King awaited their pleasure, so that he could escort them to the banquet. Quickly quaffing down her wine, Mrs Longton, followed by Lizzie, walked serenely out of the room and the three of them made their way to the Kings apartments.

As Lizzie and Mrs Longton entered the King's room they saw him and Princess Elenya standing by the fire place deep in conversation. They turned and smiled at Lizzie and her grandmother.

"You look very pretty," Elenya nodded at Lizzie. "And Mrs Longton, wow!" she added with a cheeky wink.

"Thanks," grinned Lizzie, taking in the picture that was Elenya. "You look beautiful." Lizzie wasn't exaggerating; Elenya did indeed look stunning. Her blond hair fell in a sheet at the back of her head and a small golden coronet held it in place, like a priceless Alice-band. Her dress of silvery grey silk was encrusted with a dazzling array of small sparkling jewels that appeared to be emeralds and diamonds.

"Elizabeth; Mrs Longton," the King greeted them both and bowed politely. He then walked over to a table on which stood a beautifully engraved silver box. Raising the lid, he lifted out a small gem encrusted tiara. Holding it lovingly in his hands, he walked over to Lizzie.

"This was your mother's," he said softly, turning the beautiful item in his hands so that the precious stones sparkled with a life of their own. "It would please me greatly if you would wear it this evening, Elizabeth." Lizzie looked at the tiara and her eyes filled with tears. This was her mother's and the thought of wearing something of hers made her presence feel close.

"Oh, thank you grandfather," Lizzie smiled, looking up at him. She turned her eyes towards the King's face as he placed the tiara on her head. She could see the sadness in his eyes but his mouth smiled down at her. It felt a little big but she didn't care a jot. As the King took his hands away and stood back to admire her, she placed a hand gently on the tiara. She was actually beginning to feel like a princess now.

"There is something else I should like to show you, Elizabeth," said the King. "Will you come with me?" Then, taking Lizzie's hand, he placed it through his arm and guided her out of his rooms and into the large entrance hall, followed closely by Mrs Longton and Elenya.

Ascending the grand staircase to the first floor, they walked towards a large pair of gilded doors that swung open as they approached. Lizzie could see that they were entering

270

a long galleried room. To one side of the room were tall windows, which looked out over the grounds of the castle. Dusk was falling and the moon and the first stars of the impending night were beginning to peer through the wispy clouds, which showed red and orange from the setting sun. Opposite the windows, rows of paintings lined the wall and Lizzie was reminded of the old family portraits that hung in the landings and staircase of Longton Hall. There was, however, one stark difference; the faces in these portraits were, by evidence of their ears, those of elves. As they walked along, the King pointed out the various faces of Lizzie's ancestors.

"That's Elverine the Wise," he said, pointing at a she-elf with soft eyes and a gentle face. "And that's Eldwin the Black; he was something of a black-sheep in the family. He wasn't exactly bad, but let's just say he wasn't always as good as he could have been," said the King with a wink. Lizzie looked into the face of the elf; he had more the look of an imp about him than that of an elf.

After several more paintings of elves, whose names Lizzie thought she'd never remember, they finally stopped and stood in front of the largest portrait amongst them. The elf in the painting was wearing a crown and his hand rested on top of the hilt of a long silver sword, the point of which was resting on the ground to his side. He looked very grand and proud, but there was a hint of humour in his face and Lizzie warmed to him immediately. There was, however, something Lizzie noticed more than anything else about this elf and that was the size of his ears. She knew that elves had long pointed ears only too well but this elf's ears were huge. A bubble of giggles threatened to escape her as she took in the picture. The elf's ears looked so funny but she knew it would be disrespectful to laugh and so swallowed hard to push the bubble back down inside.

The King gazed down at her and, as if reading her mind, said, "You're probably thinking what big ears he has," he

271

grinned, "but let me explain. I know, from what Elwood has told me, that the children in your village are unkind to you and that one of the insults they throw at you is that of calling you Lizzie Long Ears."

At hearing her grandfather uttering her hated nickname, Lizzie flushed red. Her ears burned and she closed her eyes against the horrible memories of her tormentors. The bubble of giggles burst inside her, leaving a hollow feeling. She said nothing and so the King continued.

"This, Lizzie, is King Eldearen the Great." Lizzie opened her eyes and looked up into the face of the elf in the picture. The King continued, "He was a good and kind King. He was wise and brave and he is revered in our world as one of the greatest Kings to ever rule over Elvedom. Many children in our world are named after him. King Eldearen was also known by another name, and if that name is given to any elf in our world it is seen as a sign of great respect because that elf has proven him or herself to be brave or good, wise or kind, or maybe all of those things."

Lizzie looked at her grandfather, quizzically.

"That name, Elizabeth, is Eldearen Long Ears." A look of surprise spread across Lizzie's face. "So, Elizabeth, if anyone ever calls you by that name again, remember King Eldearen and take it as a huge compliment, not as the insult it was intended to be. You are Eldearen's descendent and you have proven today that you are worthy to wear that name – Elizabeth Long Ears." He smiled at her.

Lizzie looked up at King Eldearen and beamed; a warm glow spread through her small body. She turned towards her grandfather, and, putting her hands on her hips, said, "Well, at least my ears aren't *that* big."

King Elfred, Elenya and Mrs Longton laughed.

"Now, let's go and party," beamed Elenya, and the small group left the gallery and returned down to the entrance hall. Through the doors to the banqueting hall, Lizzie could see several long tables adorned with silver, crystal and flowers. Large silver candelabras with hundreds of flickering candles lined each of the tables, shedding their light over the proceedings. Dozens of elves were already seated and were chatting animatedly amongst themselves. As the royal party entered, the company fell silent.

With Princess Elenya and Mrs Longton walking grandly in their wake, Lizzie and her grandfather proceeded down the hall to the top table, until they stood behind it and looked out upon the assembled elves before them.

The King then raised his hands in greeting. "My brethren, kinsmen and women, welcome. You know why we are gathered here this evening, but suffice it to say, my daughter Elenya," he waved a hand in Elenya's direction, "and granddaughter Elizabeth," he turned and indicated Lizzie in the same way, "have returned the Harp of Elvyth to our safe keeping." The hall erupted in cheers and whoops of delight as each elf applauded enthusiastically. Lizzie couldn't help but break out in a huge beaming grin. Waving his hands up and down, as a sign that the elves should quieten, the King continued.

"Tonight is a time for celebration. So, without further ado, let us eat, drink and make merry." With that, the musicians struck up the strains of a beautiful ballad and the King and his party sat down and the banquet commenced.

Whilst a team of liveried elves expertly and unobtrusively served the food and drinks, Lizzie looked around the room, seeking out her friends. She looked along the table to her left and saw Eloise peering around her father and waving frantically in Lizzie's direction. Lizzie waved back at Eloise, who was smiling from ear to ear, her pretty brown face glowing with happiness. Lizzie then looked along the table to her right and could see Elrus sitting between his father, Elmer, and mother, Elmara. He was leaning around his mother and appeared to be deep in conversation with Max who was sitting between Elmara and Marvin.

Lizzie sighed happily and tucked ravenously into the food placed in front of her. She hadn't realised how hungry she was until she dipped a chunk of the soft warm bread into a thick creamy soup and popped it into her mouth. After the soup came a wonderful fish dish, followed by roast venison with all the trimmings. When the last course, a concoction of fresh fruits and thick clotted cream, was finished, Lizzie felt as though she was fit to burst.

When the meal was finally over, the tables were quickly moved to the sides of the hall for the entertainment and dancing to commence. Whilst their food slowly digested, the guests were entertained by jugglers and acrobats, dancers and singers, and Lizzie cheered and clapped as hard as everyone else. Then one of the singers announced that the dancing was to commence. Eloise came running over to Lizzie.

"Come on, Princess Elizabeth, let's dance," she cried excitedly. "We love dancing in Elcarib." Lizzie, grinning wide, ran hand in hand with Eloise down to the dance floor; laughing as they passed Elrus and Max. Elrus jumped up and called, "Hey wait for me!" Then, turning to Max, said, "Come on mate, shake a leg."

Max looked horrified and shook his head emphatically. "No thanks. Not just now," he mumbled, looking down at his hands, his face burned in embarrassment. Elrus laughed loudly.

"You don't know what you're missing," he cried as he turned and ran after the girls.

Elrus, Eloise and Lizzie threw themselves into the dancing with gusto. It was like the day that Lizzie had first met Elrus when they had danced at his village feast. They whirled and twirled, twisted and swung around the dance floor with abandon. Lizzie had the same feeling of complete freedom that she'd felt at the village feast. It helped to see everyone else on the floor dancing in the same exuberant way. Lizzie looked across and saw her grandmother and grandfather dancing an old-fashioned waltz quite out of time with the wild jig that was playing. Then she spotted Elroy swaying his hips rhythmically whilst he danced with a beautiful dark skinned elf that shimmied and shook her lithe body with effortless ease. It was almost as if everyone was hearing completely different music being played at the same time.

During a break in the music, Lizzie looked up and saw Max sitting alone watching the dancers. He was moving his head from side to side in time to the beat and smiling shyly. As the music struck up again, she went over to Max and sat down next to him.

"Aren't you going to come and join in, Max?" she asked gently.

Max shook his head. "No, no thank you, ma'am," he stammered. "It's not really my thing," he said looking down and picking at his finger nails.

"It's great fun you know," Lizzie continued.

"Yes, yes I'm sure it is but it's not for me," he said shyly. Lizzie was sure he really wanted to join in but was too self-conscious so she persisted.

"Look, Max. The first time I danced like that was when I met Elrus at his village just a couple of days ago. I felt really stupid and embarrassed because I'd never danced like that before. In fact, the only time I'd ever danced before was on my own at home, or maybe sometimes with my gran or Mary around the kitchen when the radio was on," she almost said to herself. "Anyway, I'd never danced with such

275

freedom. Just come and have a go, no-one's going to laugh at you, promise, and remember what Flaxon said." Max looked up at Lizzie quickly, unsure of what she meant.

"Nothing ventured, nothing gained," she grinned.

Max smiled at her. She was right, of course. What was there to be scared of in dancing a few silly dances? He'd been into the bowels of Eldorth's castle, for heaven's sake, he thought to himself. Then, smiling bashfully, he nodded at Lizzie. "Okay," he agreed and, standing up, followed her down on to the dance floor. Upon reaching the others, Elrus clapped Max on the back encouragingly. Lizzie suddenly grabbed Max's hands and began spinning him around the floor and, laughing all the while, the four friends danced the night away.

The banquet went on into the small hours until finally, happy, exhausted and dishevelled, the revellers retired to their homes or bedchambers, and a weary Lizzie fell into bed and into a dreamless sleep.

Chapter 26 – Homeward Bound

Lizzie and her grandmother rose late the next morning and, having eaten a leisurely breakfast, the two of them made their way to the King's study. As they entered his room, the King was sitting behind his huge desk, a silver fountain pen in his hand. He put down the pen and closed a large leather-bound book he'd been writing in and stood up to greet them.

"Good morning, Mrs Longton," he said, bowing his head and, turning to Lizzie, said, "Elizabeth. I hope you both slept well."

"Very well, thank you, Your Majesty," said Mrs Longton.

He walked around the desk towards them and took Lizzie's hands in his own. "I have spoken with Marvin and instructed him to arrange for you both to return home to Longton Hall today," he announced. Lizzie looked at him in hurt surprise.

"So soon?" she asked. "Can't we stay here?" The King shook his head sadly.

"No, Elizabeth. It is better for you to return to your home in the human world. It is still not safe for you to stay here with Eldorth at liberty. There is no doubt he knows of your existence now and we are sure that he will attempt to do you harm," the King said sadly. "He will be very angry at having had the Harp snatched from under his nose, and we cannot be sure what he might do by way of retribution. It will, therefore, be safer for you living with your grandmother in your own world."

Lizzie plonked herself down on one of his sofas, disappointment etched on her face. "But this is my world now," she groaned. Her grandmother watched her granddaughter gloomily and then turned to the King.

"Will we be safe there?" she asked him. "I mean, there's no way that Eldorth can get into our world, is there?"

The King shook his head. "He does not have the means of doing so," stressed the King. "Not yet anyway. We know that he is gaining in power but it is not yet sufficient. The retrieval of the Harp of Elvyth will have been a set-back for him but I'm sure that he will endeavour to increase his power by other means. Our intelligence suggests that he does not yet have the knowledge of how he may break through to other worlds. So, it is imperative that we arrange for yourself and Elizabeth to return home as soon as possible."

Lizzie sat forward on her sofa, a puzzled frown on her face. "Grandfather," she began. "There's something that doesn't quite make sense."

"What's that, Elizabeth?" asked the King.

"If Eldorth isn't able to travel to other worlds, how did he get the sacred relics hidden in them?" she asked.

The King looked impressed. "Well done, Elizabeth. You're using your keen intellect to think things out and question them. In answer to your question, we believe that Eldorth has used couriers to take the relics into these other worlds. Who these couriers were, of that we are unsure."

"Couriers?" queried Lizzie.

"Yes," replied the King. "People or creatures that were passing over to the nether and spirit worlds and could carry the relics with them. We think Melificent used her dark powers to enable these couriers to pass over, taking the relics with them. As for how the relic was taken into the human world, well, we have yet to discover how that was achieved." The King looked pensive.

"So....," said Mrs Longton slowly. "Eldorth has had a courier that has travelled to the human world? But I thought you said that he didn't have that power?"

The King looked at Mrs Longton, and seemed a little unsure of himself before stiffening his back in resolve and saying, "We feel confident that Eldorth himself cannot pass over to the human world but he has, at some time, known someone who could and that is what we need to discover. It is something that my people and our allies are still working on."

He sat down next to Lizzie and placed a hand on her shoulder. He looked deep in her eyes.

"My dear Elizabeth, I have waited so long to be able to tell you the truth about your heritage and at last it is done. I know that you feel I should have contacted you sooner but I was unable to do so for the reasons I've explained," he said gently. Then, turning to Mrs Longton, he smiled and said, "It could also be argued that my method of enticing you both here to Elvedom was somewhat underhand." Mrs Longton gave him a wry look. "But," he continued, "There seemed no easy way in which to do this. If I had just turned up on your doorstep and announced I am Elfred, King of Elvedom, you would have dismissed me as a madman. In the end, I hope you agree that all has worked out well."

Lizzie nodded emphatically. "Oh yes, Grandfather," she said brightly.

"There is one final thing that I must tell you before you go home. There has never seemed to be a good time to explain but it must be now. It is about your father," both Lizzie and Mrs Longton's eyes snapped to the King's face. The King took a deep breath and asked Mrs Longton, who was standing rooted to the spot, to sit down.

"Elizabeth," he began. "You have, I am sure, always wondered why your father has never been home to see you

279

since the night of your birth, nor to have ever written to you or made mention of you in his letters. Lizzie nodded slowly, not taking her eyes from the King's face.

"Well, he has done so because he was told that was what he must do," explained the King.

Mrs Longton felt anger well up in her. "Who told him to do that?" she asked hotly.

"I did," said the King sadly.

"You did?" Mrs Longton asked; she was now confused. The questions tumbled out of her. "You asked Tom? But how? Why? Tom knew of you?"

"Yes, Mrs Longton. Tom knew of me. He knew about Elethria's real origins and of the curse she was under, but he was sworn to secrecy. He could not even divulge the secret to you. In any case, would you have believed him?" the King smiled. "But there was good reason for him to know and keep the secret safe. When Elethria became pregnant with Elizabeth, she knew that she had taken a terrible risk, but she wanted your son's child more than anything else because she loved him more than life itself." He looked sadly at Mrs Longton. "She turned to me and told me about the pregnancy and that she had told Tom about her past. He did not doubt her but he became frantic for her and the baby's safety. I met with Tom and was glad to have done so; he is a good man." Mrs Longton's eyes filled with tears; Tom, her Tom, had known all along.

"Tom was made to understand that I, with the help of Marvin, we would do all we could to save Elethria and the child. He knew that we could not guarantee success as dark curses are almost impossible to counteract a curse and I explained that we may only be able to save one of them. I told him that if the worst happened and only the child survived then he must go away and leave it in your care. It was the only way that the baby could be hidden and

280

protected against Eldorth or his spies." The King looked at Lizzie and smiled, "If your father was known to be bringing up a child, it would also be known that that child was Elethria's and so you would have been Eldorth's target. Without Tom around you were anonymous."

"So can Tom now meet Lizzie," asked Mrs Longton, swallowing hard, and looking excited at the prospect of a meeting between her son and granddaughter.

The King shook his head sadly and said, "I'm afraid not. Not yet. He must stay away from Elizabeth until the other relics are retrieved. Tom told you the truth when he said he was away excavating for ancient relics, as it is he who is currently trying to find the sacred relic in your world." He turned again to look at Lizzie, who was sitting just staring at her grandfather in silence. "You see, Elizabeth, your father wanted you as much as your mother did and it has been more difficult for him to stay away from you than you will ever know. But I have been in regular contact with him and kept him up to date on your progress over the years from the reports I received from Elwood."

Lizzie suddenly seemed to find her voice, albeit a very small voice, "So, daddy really did want me?" she asked. The King nodded.

"I knew it deep down really," Lizzie said, looking into the King's face and then into that of her grandmother. "Even though my mind kept telling me if he really wanted or loved me he'd come and see me or write to me; in my heart I knew."

The King smiled. "I am sure that you will meet one day soon," he said.

Suddenly there was a huge sob from the chair opposite them as Mrs Longton finally gave way to her grief and relief. Crying almost uncontrollably into a large white handkerchief that was hurriedly scrabbled from her handbag, she blew her nose loudly into its folds. Lizzie ran over and threw her arms around her grandmother's neck.

"It's alright, gran. You see, you always told me the truth. You always said he loved me and wanted to be with me but his work kept him away. I know you thought you were lying, but actually you weren't."

Mrs Longton peered tearfully over the top of her handkerchief at Lizzie's excited face, then, lowering it and smiling weakly, she said in a choked voice, "Yes, I suppose you're right, darling." She then turned to the King.

"Thank you so much for explaining about Tom. You have no idea how difficult it has been these past eleven years. I couldn't believe it when Tom walked away that night. Each time a letter arrived, I thought that maybe this time he would ask after Lizzie, or maybe even say he was coming home. I couldn't understand how he could stay away. I mean, look at her," Mrs Longton reached out and cupped Lizzie's face in her hands. "She's so beautiful and clever and he would be so proud of her." Looking back to the King, she asked him if he would be contacting her son again soon.

The King nodded. "Yes I will and before you ask, I will tell him all about you and Elizabeth and your visit here. He already knows how beautiful and clever she is and is deeply proud of her." Then, looking hard at Lizzie, said, "It'll be interesting to see what he makes of your visit to Eldorth's castle given your antics."

"Would you also give him Lizzie's and my love and tell him we miss him," asked Mrs Longton, dabbing at her eyes with the soggy handkerchief.

"Indeed I will," agreed the King.

Lizzie smiled happily as a warm glow spread through her body. Her father loved her and wanted her; this was the happiest day of her life. That happiness was dampened a little when the King said, "Well, it is time that you returned home."

Seeing the look of disappointment on Lizzie's face the King continued. "It is only for now, Elizabeth. It is important that your education in our ways continues. I have, therefore, arranged for Elwood to continue to watch over you, but now he will also instruct you on anything you ask him. I trust that is acceptable to you, Mrs Longton?" Mrs Longton nodded.

"Of course, and he'll stay with us at Longton Hall," she said. "My only concern is won't he be a bit obvious? I mean what with his pointed ears and penchant for wearing green."

The King laughed. "You can always explain him away as being a cousin or some other relative of Elizabeth's. I shall ensure that Elwood understands that he needs to tone down the green outfits so that he is a little less conspicuous whilst he's visible in your world."

*

The preparations were soon made and within the hour, Lizzie and her grandmother along with Elwood were set for their return to Longton Hall.

Marvin met them in the King's rooms and informed them that he had arranged for a temporary Threshold to be formed that would take them directly from Elvedom Castle to Longton Hall. As they entered Marvin's rooms on their way to the Threshold, they were met by Elenya, Elrus, Eloise and Max who were waiting for them. Elenya was the first to step forward and take Lizzie in a huge hug.

"Well, little niece, time to go home, eh?" she said, smiling down at Lizzie's upturned face.

"Yes, but grandfather says that I can come back soon," said Lizzie.

"Good. In the meantime, don't forget you have the locket if you need us," Elenya grinned.

"But will it work in the human world?" Lizzie asked, looking up at her aunt and taking the locket hanging from her neck in her hand.

"Of course it does. Your mother used it all the time to contact me and dad," Elenya reassured her. Lizzie smiled happily and gave her aunt a final squeeze then, letting her go, she turned to her three new friends. "I wish you could all come with me. I could do with a few friends where I live," she said, with a hint of sadness.

"Well, don't forget to invite us to come and see that telly of yours some time," Eloise reminded her, taking Lizzie's hand in her own. Then, looking sideways at Marvin, and nodding in the direction of curtains hiding the Threshold, she whispered, "Perhaps Marvin can arrange one those again soon." Lizzie grinned at her and they hugged. Lizzie then turned to the boys and firstly hugged Elrus and then went to Max who looked down shyly. Lizzie knew he'd be mortified if she hugged him, so she stuck out a hand for him to shake instead. Taking her hand warmly in his he shook it heartily, a smile lighting up his face.

"I shall miss you two so much," she said to them both. "But I'll see you again soon, I promise."

"You can count on it," chirped Elrus, cheekily.

When Lizzie and Mrs Longton had at last said their goodbyes, Marvin drew back the velvet curtains and revealed the old battered door that lay behind it. Marvin slowly opened the door and with a final look over their shoulders, Lizzie and her grandmother, together with Elwood, stepped over the Threshold.

Lizzie and Mrs Longton got back to the normality of being at Longton Hall surprisingly quickly, given that Elwood was now a permanent fixture.

As the King had suggested, they explained away his presence to Bob and Mary Crowther as a distant cousin of Lizzie's mum, Ria, who had, by some rare coincidence, just happened to be staying in the same hotel. Mary had looked a little suspicious but said that she could see the family resemblance - trying hard not to stare at Elwood's ears. Over the following days, she had bombarded Elwood with questions about his family and Elwood had enjoyed himself immensely coming up with more and more elaborate fibs every day. How he remembered what he'd said and didn't trip himself up, Lizzie wasn't sure, but she was impressed all the same; although she did begin to wonder if she'd believe anything he said ever again.

Elwood had at least changed his wardrobe so that he now dressed predominantly in more muted colours, such as browns and fawns, but there was always a touch of green in there somewhere. Sometimes it was a green jumper or just his socks. Lizzie was sure on the days that there she was unable to see any green in his attire, he was probably wearing green underpants.

Lizzie spent much of the remaining few days of the school holidays going on long walks with the dogs, Basil and Rathbone, and Elwood. She enjoyed telling Elwood all about the area in which she lived and she introduced him to some of the shopkeepers in the village. Most people politely tried to avoid staring at his ears, although there were some double-takes when they first met him. Lizzie was glad that there was no sign of the dreaded Bray twins, as they were off on some foreign holiday with their parents – something they'd been bragging about for weeks prior to breaking up for Easter.

Elwood especially enjoyed visiting the library and talking to Miss Bookham, the librarian, about his wealth of knowledge. Lizzie couldn't help but smile at his lack of modesty and Miss Bookham's look of resignation. Mrs Longton also took Lizzie and Elwood on a few trips out into the Sussex countryside in her old Jaguar car, which she was relieved to see had been returned to the Hall from the car-park at Markham station sometime during her and Lizzie's absence.

In the evenings, when Bob and Mary had returned home, Lizzie and her grandmother would sit and talk to Elwood about Elvedom. He happily answered their questions about everyday life there and told them stories about its history and folklore.

One of the first things Lizzie had done when she returned home was run to her room and open the inlaid wooden box that sat on her dressing table. It was her treasure box and contained all sorts of things she had either collected or been given over the years. In the bottom layer of the box she found the thing she was looking for; her mother's locket. She took it out and examined its beautiful swirling engravings. Then, remembering what her aunt had shown her, she rubbed her thumb over the catch three times and flicked it open with her thumb nail. The locket finally flew open.

Inside, Lizzie saw the same image of her grandfather as the one she'd seen in Elenya's locket. She smiled down at it happily. In the frame on the other side of locket was a portrait of Elenya. Lizzie looked at it in surprise but then laughed as she thought, it made sense; her mum would obviously not have a picture of herself, but of someone she would wish to talk to; and who else but her sister? She took the locket and ran back downstairs to show it to her grandmother and Elwood.

Mrs Longton said that it was important for Lizzie keep the locket close and that she should wear it always. The only

286

problem with that was that Lizzie wasn't allowed to wear jewellery to school, and so Mrs Longton sewed a special pocket onto the inside of Lizzie's skirt so that the locket could be concealed safely inside.

Lizzie went back to school on the Monday following their return from Elvedom Castle, and one of the first tasks the teacher gave the class was to write an essay about how they'd spent their Easter holidays.

Lizzie was tempted to write the truth about her exciting adventure during the holidays and how she'd met her grandfather and aunt and how they were elves, thereby, making her a Half-Elf. But then she thought she'd better not as she'd probably get told off for having too vivid an imagination or worse, telling lies. So, she just said that she'd stayed at the Hall, reading books, watching telly, playing with her dogs - Basil and Rathbone - and doing some gardening with Bob who helped out at the Hall. Miss Finley, her teacher, read the essay sadly. Poor Lizzie Longton, it was the same story every holiday, if only she could make some real friends, she thought.

Things were still bad between Lizzie and the other children. No-one played with her or spoke to her. Any words mentioning Lizzie were spoken with venom, as she could hear Regina and Veronica Bray making cruel jibes about her skinny legs or stupid ears. Lizzie's already acute hearing seemed to be getting even sharper, because they picked up on things even if they were said quietly behind her back. She would hear the other children laughing at the horrid comments and her face would burn with embarrassment and hurt. But then Lizzie would think about what her grandfather had said about Eldearen Long Ears and would smile secretly to herself.

As she left school that first day, Lizzie began to walk home. As usual, she made sure that she got away before everyone else so that the other kids didn't corner her somewhere, but as she reached the corner of the street she heard feet running behind her. Turning quickly, she could see Regina and Veronica and some of their gang running in her direction calling out names again. As they started singing out, "Lizzie Long Ears, Lizzie Long Ears," Lizzie suddenly felt a surge of inner strength. She'd gone to Eldorth's castle and retrieved the Harp of Elvyth. If she could do that, then she could do anything.

Lizzie turned and stopped. Taking the same stance as her grandfather had when she and her friends had returned after their adventure, she stood – legs apart and hands on hips - and faced her tormentors. The suddenness of her actions seemed to confuse the gang and they screeched to a halt; the ones behind crashing and banging into Regina and Veronica who'd been leading them and almost knocking them over. They stared at Lizzie and she stared back. Regina opened her mouth and began, "Lizzie..." but got no further when Lizzie shouted at them.

"You know something, you're really stupid. You don't scare me. I can beat you at anything you ever try to do. So just bog off!" she stormed. The looks on the faces of the bullies was a picture and Lizzie burst out laughing as Regina and Veronica's jaws dropped open with the shock of actually being challenged. Lizzie turned on her heels and began to stride purposefully away when Regina suddenly found her voice. "You're gonna get it, you stupid Long Eared freak," she screeched.

Lizzie turned again, a broad grin across her face. Raising herself up as tall as she could, she said, "And proud of it." Then, turning once again, she skipped off down the street.

The twins and their gang stared after her, too shocked by her unexpected outburst to respond further. Then Lizzie's lovely long ears could hear the twins ranting behind her.

Lizzie smiled as she began to run towards home. Placing her hand on the pocket holding her locket, she felt it begin to glow warm and vibrate beneath her palm. Lizzie began to run faster than she ever had in her life. Her adventures had just begun.

The Dragon Flyers – Book 2 of the Long Ears Legacy

Back home and faced with having to cope with her lonely life in Chislewick, Lizzie Longton is thrilled by a surprise visit from her new friend Elrus of Elvenholme. However, the visit is cut short by an urgent summons by Lizzie's grandfather. King Elfred.

Upon her return to Elvedom, Lizzie learns that the whereabouts of another sacred relic, The Chalice of Elaria, has been discovered. Plans are put in place to retrieve the Chalice and so Lizzie, together with a select party of trusted companions led by her aunt Elenya, travel on a secret mission to secure the help of specialist forces, based in the Mountains of Snow.

On her journey through Elvedom, Lizzie learns more about the new world she is now part of and discovers things about herself that she could never have dreamt possible in her wildest imagination.

The Dragon Flyers - Book 2 of the Long Ears Legacy is available from late 2013.

About the author

Since childhood, I have dreamt of being a writer and have always written stories, poetry and plays. Then life, and the need to earn a living, got in the way and so I've had careers as a Human Resource Manager (for a world renowned public transport system in London), self-employment and currently as a college administrator.

The decision to finally follow that dream came about when I suffered the tragic loss of my youngest brother, followed much too soon afterwards by my beloved dad. These two life altering events proved that life is much too fragile and precious to waste it wondering "what if?"

Like most authors, even those writing of a fantasy world, I called upon my own life experiences and the traits and personalities of loved ones (and not so loved ones!) to create a whole new existence.

The Harp of Elvyth is my first full length children's novel and is book one of a planned series of books called The Long Ears Legacy. It follows the adventures of little Lizzie Longton as she makes her way in two quite different parallel worlds.

A born and bred Londoner, I now live in Surrey England with my husband, my teenage son and daughter (who might recognise bits of themselves in the stories!) and our two dogs Wilma and Wally.

Debbie Daley

Lightning Source UK Ltd.
Milton Keynes UK
UKOW05f0503191113

221358UK00002B/12/P